THE
GOBLIN
GATE

THE GOBLIN GATE

HILARI BELL

HARPER TEEN
An Imprint of HarperCollinsPublishers

HarperTeen is an imprint of HarperCollins Publishers.

The Goblin Gate
Copyright © 2010 by Hilari Bell
For information address HarperCollins Children's Books, a division of
HarperCollins Publishers, 10 East 53rd Street, New York, NY 10022.
www.harperteen.com

Library of Congress Cataloging-in-Publication Data
Bell, Hilari.
    The goblin gate / by Hilari Bell. — 1st ed.
        p.   cm.
    Summary: Jeriah uncovers a web of political intrigue while trying to
obtain a spell from Master Lazur that might allow him to rescue his brother
Tobin from the Otherworld, where he was taken by the beguiling hedgewitch
Makenna and her legion of goblins.
    ISBN 978-0-06-165102-1 (trade bdg.)
    [1. Fantasy.   2. Witches—Fiction.   3. Knights and knighthood—
Fiction.   4. Goblins—Fiction.   5. Magic—Fiction.]   I. Title.
PZ7.B38894Gnm 2010   2009039666
[Fic]—dc22   CIP
                                                                   AC

Typography by Hilary Zarycky
10 11 12 13 14   CG/RRDB   10 9 8 7 6 5 4 3 2 1

First Edition

For Anna-Maria: without whose help
this book would never have reached publishable form.
I owe you big-time for this one.

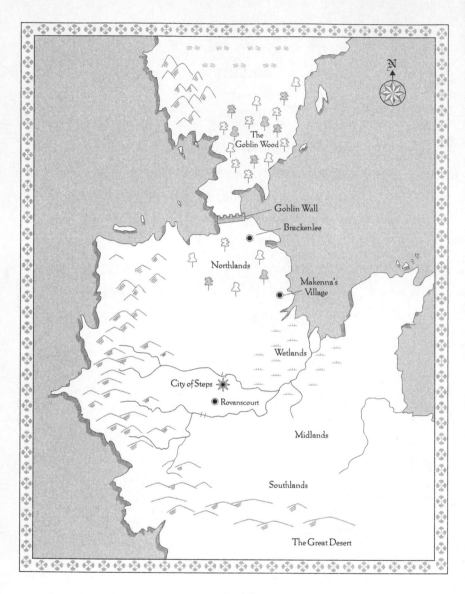

The Goblin Wood

Goblin Wall

Brackenlee

Northlands

Makenna's
Village

Wetlands

City of Steps

Rovanscourt

Midlands

Southlands

The Great Desert

REALM OF THE BRIGHT GODS

CHAPTER 1

Jeriah

"IT WILL BE DAWN SOON," Jeriah told the priest who rode beside him. "If we haven't caught them by then, won't we have to rest the horses?"

The lessening of darkness through the trees to the east surely signaled the beginning of the end of the worst night of Jeriah's life—and not only because of the difficulty of keeping his mare from stumbling in the wavering light of moon and torches.

"We'll catch up with them soon enough," Master Lazur replied. "They only had a forty-minute start, and they've delayed several times, waiting for others to join them."

One of the people they were chasing was Jeriah's brother.

"The goblins must have bespelled him." Jeriah had been pursuing this argument all night, whenever he managed to maneuver Glory up beside the priest's horse. "Just as I was bespelled when I led them to your tent."

"Then why didn't his mind and will return to him when he crossed the charmed iron that protected my tent?" Master

Lazur demanded. "As yours did."

"Maybe the spell on him was different. Deeper, or on him longer. Or maybe he was drugged! Tobin led you to the goblin village just a few days ago. Why would he help us find the goblins and capture the sorceress, and then help them escape?"

"I'll ask Tobin that," said the priest. "And if he was acting under compulsion, no harm will come to him. But first we have to catch them."

The priest urged his horse forward to speak to the chief tracker, though the man hadn't signaled that he'd seen anything new. If Tobin hadn't been bespelled or drugged, he would probably hang. Or was it a hanging offense to help a murderess escape the church's custody if you hadn't killed anyone yourself?

Jeriah feared he was going to find out, because no matter what he'd told the priest, he didn't believe Tobin had been bespelled. Not bespelled, or drugged, or even smitten silly by the sorceress' remarkable beauty.

He'd acted too swiftly, too intelligently on that lightning raid to steal Master Lazur's books . . . and what in two worlds had he wanted the priest's spell books for?

He hadn't said. With Jeriah bound and gagged at his feet, Tobin hadn't said anything that mattered except that he'd explain someday. A lot of good that did! His brother would be explaining to a judge if they were caught.

And they probably would be caught. Jeriah had tried to

delay them, but Master Lazur had been watching. If he'd done anything too conspicuous, the priest would have left him behind. One of the knights of legend might have managed it, but Jeriah had found that stopping a troop of armed soldiers, when you yourself had only a horse and a sword, wasn't possible in the real world.

His subtle attempts to delay the troop's departure, and the tracks he'd managed to scuff over "by accident," hadn't done anything but draw so much of the priest's attention he hadn't dared do anything more. He had to be present when they caught up with Tobin—that would be his best chance.

The trees were thinning, and glow from the brightening horizon began to dim the moonlight. The troop picked up its pace, trotting now, despite the horses' weariness. If Tobin could stay ahead of them for just a little longer, they'd have to stop to rest their horses. But the sky was growing lighter . . . in the south? What—

Master Lazur shouted, urging his horse to a canter, and the rest of the troop followed.

Glory began to canter too, without even a touch of Jeriah's heels, and he kept his eyes on the growing light ahead of them. Blue-white, not at all like the thinning gray to the east where the sun would soon rise.

Magic. The sorceress must be casting some spell, and the back of Jeriah's neck prickled with primitive fear.

He urged Glory to a gallop, cutting through the rest of the troop. Master Lazur cast him a wary glance as Jeriah pushed past him, but Jeriah hardly noticed. The trees were thinning. . . .

Then he saw her. The great wall that divided the Goblin Wood from the rest of the Realm stretched out over the low hills, glimmering silver in the moonlight. The ragged gap where the road broke through was filled with a glowing sheet of light, which rippled and shifted as if tossed by a wind he couldn't feel.

The sorceress stood in the center of the gap, and those same currents set her dark hair swirling about her. Her back was to Jeriah, and beyond her . . .

Goblins streamed toward the gap, dozens, hundreds of small bodies, so many they might even have been able to overcome the priest's troop. But when they reached the light, they vanished.

Jeriah didn't care if all the goblins in the Realm escaped— he'd just seen Tobin, standing on the far side of that shimmering curtain. He tapped Glory's ribs with his heels and she thundered down the road. The sorceress would be gone by the time he got there, but that didn't matter either.

If he could just reach Tobin before the rest of the troop, tell him to say he'd been drugged and bespelled! Tell him to lie. . . . Tobin was a terrible liar. Tell him to act drugged, confused, and let Jeriah do the talking. Jeriah would knock Tobin out if he had to, in order to handle those first critical minutes of questioning.

The flood of goblins into the light had slowed; the last of

them would soon be gone.

The sorceress bent to pick up a pack—the pack that held Master Lazur's spell books. Soon she too would step through the gap, taking that alarming spell with her, and all he had to do was reach Tobin before—

The sorceress turned toward the light and disappeared. Jeriah was close enough now to see the expression on his brother's face shift from grief to decision. And when Tobin decided, action followed. Jeriah cried out then, a wordless shout of protest, warning, but it did no good.

Tobin took three running strides, plunged into the fading light, and vanished.

The glowing field wavered and blinked out, just seconds before Glory plunged through the place where it had been. Jeriah dragged her around to look back. Arcane symbols covered the shattered gap in the wall, but not even a flicker of light remained. No sign of his brother. Nothing but the dawn breeze rushing through the ragged stones, and the thud of slowing hoofbeats as the troop drew near.

"Tobin!" Even as the scream burst from his throat, Jeriah knew it was useless.

He glared at Master Lazur when the priest rode forward. The rest of the troop stopped before they reached the gap, but the priest rode right through to examine the scrawled signs. Fury warred with respect in his expression. "How did she do it?"

Jeriah didn't care. "Where are they? Where's my brother!"

"In the Otherworld. You remember the dimension from which I got the stone we used to locate the goblin camp?"

"But you said it took half a dozen priests to open a gate to the Otherworld—she was only a hedgewitch! How could *she* do it?"

"A very good question." Respect was winning. The priest climbed out of the saddle and laid his hands flat against the stones. "Ah, yes."

"Ah, yes what?" Jeriah demanded impatiently.

"The wall is a power sink. I knew that—or I would have, if I'd been thinking in terms of history. There must have been two hundred years of accumulated power in those stones. No wonder she could do it. How very bold."

"Then you can do it too. Open a gate so we can go after them."

"Jeriah." The grave sympathy in the priest's face turned Jeriah's blood to ice. "In the first place, I can't. The girl drained its power when she made the gate. And so large! I didn't know that was possible. In the second place . . . they're gone now. The sorceress and her goblins. Your brother rid us of them, as completely as if he'd killed them. And he gave his life to do it. He's a hero, and I shall see he gets full credit. But I'm not about to give them a chance to come back."

"What do you mean, gave his life?" Jeriah heard the hysterical edge in his voice, but he couldn't control it. "He's still alive in there. He's still—"

"He's gone. And we might as well go too. We can water the

horses, and rest them at that stream we pass—"

"You're *leaving*?" Jeriah's voice cracked on the word. "You can't leave! Tobin's . . . You have to bring him back!"

"I can't." Master Lazur laid a hand on Jeriah's elbow. "I'm sorry. We'll go back to the settlement, and—"

Jeriah used the hand on his elbow to get his own grip on Master Lazur's arm, then catapulted out of the saddle and knocked the priest flat on his back in the dusty road.

"We're not going anywhere." He straddled Master Lazur's body, one hand twisting the priest's collar tight. His other hand fumbled for his knife hilt. Master Lazur moved beneath him, starting to struggle for air. "Not till you cast that gate, so we can get Tob—"

Half a dozen hands seized him—Jeriah yanked out his knife and pressed it against the priest's throat.

"Back off," he snarled. "Back off or . . ." Or what? If he killed Master Lazur, he couldn't bring Tobin back. But the guards didn't seem to know that. Their grip on his arms, his collar, slackened and fell away.

"You're going to cast that gate," Jeriah told the priest. "You're going to cast it now."

"Or what? Cutting my throat won't get your gate cast."

Master Lazur's voice was calm, but Jeriah could feel the tension in his body. And he was right—if Jeriah killed him, the gate would never be cast.

"But why not open a gate?" Jeriah tried to speak calmly too, but his heart hammered against his ribs. Awareness of the hovering guards prickled along his nerves. "I'll go in, tell Tobin he's in danger, and we'll come right out."

"If it were that simple, I might consider it." The priest's voice was almost gentle, but his eyes flicked aside, searching for his guards. "But one of the many problems with the Otherworld is that when you open a gate, even if you're in exactly the same place in this world, it appears in a different place there. If I opened a gate right now, on this road, it might appear in the Otherworld hundreds of miles from where your brother is."

A chill brushed Jeriah's heart. "That's a lie. That has to be—"

"I'm sorry. It's not." Master Lazur's gaze caught his, holding it.

"Then I'll just have to go into the Otherworld and find him. Let the sorceress open a gate to send us back! You could do that, couldn't you?"

Lazur said nothing.

"You can do that. You will." Jeriah bore down on the knife.

"Wait! Listen to me," Master Lazur said hastily. "I might be able to cast the gate, but if I did, I'd be signing your death warrant! Because she *won't* be able to open a gate to let you out."

"She found a power sink, she managed it once before," Jeriah said. "She can do it again. All you have to do is—"

"Watch the knife," Master Lazur said sharply.

Jeriah took a shuddering breath and tried to still the trembling in his hands. "If she opened a gate here, she could—"

"You're wrong," the priest said. "The Otherworld drains magic even faster than it drains life. Within a few days, she'll be unable to cast any spells at all. That's why I can be so certain that she and her goblins aren't coming back. Unfortunately, that applies to your brother too."

"You're lying!" Jeriah shouted. "You—"

He'd forgotten about the guards. A hard hand closed around his knife wrist, and more hands yanked him away from the priest. A hard cuff made his ears ring, and his thoughts hazed over. Every thought but one—Master Lazur had to cast the spell or Tobin would die. He couldn't die, he couldn't, he couldn't . . .

"You're lying!" Jeriah's throat was tight with strangled sobs. Tears and snot ran down his face, but the hard grip on his arms didn't slacken. "That girl, the sorceress, why would she have gone there if it would kill them all? She wouldn't have. You can—"

"She didn't know," said Master Lazur. "Only a handful of priests were involved in the experiments from which we learned . . . well, we learned a lot about the nature of the Otherworld that isn't really relevant now—except that your brother isn't coming back."

"But if they started to die the moment they stepped through that light curtain thing, why didn't they just turn around and step out?"

"Because the Otherworld doesn't kill immediately," Master Lazur told him. "It won't kill those who have innate magic, and even your brother will survive for a bit over two months."

"Two months? That's plenty of time. Tobin was working for you. He got rid of that accursed sorceress for you. You can't just let him die!"

He was shouting by the time he finished, beginning to struggle again. The guards' grip tightened. They were about to drag him away!

"No," said Master Lazur abruptly. "He's right. I owe him the truth, at least." His gaze turned to Jeriah. "But you have to behave yourself. Can you?"

Fighting the guards wouldn't get him anywhere. Fighting Master Lazur wouldn't either. Calm, calm. He needed the priest's cooperation.

"I'm sorry," he muttered. "That was stupid of me. But a few people recover from any illness. Even plagues. You can't *know* that he's going to die."

His voice cracked on the word, but Master Lazur looked up at the guards, and the grip on Jeriah's arms loosened.

"This isn't a normal illness," the priest told him. "It's a magical effect, caused by the very nature of the Otherworld. I admit I worked on some spells that might protect against it, but they were all theoretical. And since they couldn't be cast without magic . . ." Master Lazur shrugged.

"Wait! You were working on spells that could protect him,

and she has your spell books. If the spells can keep his life from being drained, maybe they could protect her magic as well. She could still send him home! Anytime!"

The priest shook his head. "She doesn't have those spells. I don't keep experimental notes in my books, only completed work. And thank the Bright Gods I have copies of my completed books back in the city! It will be good to be home again."

"Where are the spells that could keep Tobin alive?"

If he could get those notes into the Otherworld in time, find his brother and the sorceress . . .

"I'm not going to answer that," said Master Lazur. "The knowledge would only torment you. In fact, I'm going to send you home. Your parents should be told as soon as possible, and as kindly as possible. You are now your father's heir. You'll need to talk to him about whether you should continue as my assistant or stay at Rovanscourt."

"But what about Tobin? I have to . . . to . . ."

To do what? Master Lazur wasn't powerful enough to cast a gate spell alone, and even if Jeriah could open a gate, how could he locate that deadly Otherworld? Or get his hands on the spells to keep his brother and the sorceress alive till they could find a way out?

If he left Master Lazur's service, the spells that might save Tobin would be out of reach forever.

"Wait, don't send me home! I want to serve the Realm." Even to his own ears, it sounded false.

"Talk to your father first."

"But—"

"I won't keep an assistant who won't obey me. Go home. Either for one month or until your father releases you."

Jeriah's fingers clenched into fists, but he couldn't let the priest dismiss him. Those spell notes were Tobin's only chance. He had to return to the priest's service, play a waiting game.

Tobin would probably die before a waiting game ended. And even if he could get the notes, how could he open a gate into the Otherworld? Much less find his brother in time?

A strangled sob tore through the constriction in his throat.

"Jeriah." Master Lazur reached out, lifting Jeriah's chin till he was forced to meet the man's eyes. "Sacrifices have to be made if good is to prevail. I can't have you opening gates into the Otherworld. There's a goblin army there, and a dozen condemned hedgewitches, and who knows what else! Even if you could open a gate, you'd never find Tobin in time. He saved the Realm. It was a noble sacrifice, even if he didn't know he was going to die. It was his choice. Let it go."

Jeriah jerked his head away and stumbled to Glory, hiding his face against her warm brown neck.

You're wrong. It's my fault he was here. It's my fault he ever got involved in this mess.

But it wasn't Jeriah's fault that Tobin had gone leaping into the light. It had all been working out fine, before his brother had gotten involved with the sorceress and her accursed goblins. It was their fault!

Jeriah heard the creak of leather as Master Lazur swung up into the saddle. He was leaving.

It didn't matter whose fault it was. They were leaving Tobin to die, he couldn't endure that, couldn't accept it, couldn't let it happen. He *wouldn't* let it happen.

No. Jeriah lifted his head, and the resolve settled into his bones like cooling iron. *No matter what it takes, I'm going to get my brother back. Alive.*

But how?

Makenna

"HAVE YOU GONE MAD?"

Makenna glared at the knight, who was gawking at the flower-starred meadow around them. To her, it looked very like the meadows in the northern woods they'd left behind . . . though she didn't recognize some of the flowers.

"Have you mislaid what's left of your tiny wits? Why in the Dark One's name did you come through? There are no other humans here! Do you have any idea how alone you'll be?"

He looked at her then, and she saw him check at least two replies before he finally said, "It was an impulse."

"An *impulse*?" Adrift in a new world, surrounded by frightened goblins who depended on her leadership, she couldn't scream and tear her hair. No matter how much she wanted to. "What a fine, sensible reason to go putting your life in danger, separating yourself from your family, from all you've ever—"

Annoyance dawned in his ordinary face. "My life was in

plenty of danger where we were. Maybe I came because I didn't want to be hanged for helping you and your goblins escape. Did you happen to think of that?"

"I told you what to say! You could have lied your way out of it."

"After all he's put us through, do you really think Master Lazur is that kind of fool?"

"No, but with us gone, he won't care enough to bother about something as unimportant as hanging you!"

"And you know him well enough to be sure of that?"

In truth, she was sure. The priest was a practical man, when all was said. Though others, the ones who weren't so practical themselves, might not have seen that as clearly as she had.

But if that was his reason, why hadn't the crazed lordling said so in the first place? An impulse. Bright Gods.

Makenna pressed her hands over her eyes and let it go.

"I don't have time to deal with this now. We need the Greeners to sort themselves into order and figure out what we can eat here. And we need someone to scout for water, and a good place to set up camp. Cogswhallop, you . . ."

Cogswhallop wasn't by her side.

"Cogswhallop . . . ?"

CHAPTER 2

Jeriah

JERIAH'S RESOLUTION HIT ITS FIRST setback almost immediately—Master Lazur refused to relent in his decision to
send Jeriah home. Jeriah argued as much as he dared, and
managed to get a few more details out of the priest. But the
dawn of the next morning saw him mounted, on the road to
the south.

It didn't matter. Impossible or not, he was going to rescue
Tobin and bring him back.

But before that, he had a promise to keep. A promise that
had taken him to this busy street in Brackenlee. At least it
wasn't out of his way.

"Excuse me, goodman. I'm trying to find a horse that
was sold here a few weeks ago. I have to buy him back. He
belongs . . . he belonged to my brother." Despite his resolve
to rescue his brother, Jeriah's voice faltered on the words.
When it came to heroic action, his record so far didn't
inspire much confidence. Not that the conspiracy's failure
had been his fault—it hadn't! But he still had to steady his

voice before he went on. "Can you tell me who might have bought him?"

"That'd likely be Lido, the blacksmith." The old man noted the past tense—sympathy softened his wrinkled face. "He buys and sells livestock. His forge is at the end of the street, off to the left. Don't you let him drive too hard a bargain, youngling . . . ah, sir."

"Thank you." At any other time Jeriah might have resented being called "youngling," but this morning he felt more like an old man than a fifteen-year-old. Jeriah clucked to Glory, and she picked her way down Brackenlee's busy main street. To go to Brackenlee and buy back his horse was the only thing Tobin had said, in that last frantic meeting, that made any sense. He'd babbled a lot about "please forgive me" and love, and how he'd explain when he got the chance.

At the time Jeriah had wanted answers to questions that mattered, like *Why are you helping the sorceress?* or even *How do you intend to get out of this without being hanged?*

Had Tobin always planned to escape into the Otherworld? He hadn't known he'd die there! Even the sorceress, curse her black heart, hadn't known. Two months before he started to die. A few weeks at the longest after that.

His brother's babbling about love and forgiveness didn't seem so irrelevant now.

To Jeriah's eyes, Brackenlee's wood-shingled buildings looked drably similar, but the thick smoke pouring from the smithy's chimney on this bright spring day made it easy to locate, and Fiddle's gray bulk stood out among the plow and riding horses in the corral. Jeriah's throat tightened again, but he managed to form Tobin's whistle. The gelding pricked his ears and trotted over, huffing in surprise when he saw it was Jeriah.

"Stupid horse." He reached out to stroke the soft gray muzzle.

"Can I help you, sir?"

The man's hair formed a spiky ring around his balding head, but muscle bulged in his shoulders.

"Goodman Lido? I want to buy this horse. How much?" The man's eyes narrowed at the noble accent, and Jeriah cursed himself for being so blunt. When he'd left home to enter Master Lazur's service, his father had given him twenty gold pieces and a small bag of silver and copper, and told him to make it last a year. He still had most of it, but . . .

"You've got a fine eye for horses, m'lord, a fine eye. Perfect conformation for a charger. And only four years old."

"He's too small," Jeriah pronounced. The horses his uncle bred were smaller than most, but they were swift, agile, loyal, sweet-tempered, and intelligent—for horses.

"He's no smaller than the lovely lady you're riding." The smith's eyes twinkled shrewdly. "And gentle as a lamb."

"Just be glad you were introduced to him," said Jeriah.

"Aye, he wouldn't let the stable boy near till I told him it was all right. But that's part of his perfect training! Why, he comes at a whistle . . . does a man know the right notes."

Jeriah gave up pretense. "He was my brother's horse. How much?" He wasn't going to leave without Fiddle, even if he had to steal him.

"Well, m'lord, seeing you're a brother . . . I might let him go for as little as thirty-five gold pieces."

"What! That's robbery! Ten."

It took a long time.

". . . sixteen, seventeen, eighteen." Jeriah counted aloud, dropping coins into the man's hand. "Will you put a halter on him, or do you charge for that too, you bandit?"

"Nay, I'll throw in the rope, and offer a free word as well. Watch out on the road, m'lord. There's real bandits out there, who'd risk a lot for a horse as fine as this. Not to mention your sweet lady." He stroked Glory's neck and she lipped at his arm, begging for a treat.

A brisk breeze shook the new leaves as Jeriah led Fiddle away from the village, and clouds were building for an afternoon rain. He couldn't return to Master Lazur until he had his father's permission, so Jeriah had to go home and get it—no matter how horrible it would be to tell his family what had happened to Tobin.

This had been his mother's scheme. How could Jeriah tell her it had gone so bitterly wrong? His father, even though he'd all but forbidden them to mention "the traitor's" name, had always loved Tobin best. His quiet older sister confided in Tobin when she wouldn't talk to anyone else, and his younger sister had loved him as much as she'd tormented him. The whole family was . . . better, when Tobin was there.

And not one of them would believe Jeriah was capable of bringing Tobin home safely. Could he even tell them about his plans? Probably not.

The prospect of telling his parents and sisters that Tobin would soon be dead was so horrible that Jeriah almost wished the smith's bandits would leap out and save him from it with a sword through the heart. Unfortunately, there wasn't much chance of that here. There were a few lawless bands in the war-torn Southlands, but they weren't likely to wander as far as the northern woods. The smith's "bandits" was probably some poor wretch who'd lost his job, and taken to robbing chicken coops.

And telling his family, no matter how much it would hurt, was the least of his problems. The first thing he had to do was get his hands on Master Lazur's spell notes—they'd probably contain some information about casting gates as well. If Master Lazur's spells could prevent her magic from being drained, the sorceress might be able to cast a gate to get them out of the Otherworld. As far as Jeriah knew, all the priests who'd been willing to fight the cadre that controlled the Landholders' Council had been executed when the conspiracy failed, and all the others were Master Lazur's allies.

Impossible . . . Fear of failure dragged at him, but Jeriah thrust it aside. He'd find someone to open the gate—because he had to, or there was no plan. So, assuming he could get into the Otherworld, he'd then need someone to help him find the sorceress and his brother. Someone who could guess where she might go. Someone who knew of a way, magical or otherwise, to locate her or her goblin . . . Goblins! Goblins might well be able to find their own kind. And goblins had magic! Perhaps they could even open a gate, if Jeriah could give them the spell.

He glanced around at the new-leafed trees, almost expecting to see goblins lurking there, in answer to his wish. Not a chance, these days. Before the Decree of Bright Magic passed, there were goblins in every wood and farm, but those who hadn't been driven out or slain avoided people now—and small blame to them. How could he convince the goblins to help him? How could he even get in touch with them?

Jeriah rode for almost a quarter mile, leading Fiddle and contemplating the question, before the answer struck him. He swore aloud and cantered back to town.

The smith was pumping the great bellows, coals glowing with each rush of air. He turned from the task as Jeriah rode up.

"Goodman Lido, who sold you this horse?"

"Why do you ask, m'lord? I've no reason to believe the beast was stolen." The smith's smile had vanished.

"He wasn't stolen, I just need to talk to the man who sold him. Please, who was it?"

"I'm not rightly sure I remember. You'll understand, I buy a lot of horses." The blacksmith edged toward the forge's door.

"Wait." Jeriah held out his hand, pleading. "By St. Spiratu the Truth Giver, I don't mean any harm to the man, or to you, or to anyone. I just want to talk to him."

"Well, if you mean no harm to honest folk, I *might* be able to remember . . ."

Gritting his teeth, Jeriah dug out two silver pieces and tossed them to the smith.

"Why, m'lord." Lido grinned. "I believe I do remember. It was Todder Yon, the tinker. He passes through here, oh, every six, nine months. He often sells horses or other stock. He gets 'em in trade, so I'd no reason to believe this one was stolen."

How often does a tinker get a knight's horse 'in trade'?

"I don't care about that. Where can I find this . . . Todder Yon?"

"That's the name, but as to where you can find him . . . Todder doesn't follow a regular route. This time he said he came from Wildford, so he's not likely to go that way. You might give Stockton a try, or Millford, or Bidlow."

"Thanks," Jeriah muttered. "I think."

The smith grinned. "Don't mention it, m'lord."

"No, sir, he's three weeks gone from here," said the plump serving maid. "But you might try Huddersfield, or Linksley, or Marbury. He doesn't have a regular route."

Jeriah groaned silently. He'd heard similar answers in every village, hamlet, and town for the past six days. Todder Yon was here last week, four days ago, hadn't been by since last autumn. Jeriah was spending silver as if his purse were bottomless, his clothes were no sooner dry than they got wet again, and he hadn't had a good night's sleep since the hunt began. He'd reached Millford just as the rain came on. When he learned the tinker wasn't there, the exhaustion of a sleepless night and a day of apprehension, both spent in the saddle, hit him like a jousting lance. He'd rented a room in Millford and tossed in the lumpy bed until dawn, then set off hopefully in search of the tinker—but he was no closer to finding him now than he'd been then. The man was elusive as a ghost!

"Will you be wanting a room, sir?" the girl asked. "We'd be happy to have you stay the night." She sounded quite enthusiastic about keeping him there, and her sidelong glace was flirtatious. "There's said to be bandits about, and it'll likely pour in an hour or two. You'd never make Huddersfield before it comes down."

"That doesn't matter." Jeriah, who'd inherited his mother's dark good looks, was accustomed to maids trying to flirt with him. Sometimes he flirted back, but now he had no time to spare. "I'm used to getting wet. Can you give me directions to Linksley?"

"Surely. Just take the west road out of town about a two hours' ride, and you'll see the Linksley road splitting off to the south. But Huddersfield is closer."

"I know." Jeriah dropped a silver piece into her outstretched palm. "I was there day before yesterday."

The rain began shortly after he turned onto the Linksley road. At least the maid's directions were better than some he'd tried to follow over the last few days.

The wind blew out of the south, pushing back his cloak and hood. Jeriah tucked the corners of the cloak between his legs and the saddle, but he had to hold the hood with his free hand to keep the rain out of his face. The hand that gripped the reins was already cold. He'd long since tied Fiddle's lead rope to Glory's saddle—fortunately, the well-mannered gelding gave him no trouble.

It was embarrassing, when you'd been dreaming all your life of knightly deeds, to discover that you couldn't track down a common tinker. Almost as embarrassing as learning that just being cold, wet, and tired all the time was enough to discourage you. Tristar of South Farring had tracked the evil Maroth all through the icy wasteland of the far north and never faltered. Jeriah had wanted to quit days ago.

Raindrops spattered his face and Jeriah pulled his hood lower. If he couldn't find a wandering tinker in his own world, how could he hope to find his brother in an entirely different one? He shook his head. These waves of self-doubt were becoming more frequent as days went by and Todder Yon continued to elude him, but he couldn't quit. If he quit, Tobin would die.

One step at a time, he told himself wearily. First the tinker, then the goblins, then the rest of it.

Branches rustled furiously as a man sprang out from behind a tree and seized Glory's bridle. She snorted and shied, and for a moment staying in the saddle demanded all of Jeriah's attention.

He dropped the reins and started to draw his sword, but hard hands clamped on his elbow. A cudgel struck his right shoulder, numbing his arm, and Jeriah yelped with the sudden pain.

There were five of them, all men, with ragged clothes and dark hair. *Bandits. Why didn't I listen?*

He kicked Glory, shouting for help. She tried to rear, but two men were hanging on to her bridle, and they knew what they were doing. Jeriah struggled to free his sword arm, and almost succeeded when Fiddle snapped his halter rope and spun to kick. But one man clung to Glory's saddle and grabbed Jeriah's wrist just as he got his hand on the hilt.

The bandits fought in silence. Jeriah would have shouted again if he hadn't been so busy gasping for breath. The thunder of his own heartbeat was louder than the thud of the horses' hooves.

A cudgel struck his ribs and pain leapt up his side. Someone grabbed Jeriah's belt and pulled; he'd have fallen if Glory hadn't spun.

But the men clinging to her bridle stayed with her, like dogs hanging on to a tugging rag. The man gripping Jeriah's sword arm stayed, and the rest closed in again.

A flash of regret almost broke through the panic that pounded through him. He couldn't afford to die. Not now!

A blow that could have broken his arm missed, smashing bruisingly into his thigh. Jeriah had come north as a priest's assistant—his armor was in a chest at home. His sword arm was pinned. Two men held Glory's head down so she couldn't fight, and Fiddle had run off. Another man grabbed Jeriah's leg and yanked his foot from the stirrups. Jeriah twisted his leg, trying to kick, but the man gripping his belt heaved, pulling him down.

Another blow smashed his shoulder; the pain was sickening. Hands shoved him, and he stumbled to his knees. He never saw the blow that struck his head, but lightning streaked across his vision and agony blotted out thought.

The lightning left darkness behind, but, slowly, his hearing returned.

". . . of you help me get this demon-cursed mare . . ." The man's voice grunted with effort.

Other voices replied, but Jeriah didn't understand what they said. Waves of pain washed through his head, but he couldn't die now. Someone rolled Jeriah over. His limbs flopped helplessly, and the surge of blackness almost sucked him down. He concentrated on the voices.

". . . only got a handful of silver," someone said. "But with what we've already got . . ."

A handful of silver. They were robbing him. Of course they were. Bandits.

". . . decent clothes . . . split up . . . mare's worth a lot more . . ."

Glory! They were stealing Glory! Jeriah did his level best to move then, to protest, but his body refused to obey and the pain in his head whited out sound for a time.

". . . get some land," one of them was saying when his hearing returned. "Far enough past the wall that those white demons will never reach us. Which reminds me, get his weapons too."

Hands fumbled at his belt, and another shaft of pain shot through Jeriah's head as his body rolled again. He wasn't aware of the sound he made till the hands searching his clothing froze.

"He's alive."

"Never said he wasn't," another voice replied. "I thought . . . take care of that while we dealt with the mare."

"But I can't just . . ."

"You said you'd take care of it."

"I thought you'd already done it!"

They sounded like brothers squabbling over who had to wash the dishes, and Jeriah wasn't even surprised when a firm voice interrupted.

"He's seen our faces. Finish him."

"Hey! In a fight, that's one thing, but I can't just . . ."

They were squabbling over his murder. Jeriah felt almost too horrible to care, but some of the argument penetrated anyway.

". . . Northers didn't save our . . . hang us in an instant if he identifies us."

"They'll be even more likely . . . What was that?"

The voice sharpened on the final words, and Jeriah frowned. There was something about their voices. An accent?

"They've spotted me!" a strange voice bellowed. "Get the troop up here! Now!"

That voice had no accent. How odd. Someone tripped over Jeriah and swore. Pounding steps. Pounding hoofbeats. The beat of pain in his head.

Jeriah slid gratefully into the darkness.

His first awareness was pain; sharp in his rib cage, an ache in his thigh. Jeriah's shoulder felt as if it might shatter if he moved. But all these pains were dwarfed by the agony in his head, which pounded all the way to his stomach with every beat of his pulse. His stomach fought back with an urgent wave of nausea, and Jeriah discovered that he could move after all—he rolled over and vomited.

As his stomach heaved itself dry, Jeriah became aware of hands holding his shoulders and a pan catching the contents of his stomach. A man's voice was speaking, though Jeriah was beyond paying attention to the words. When he finished, the hands eased him down. There was a pillow, thank the Bright Gods, beneath his aching head and blankets above and below him. But the surface under the blankets was hard and lumpy. Why was he lying on the ground?

Footsteps moved away, taking the acrid smell of vomit with them, and Jeriah caught another scent—the medicinal smell of the bitter tea his mother gave him for headaches and bruises. Demon's teeth, he had both!

Jeriah tried to open his eyes, but the sunset's golden light sent spikes of pain through his skull. He could hear movement, rattling metal. Then the steps approached, and a gentle hand lifted his head.

"Come on, lad, let's give it a try."

He sipped gingerly—the tea was stronger than any he remembered—but he kept it down, and the stranger showed no impatience. "Good, lad. That'll help."

When Jeriah turned away from the cup, the hands laid him down again and the footsteps moved away. He listened to the slosh of water, a few clanks, the rhythmic thunk of an ax in wood. The light on the other side of his eyelids was dimming. He really should try to see who it was. He was still thinking about it when he fell asleep.

The pain of rolling onto his sore shoulder woke him, and Jeriah opened his eyes before he had time to think. A large fire danced beside him, warding off the chill. The sky was dark, with stars glittering amid bits of drifting cloud.

On the other side of the fire a man leaned against a large pack. His hair showed more gray than brown, and fine lines creased the skin around his eyes. When he saw Jeriah looking at him, he rose and came to kneel at Jeriah's side. "So you've decided to join me. I'm glad to see it. For a while, I thought you might not! How's the head?"

"Better," said Jeriah. It still throbbed, but he could think and function. He raised his left hand, since his right shoulder hurt, and found a swollen lump above one ear.

"Aye, it's a nasty one. Look at me, lad." The man held up a finger and watched Jeriah's eyes track it. "You're seeing all right? Good. What's your name?"

"Jeriah Rovan. I was on my way to Linksley when they—Glory! Where's Glory?"

"If Glory's a pretty brown mare, she's tethered over there with the gray fellow."

Jeriah slowly turned his head in the direction the man pointed. Fiddle was watching them, but Glory stood with her head down, sleeping. There were no other horses. And where were the rest of his rescuers?

"Is the rest of your troop still chasing the bandits?" Jeriah must have been unconscious for hours. He was surprised the bandits could elude an armed troop this long. Though the stranger wasn't wearing the sunsguard red tabard, or any other kind of uniform.

"You were awake to hear that?" The man poured Jeriah a tin mug of healing tea. "Keep sipping on this. I didn't think you were conscious when I first showed up. In fact, if I hadn't heard them say otherwise I'd have thought you were dead! But as for my troop . . . you're looking at it."

Jeriah stared. "You're telling me that you drove off those bandits? There were five of them! And you're not—" He stopped, fearing to insult the old man, but the stranger was smiling.

"No, I'm not a knight. Or even a fighter, unless I have to be. I just fired a couple of crossbow bolts into the trees beside them, and started shouting for the rest of 'the troop' to come to my aid. And using that for a hand warmer won't do a thing for your headache." He gestured to the mug.

"They fell for that trick?" Jeriah wanted to laugh, but his head was throbbing. He took a cautious sip. Not too hot, and although his stomach complained, the tea stayed down.

"Why not?" the stranger asked comfortably. "They'd finished stripping you and were having a demonish time with the mare, so they were ready to give up."

"It was lucky you came along at the right moment."

"Ah . . . not exactly. I waited till I thought they'd be willing to leave before I tried it."

"You waited? You just sat there and watched them rob me?"

Jeriah started to sit up, but a pulse of pain in his head sent him back to the pillow in a hurry. The stranger's ruse no longer seemed funny.

"Timing is important in these things. And there were five of them. Speaking of timing, I'd give that tea a few more minutes to work before you get lively."

"You may be right about that." Jeriah still didn't care for the stranger's tactics, but there was no point arguing. "Besides, the smith in Brackenlee warned me there were bandits in the area. But I didn't believe him, so I wasn't paying enough attention." Which meant part of this was his own fault.

"I must admit," said the man, "I was surprised to see 'em myself. In the Southlands, that's something else, but this far north . . ." He shook his head. "What's the Realm coming to?"

A wisp of memory tickled Jeriah's aching brain.

"They were going to steal Glory."

"Aye, but they didn't," said the stranger soothingly. "You've no need to worry."

"No, it's not . . ." Jeriah pressed his hands to his head, trying to force the memory through. "They said something about a demon mare. . . ."

"I'm not surprised. She put up quite a fight."

"No." Jeriah gulped down the last of the tea, hoping it would help his head. "It was something else about demons. White demons."

A frown creased the man's brow. "White demons. Isn't that what Southlanders call the barbarians?"

Five ragged men, all with black hair. Had they also had the swarthy skin of Southlanders? Jeriah couldn't remember.

"Seemed to me," said the stranger, "that they were speaking with a bit of an accent. Wasn't one I placed, but my territory's here in the Northlands."

Had the men been speaking with a Southland accent?

Jeriah couldn't remember. "What would Southlander bandits be doing this far north?"

"I haven't heard of them spreading up this far, but . . ." The stranger picked up one of his pots and refilled Jeriah's cup. "Do you know about the surprise attack the barbarians made on the border last month?"

"I heard something about it." Jeriah blew on the tea, then sipped. Both his stomach and his head were beginning to settle.

"It was after our army had withdrawn for the summer," the man continued. "Being desert folk, the barbarians had never attacked in the hot season before. Thousands of Southlanders were driven out of their homes, all in one night, with no chance to take stock, or seed, or tools. They've nothing to start over with, and not much to lose. And they're the lucky ones! The only reason the barbarians take prisoners is so the meat won't spoil before they're ready to eat it."

Jeriah shuddered. In the army they said that a quick death by your own knife was better than capture by barbarians.

"Aye." The old man's face was sober. "It's bad. And if the lawlessness is spreading this far, soon no road in the Realm will be safe!"

"This one certainly wasn't," Jeriah said bitterly. "And I can't afford . . ." He didn't mind losing his silver. It was the delay that mattered.

"They were still cutting the packs off your saddle when I arrived," said the stranger, misunderstanding that unfinished sentence. "So anything you had on the horses you still have. I'm afraid what you carried is gone."

Jeriah glanced down at himself for the first time. He was dressed in an unfamiliar homespun tunic, worn to softness. He looked around but saw no sign of his belt, boots, or sword. Or purse. "My sword's the worst loss."

"Do you need money? I can lend you a bit to get on with."

"Could I sell you some spare tack instead?" Jeriah asked. "I didn't have much money left. At least now I won't have to tell Father that I spent the rest. How did you catch Glory? She doesn't let strangers handle her."

"It took a while, but once the gray fellow came back and she saw he trusted me, she decided I was all right."

"But he's trained the same way. He shouldn't have trusted you either!" Jeriah's eyes darted around—tin pots, tin cups and spoons. The big pack. Was it possible . . .

"Ah, but he and I had met before." The man nodded, confirming of Jeriah's dawning suspicion. "Yes, I'm Todder Yon. I understand you've been looking for me."

It couldn't be a coincidence. "How . . . ? What . . . ? Were you following me?" Jeriah demanded. His head was throbbing again.

"Aye. After hearing in three different towns that a young knight was trying to track me down, I got curious. So I came after you. What do you want of me, Jeriah Rovan? Not"—his eyes strayed to Fiddle—"that I can't guess."

The wrinkled face held nothing but kindness and sorrow, but Jeriah was suddenly aware that he had no sword, and his right arm was all but useless. If he had intended harm, he'd have been helpless to pursue it. A chill of wariness brushed him. This man was no fool.

"I need you to help me get in touch with some goblins." Jeriah rose carefully to his knees, leaning forward, though the movement made his whole bruised body ache. "I need their help. It's a matter of life and death."

"Lad, the goblins aren't dealing with humans these days. I hope it's not really a matter of life and death, because if it is, you've got a problem."

Jeriah clutched his throbbing head in both hands. How to persuade this man?

The tinker sighed. "Lie down. You getting sick won't save anyone."

Jeriah stiffened his spine and remained upright. The tinker's expression was quietly unyielding, but he'd been kind to Jeriah. Surely if he knew the truth . . . Would he want the truth? Maybe enough to trade for it?

"You were a friend of hers, weren't you? The sorceress?"

"Mistress Makenna? The one who's been condemned to death? And whose accomplices they might hang too, just on principle? Certainly not."

Jeriah gritted his teeth. "All right. If you had been her friend. Or if you were her enemy. Or even if you only traded gossip in the villages around here, would the truth about what happened to her be worth something to you?"

"I've heard rumors in half a dozen towns that she and her goblins have vanished," the tinker admitted. "Half a dozen different rumors."

"I saw them disappear with my own eyes."

The tinker snorted. "And how did that come about? If you're going to make up tales, you should at least make them plausible."

"I came north as Master Lazur's assistant," Jeriah told him.

"Oh, then I'll certainly trust you."

"You can," said Jeriah grimly, "because when she vanished, she took my brother with her. And if I don't get him out of the Otherworld in two months, he's going to get sick and die."

Less than two months, now. He shivered.

The tinker was frowning. "Still, Lazur's assistant . . ."

"It was . . . a new position for me," Jeriah told him. And not entirely voluntary, but he had no intention of sharing that with a stranger.

"Hmm. Maybe we can trade a thing or two," said Todder Yon slowly. "The true tale of what happened to the sorceress and her goblins, that'd be of some value in the towns I visit. That's my only interest, mind."

Jeriah nodded eagerly. "And in exchange, you'll put me in touch with the goblins?"

"I told you, they're not inclined to trust any human these

days—including me! I'll give you as fair an exchange for your information as I can, but I make no promises as to what the goblins will do! In fact, I doubt you'll ever see a sign of them."

It wasn't much, but it was more than Jeriah had now and the story cost him nothing. Not even time, for it would be at least another day before he could ride.

"I can only tell you what happened from my point of view," Jeriah warned him. "And there's plenty I don't know! The first I heard of the sorceress was when Tobin was sent into the north, several months ago, to help Master Lazur capture her and destroy her goblin army."

"Getting rid of a sorceress and a whole goblin army seems quite a task for one lone knight and a priest! If you don't tell me the truth, the whole deal's off."

"It is true! Tobin wasn't supposed to get rid of them by himself. His part was to allow the goblins to capture him, so their camp could be located. Master Lazur brought a whole village of settlers, and several troops of the church's guard, into the wood to actually capture the sorceress and wipe out her army. I came north with them."

"So your brother, he got himself captured and then betrayed them?" The tinker's face had hardened.

"She was delaying the relocation," said Jeriah firmly. "And since the barbarians just captured over half the Southlands, no one can deny that Master Lazur is right about that! Tobin was a hero! At least he should have been. It went perfectly, all according to plan, but then he went crazy! We had captured the sorceress, holding her in charmed iron so the goblins couldn't free her, but Tobin sneaked into camp and got her out. And I don't understand that at all! He acted like he knew what he was doing, but the goblins bespelled me to get them into Master Lazur's tent. Could the sorceress have bespelled Tobin as well?"

"I doubt it," the tinker said dryly. "Spells that can compel a person against their conscious will are difficult to cast, and very hard to maintain for more than a few minutes. Even for a hedgewitch, Makenna didn't have much magical ability. It's more likely that your brother found destroying 'the goblin army' more than he'd bargained for."

"I saw hundreds, maybe thousands, going into the Otherworld," said Jeriah defensively. "So I don't think Master Lazur put much of a dent in their numbers."

"I heard she'd cast a gate." The tinker's voice was soft with wonder. "I thought it had to be a tale. Are you sure . . . ?"

"There was a big shimmery patch of light across the road," Jeriah told him. "And when people stepped into it, they vanished. Master Lazur said it was a gate to the Otherworld. And I don't think he was lying."

"But the legends say that only the saints themselves have the power to do that!"

"Master Lazur told me she drained magic out of the great wall," Jeriah told him. "A power sink, he called it."

A smile lit the tinker's face. "How fitting. That wall was

originally built and charmed, all those centuries ago, to keep the goblins behind it. It was the church's first attempt to rid the Realm of them. You'd think they'd learn, wouldn't you?"

"That doesn't matter," said Jeriah. "It's now—"

"Seeing as how you want to talk to some goblins, I'd say it matters a lot!"

"I don't *want* to talk to them," Jeriah corrected him. "I don't have a choice."

"Seems to me," Todder said slowly, "that your brother went of his own will. And finding him once you get to the Otherworld is the least of your worries. Or at least the last. How—"

"I'll take care of the rest of it," Jeriah interrupted. "But I need your help if I'm going to find the goblins in time. Can't you just take me to the ones who knew her best? For Tobin's sake?"

He was begging now, but he didn't care.

"You're not thinking, lad. By your own account, the goblins who knew her best went with her."

"Surely some of them were left behind!"

"That might be, particularly if they left in as big a rush as you said. And some may not have wanted to go—they're independent little creatures. Makenna's the only person I've ever heard of who's organized and led them."

Seeing the respect in Todder's face, it occurred to Jeriah that the tinker might not be quite as helpful as he sounded. He obviously cared about the sorceress. Why should he trust

Jeriah, after all? He took a deep breath and forced himself to let it out slowly.

"If you worked with her, you must have known her goblin allies pretty well."

"Not really. In fact, the only goblin I saw more than once was Cogswhallop, who was her second-in-command. The only thing they needed me for was to deal with other humans, to sell things for them"—he gestured at Fiddle—"and buy the things they couldn't make."

"So how did you contact them?"

"That was easy. All you had to do was pass the wall and they'd contact you. But your Master Lazur went and changed that. The Goblin Wood is probably the worst place in the Realm to look for goblins right now."

"Then how can I contact them?" Jeriah demanded. "Much less find one who knew the sorceress?"

Todder shook his head. "I can't make you any promises about the first part, but if you can talk to one of them, you can send word to the rest. The lass could get news from any corner of the Realm if the goblins knew it, and the Hierarch's messages traveled slower than hers. As for how to contact them, my best suggestion is to use the traditional method."

"What's that?" Jeriah asked.

"You put out a bowl of milk."

"That's it?" Jeriah stared. "That's your best suggestion?"

The tinker's face was grave, but his eyes twinkled. "The

good news is that it doesn't matter where you try it—there are goblins everywhere."

"But—"

"I'm sorry about your brother, but that's all the advice I have to offer. I warned you it wouldn't be much." The humor had vanished from the tinker's face. And he'd made no promises. Jeriah was on his own. But at least there were goblins elsewhere in the Realm, and if he could contact them anywhere . . .

"Then I might as well go . . . home. Oh, Gods."

Todder Yon was too kind to laugh.

Tobin

TOBIN WAS CROSSING THE MEADOW to report to Makenna when he met Firka coming up the path. The goblin woman carried two human-size mugs of tea.

"She's not stopped for a minute, much less a bite, since breakfast." Firka sighed. "But you might as well drink yours. And don't go telling me how busy you are, because I don't care!"

"Give me her mug," Tobin said. "I'll get her to drink it."

It had delighted him, over the past week, watching the subtle way the goblins took care of Makenna—and she needed it!

They hadn't been in the Otherworld for a full day when she'd announced that if this place was habitable, she was going to find a way to open some gates and invite every goblin in the Realm in to join them. A whole empty world for the goblins' sanctuary.

It gave the grieving goblins hope, for many of them had left parents, siblings, and close friends behind. It comforted

Tobin too—and he knew how precarious that promise was. He had watched her creep out of the lean-to they shared to read Master Lazur's spell books by moonlight.

She was too busy to read them during the day.

The goblin Makers who were laying out the new village sat with her now. The plan for the new village had been marked on a large stretch of smooth sand, since they had no paper to spare. Thadda, the best of the goblin Weavers, was waiting for the planning session to end, her apron full of some new plant fluff.

Tobin came up behind Makenna and looked over her shoulder at the drawing. It would be a big village, with plenty of room to grow. Someday it might grow into a goblin city, but for now . . .

"Just the houses we need," Makenna was saying. "We'll sit through at least one winter, make sure they're not too severe, before we bring others in, so guest shelters can wait. The Greeners say they can get two harvests in before the cold comes, so shelter and food storage are the first priorities. I only want to make sure we're laying things out with the future in mind, so that we won't find ourselves tearing houses down in order to build mills next year."

"Then I think we're ready to start," the Maker told her, rising to his feet. "I'll give Master Tobin his turn now." He nodded politely and departed.

Makenna looked up at Tobin. "You're finally back? You'll have to wait a bit, for Thadda's . . ."

Thadda had noticed the tea mugs in Tobin's hands and disappeared some time ago.

"She's been waiting to talk to me for half a hour!" Makenna started to her feet to go look for the Weaver.

Tobin handed her a mug and sat down on a rock beside the village map. "She won't come back till you've finished, so you might as well drink it. They're right, you know. You work too hard."

"I'm not working hard enough." But she sat down and sipped the tea. "We're all assuming that the seasons in this world are like the ones we're used to, but what if instead of having all summer before us, we find winter sets in next month?"

"Then working yourself into the ground won't have done any good, because the crops are growing as fast as the Greeners can make them. And if the seasons are the same length as back home . . . working yourself into the ground still won't have done any good. I was raised on a country estate. You can't rush the ripening of crops. Or much of anything, really."

She cast him an amused glance. "I was raised in a war, where rushing a march can get you to the perfect site in time to ambush your enemy. And win because of it."

"Not if your enemy is winter, and it's your harvest doing the marching."

She'd leaned back against the rock behind her and was sipping her tea. Relaxed, for once. Thadda would be proud of him.

"You took longer than I expected, checking out that bog," she said. "Did you find something?"

"No danger of any kind," Tobin told her. "And the Greeners found a root that tastes almost like a potato. We've all been eating them, and none of us have died yet, so you can add one more item to the things-we-can-eat list."

"I hope it tastes better than some of the others," Makenna said. "Nothing dangerous?"

"Not a thing," Tobin repeated.

"If there was, if some swamp monster rose out of the muck and gnawed on your bones, it would be your own fault, anyway. You're the one who insisted on coming along."

"All my fault," Tobin agreed, and suppressed a smile when she scowled at him.

She had stopped asking why he'd come through the gate, but she kept throwing out those hinting jabs.

Tobin wasn't sure she'd ever figure it out, and he enjoyed keeping her guessing. She was a bit too compulsive in her desire to know everything, to control every aspect of this new world. It made her a great general—but his job was to keep her human, as well.

He hid another smile and sipped his tea.

CHAPTER 3

Jeriah

HOME. IT WAS LATE AFTERNOON when Jeriah pulled Glory to a stop at the top of the hill, gazing over the patchwork of scattered trees and greening fields that nestled in the curve of the Abo River. On a rise several miles to the south stood the mellow stone square that was Rovan Manor. Tobin, the heir, had loved this view, even in winter. Even in the early spring, when the fields showed nothing but mud. Even in the rain, he'd sit here. The memory held more amusement than grief. Jeriah refused to think of his brother as dead, or going to die; Tobin was merely missing, in need of rescue.

It was going to be ghastly, letting his family think Tobin was truly gone. But if he told them his plans, first his father would forbid him to risk it. "You're my only living son. You have no right to take that chance." Then Tami would insist on going with him, and Senna would criticize his tactics. Jeriah's lips twitched—maybe that was why the knights of legend always worked alone. Only his mother could be counted on for practical advice.

He lifted the reins, and Glory started down the hill, scenting her barn and the journey's end.

Jeriah was riding into one of the scattered groves when the sound of cantering hoofbeats reached his ears. His hand went to the knife Todder had traded him. Jeriah had encountered several bands of refugees in the ten days it had taken him to get home. Ten days, pushing the horses as hard as he dared. Over a quarter of Tobin's two months was gone—but he couldn't return to Master Lazur until he got his father's permission. The ragged refugees he'd met hadn't delayed him, but Jeriah had learned the hard way that he might not always be so lucky.

It was only his father who rode around the bend. *Only his father?* Considering the news he carried, Jeriah would rather have faced bandits.

"Jeriah, what brings—" Then his father recognized Fiddle, and his open expression hardened. His horse's legs were muddy, and his boots even muddier. He must have been out in the fields and seen Jeriah lingering on the hilltop.

The old man rode up and pulled his horse to a stop. The lines around his mouth looked as if they'd been carved with a chisel. His eyes traveled from Fiddle to his second son's face. "Dead?"

"Well . . . ah . . . he's gone. No, I don't mean—"

"Don't dance with it. Is he dead?" That clipped voice had always reduced Jeriah to incoherence.

"It's not that simple." As clearly as he could, Jeriah

explained how Tobin had followed the sorceress, and what Master Lazur had told him about the Otherworld. The lines in his father's face grew deeper, but he showed no other sign of grief. Jeriah was beginning to wonder if the old man was made of stone—Tobin was his favorite—when he saw that his father's hands, tight on the reins, were shaking. His voice dried up and stopped.

"Perhaps it's for the best." His father's voice roughened and he cleared his throat before he continued. "He was a traitor. Now that can be forgotten—at least by some. Will you break the news to your mother and sisters? Or would you rather I do it?"

Jeriah would a thousand times rather have had his father do this, but . . . "I saw what happened. They'll want to hear it. I think I have to. For Tobin's sake."

He owed his family that much, at least.

Air rushed into his father's lungs—had he dreaded that task as much as Jeriah did?

"In that case . . . there are things I still need to do today. Will you need me for this?"

Jeriah stared. It might be easier for him to lie to his mother and sisters without his father looking on, but . . .

"Don't you want to be there? I mean, isn't it your . . . ?"

Responsibility.

"Necessary work doesn't stop, even for death." The words were hard, but the trembling in his father's hands had spread to his voice.

Jeriah couldn't remember his father shirking any responsibility, no matter how painful. Seeing him try to avoid this one told Jeriah exactly how much the news of Tobin's death had hurt.

He couldn't do this to his family. The price of this lie was too high.

"Father, there's—"

"Work." The old man's face started to twist, the stone shattering. He spun his horse and cantered off.

"—something I have to tell you," Jeriah finished, gazing at the empty road.

When he'd last come home—was it only a few months ago?—he'd planned to tell his father the truth, send him to get Tobin out of trouble, and then flee for his life. Had he met his father on the road that day, it would probably have happened just like that. Instead, Jeriah had seen his mother first.

His mouth tightened as he remembered waking in the locked attic, dizzy, disoriented, his mouth thick with the metallic taste of the drug she'd put in his tea. He remembered his fury and alarm when the girls told him, through the crack beneath the door where they pushed in bread, cheese, and nearly empty waterskins, that his mother intended that Tobin would continue to take Jeriah's place, and his punishment. "Because the courts let heirs off much more lightly. You know that."

It was true, but the thought of Tobin paying for his

mistakes was intolerable. Jeriah had twisted the hinge off a trunk and filed away the wood around the latch till he could break down the door, but it had taken days.

By the time he'd reached the city, he'd been too late to do anything except pick Tobin up, in the field where the guard had dumped his unconscious body, and clean and treat his lacerated back.

Jeriah's hands clenched on the reins, then loosened as he remembered Tobin trying not to laugh when Jeriah told him how Mother had drugged his tea. He'd made Jeriah promise to get the drugs away from her, and that wouldn't be easy.

Jeriah wanted to tell their father the whole story, but Tobin begged him not to. A priest Mother knew had offered Tobin a chance to redeem himself, to win back his rank and honor. All he had to do was lead Master Lazur to the lair of a sorceress.

. . . I'm not a hero. I'll be careful, and I'll come back. I promise . . .

But Tobin hadn't been careful, and he was going to need help getting back. Jeriah's father would never allow his only remaining heir to go adventuring in the Otherworld. If Jeriah didn't lie to his family, Tobin would die, so he had to lie, no matter how much it hurt. Anything to bring Tobin home.

Once Tobin was back, none of it would matter. He would tell his father the whole truth as soon as his brother was safe.

He rode into the courtyard, wincing at the curiosity and alarm on the faces of the grooms who took the riderless

Fiddle. It wasn't only because Tobin was the heir; the servants loved him for his own sake.

Jeriah climbed the worn stairs, dread slowing his steps. The huge doors opened before he reached them and Tamilee catapulted into his arms, all knobby elbows and flying ginger hair.

"Jeriah, Jeriah, how long can you stay? Is Tobin with you? Did you beat the barbarian goblins?" Ten-year-old Tami had a hard time keeping his mother's complex schemes straight.

Sennahra had followed Tami into the hall, her serious face lit with a smile that almost made her pretty, but it began to fade the moment she saw Jeriah's expression. "What is it? What's wrong?"

Tami looked at him more closely then, her thin body tensing. "Is something wrong?"

Freckles stood out against Senna's suddenly pale skin. "Tobin?"

Jeriah knew that even as she asked, she was waiting for him to deny it. Willing him to deny it, her fear growing as the silence stretched.

He couldn't do this, he couldn't. . . .

If he didn't, Tobin would die. For real.

"I'm so sorry," Jeriah whispered. "So sorry. Tobin . . . he's gone."

His mother knew the moment she saw his face. Senna had taken them all up to the solarium. His mother sat on a bench between two tall windows, a basket of thread in her lap, and Jeriah saw her expression change even before Tamilee burst through the door and threw herself into her mother's arms, sobbing with childish abandon.

"Tobin." His mother was so pale, Jeriah feared she might faint, and for the first time in his memory she said nothing more, only stroking Tami's hair as Jeriah repeated the same story he'd told his father. It was no easier the second time, and he wondered how many times he'd have to repeat it.

Their grief waked his own, constricting his throat till his voice husked into silence.

Tami was the one who broke it. "Will it hurt? When Tobin gets sick?"

Jeriah flinched. "No," he said firmly. This was one lie he had no trouble telling. "He'll just get tired, then he'll fall asleep."

Would the life-draining effect of the Otherworld hurt his brother? Jeriah had no idea, but from what the priest had said, it didn't begin immediately, and he intended to get Tobin out long before he fell ill, so it wouldn't matter.

"He won't be hurt. I promise."

His mother's face was wet with tears, but her voice hardly quavered as she finally spoke. "Senna, dear one, will you take care of Tami for a while? Can you manage?"

Sennahra's swollen eyes sharpened. She knew that note in her mother's voice as well as Jeriah did, but she pulled Tami gently from her mother's arms and led her toward the door without protest. Senna been born between Tobin and Jeriah, but she sometimes seemed older than both her brothers.

Jeriah took a deep breath and turned to face his mother. She was going to be harder to lie to than Tamilee. In fact, he wasn't sure if he should lie to her—sometimes his mother had ideas. Her eyes were as red as Senna's now, but not even weeping diminished her dark loveliness.

"Mother, I'm sorry."

"*You're* sorry." She pulled out a kerchief and blew her nose. "I don't know what you have to be sorry for since it was *my* scheme from the beginning. I meant for him to redeem himself, not get lost, but since he has, we shall simply have to get him back! He's not dead now, and he won't be for over a month, so we've plenty of time. And I don't know why I'm crying in this absurd way. I *never* cry, unless I can use it to get something I want."

Jeriah began to laugh, and she wiped her face firmly and put the kerchief away.

"I knew I could count on you," Jeriah told her. "You never give up."

"Well, I should think so. Giving up would get me nothing but a dead son. And"—her voice quivered—"I couldn't bear to have *him* dead, any more than I could let *you* die. Why don't we follow him into this . . . this Otherworld and bring him back?"

"There are problems with that." His mother paid close attention as Jeriah repeated everything Master Lazur had told him about the Otherworld. She was calm but her face was still pale, so he made her a cup of tea. And one for himself—Jeriah had resolved to never let her make tea for him again. He didn't tell her his plans; she might come up with a better idea on her own. And she, of all his family, knew how to lie. She was silent for a time when he finished.

"It's complicated, isn't it?" she said thoughtfully. "Clearly, the first thing we need is magical help, not only to open this gate thing, but also to find Tobin once you get in."

"Yes, I'd realized that. I don't suppose you know anyone who can work that kind of magic."

"Of course, dear one, and so do you. I'm surprised you didn't think of it, for Timeon admitted he was an expert on gates."

"Tim—"

"Timeon Lazur." She smiled, the first time she'd done so since Jeriah came in. "I've known him for years. He was an ambitious young priest when I was lady's maid to the Hierarch's mother."

This was one notion Jeriah had to dispel. "Master Lazur won't help. He wants to keep the sorceress and the goblins in the Otherworld. He won't open a gate, or permit anyone else to do it. He wouldn't even tell me where he's stored the spell notes that could keep Tobin alive."

"Then he'll have to change his mind. I'll take care of that—all you need to do is be ready to go after Tobin when I've set it up. In fact, I'll write to Timeon right now. If he's going to be stubborn, this may take some time, and we don't have much to spare."

"You're not listening. He won't—"

"He told *you* he wouldn't. But Timeon Lazur can always be persuaded . . . or pressured, if need be." She paused on the way to her writing desk and patted his shoulder. "You just have to know his weakness."

"What weakness?" Jeriah asked nervously. Confiding in his mother had seemed like a good idea a few minutes ago, but now . . .

"You know the answer to that already, dear one," his mother said. "What's the one thing Timeon cares about more than anything else in the world?"

Jeriah's alarm grew. "The relocation. But how can you use that—"

She rose and went to her desk, picking up a quill. "You can leave that to me. Although it may take some . . . Hmm. Never mind. I'll manage."

Jeriah shivered. His mother had always preferred to keep her schemes to herself—some were even good schemes. She was beautiful, clever, and ruthless. But Master Lazur was more clever, much more ruthless, and beauty didn't matter to him.

On the other hand, matching wits with his mother might keep the priest from noticing what Jeriah was up to.

Thank the Bright Gods he hadn't told her about his plans.

"Very well. I'm glad you can persuade him—I had no idea who I could find to open a gate for me."

"Don't worry." She was already writing. "I can handle Timeon."

Jeriah doubted it. "That's settled then. But what are we going to tell Father?"

The quick pen paused. "We'd better not tell him anything. He's a very good man, but sometimes, in matters like this, it doesn't work out well if one is *too* good. Besides, I'm afraid he might not entirely understand the situation."

"He never does," said Jeriah wearily.

"Well, dear one, it's a little unreasonable to expect him to understand, when you consider that you and I and Tobin have all been lying to him from the very *start*."

She returned to her letter, and Jeriah went to his own room. He asked one of the maids to send up a meal, claiming he wanted to go to bed early since he was tired from the long ride. He was tired, but he wanted to make contact with the goblins as soon as he could.

The woman accepted his request without a blink, though four in the afternoon was far too early for bed. His father had chosen to be alone with his grief, and Senna was probably avoiding everyone right now.

His meal finished, Jeriah lay tossing on his bed, but eventually the fatigue of the journey caught up with him and he dozed. A good thing, too. He had plans for tonight.

Jeriah crept down the stairs, automatically avoiding the second and seventh steps, which creaked. He wondered if every child who grew up in this house learned that trick. Tobin had shown him the noisy steps when he was very young—though Jeriah had come up with most of the pranks that made the knowledge useful.

The banked embers in the big hearth provided enough light for Jeriah to find his way around the kitchen. He took a large bowl and filled it from a jar in the pantry, where the milk had been left for the cream to rise. He hoped none of the servants would be blamed for the theft, but the cows were let out to graze at night, and it would take too long to catch and milk one.

How long would it take the goblins to discover the bowl?

Jeriah carried the milk out to the vegetable garden behind the house and set it near some bushes.

The night was crisp and still. Jeriah started to shiver, even as the quiet soothed him. He thought about returning to the house for his cloak but decided against it—the goblins might come while he was gone. Besides, the chill would keep him awake.

The gardener's shed he'd chosen for his hideout held a pile of empty sacks. Jeriah dumped several on the floor and wrapped another around his shoulders. Then he propped the door open so he could see the bowl. He sat down on the sacks to wait.

As the night grew colder, Jeriah was forced to use more of

the sacks to cover himself so the goblins wouldn't be warned away by his chattering teeth. Clouds drifted over the moon, leaving the bowl in shadow. A rabbit hopped into the lettuce bed, nibbled for a time, and departed.

Jeriah's mood passed from anticipation to boredom to weary resignation. He had napped that afternoon, so he was surprised when a wave of drowsiness washed over him. He yawned and leaned his head against the wall, just for a moment.

He woke with a start and lay blinking. A rooster crowed—that was what had roused him. Why was he lying on a pile of sacks? Memory returned, and he sat up and looked out. Dawn light spilled through the garden. Even at this distance, he could see that the bowl was empty.

"Dung!"

They'd bespelled him! Those cursed goblins had bespelled him again, and this whole night had been wasted. But at least they'd found the milk, so he supposed he had made contact, after a fashion. Tomorrow night he'd speak to them. Jeriah rubbed his face, and the blanket slid from his shoulders. Blanket?

It was a horse blanket from the stables—wool, which was why he wasn't freezing. But Jeriah hadn't brought it. And he certainly hadn't brought the cushion from his mother's solarium.

Jeriah had heard the old stories, that if you did favors for the goblins they'd repay you, but he'd written them off as nursery tales.

"Repay you with spells and deceit!" He said it aloud, in case some goblin was listening. Never mind. Tomorrow he'd be ready for them.

He got the blanket back to the stable without waking the grooms, but the cook's helper almost caught him replacing the hastily rinsed bowl. At least putting the pillow back wasn't a problem—his mother wouldn't be up for hours.

Jeriah stripped out of his tunic and crawled into his own bed, grateful for the softness of his mattress after a night on the rough sacks. He was just dozing off when his father knocked on the door.

Makenna

". . . ARE THE ONLY WILLOWS growing anywhere near us . . ."

". . . potato roots not only taste good, they're good for . . ."

". . . if you go disturbing their ground, willows won't . . ."

". . . those potato roots grow fast, too! They're . . ."

Makenna drew in a breath to shout down the whole mob, but before she could speak . . .

"Be quiet, all of you. Mistress Makenna can't hear if you're talking at the same time."

Makenna stared. She hadn't known the lordling could produce that commanding voice. He hadn't even raised it, but the squabbling goblins fell silent as he came forward and knelt between the Greeners, who wanted to plant potato roots in the stream's marshy bend, and the Makers, who wanted to use the willows growing there for baskets.

She felt a tug on her britches, and looked down into the lumpy gray face of Harcu, the chief Stoner. "Rock funny," his deep voice rumbled. "Not right."

Makenna sighed. "I'm sure it's not. Nothing else seems to be. But you're going to have to wait your turn."

"One at a time," Tobin added firmly.

Cogswhallop would have threatened to crack a few heads to emphasize the order, but Cogswhallop wasn't there—and his absence was like a cut still seeping blood.

No one knew what had kept her small lieutenant from following her through the gate, though the absence of his family was a pretty good clue. He'd been right beside her, organizing the frantic exodus as she cast the gate spell. He'd been at her side for the last six years.

Some thought they'd been captured by the soldiers, but Makenna didn't believe it. Cogswhallop was more than a match for Lazur and all his men—even Daroo was. No, Cogswhallop was safe in the Realm—no doubt working to rejoin her, just as she was trying to figure out how to open a gate to reach him.

But in the meanwhile, Tobin was doing a pretty good job of taking his place.

Makenna had assigned Miggy as her second-in-command. He was slowly growing comfortable in the role when things were peaceful, but he wasn't happy about it when trouble broke out. And that was when Tobin took up the slack.

A small, petty part of her resented a human stepping into Cogswhallop's shoes . . . but the rest of her was deeply grateful that he did it so well.

"Harcu," she said, "if the rock here's not right, then you'll either have to make do or get good rock somewhere else, because those foundations need to go in. You're doing a fine job. I don't want you stopping now. As for the rest of you"— she glared at all of them, impartially—"one reason we settled here was because we didn't want a lot of marsh nearby. Food is a priority."

The Greeners smirked.

"Food won't do you much good," one of the Makers snapped, "if you don't have baskets to store it in. What are you going to do when all that grain you're planting is ready to harvest? Put it in your pockets? We—"

"We need baskets too," Makenna agreed. "And willows can't be grown in a minute. So like it or not, you're all going to share that marsh. The Greeners will plant as near to the willows as they can without disturbing them, but they'll leave paths through their root beds so the Makers can harvest the willows. And the Makers will stay on those paths! That way . . ."

CHAPTER 4

Jeriah

"SEE THESE ROOTS?" HIS FATHER held out a young corn-stalk, roots attached. "White and firm, like they should be. Last year we had too much water in this field and lost half the crop. The first sign of the problem was in the roots. You can't just pay attention to the part of the plant you can see—you have to . . ."

Jeriah's father had been going on like that all morning. He yawned.

"Am I boring you, Jeriah?"

His mouth snapped shut. "No, sir. It's just . . . I'm sorry, I didn't get much sleep last night."

His father's lips tightened, deepening the lines around his mouth. "*I'm* sorry, son. I shouldn't have . . . I didn't get much sleep either." He knelt to replant the corn sprout, hiding his face.

The speed with which his father had set about training his new heir would have hurt, if his grief for Tobin hadn't showed so clearly. Jeriah's father had always considered

63

him . . . not incompetent, not really. Just lightweight. Not to be taken seriously. Unreliable, compared to his sensible older brother. Since Jeriah didn't want the estate, that suited him fine. But until Tobin came back he was stuck with it, so he might as well do his best.

"Um, why did you let so much water into this field? I thought old Woder measured inflow to the last drop." He gestured at the gate in the low dike that held back the river. His great-great-grandfather had married a woman from the wetlands and built the dikes and gates, creating acres of fertile land in what used to be the river's flood plain.

"We were trying to water this field with a ditch from the next gate down. We still are, in fact, and judging by these roots we're doing better this year. Come with me and I'll show you why. This is something you should know about."

His father strode off toward the nearest sluice gate and Jeriah followed, slipping in the muddy furrows.

"Look at the wood of this gate, Jeriah. What do you see?"

"Well . . ." He examined it, fishing for an answer. "It's damp. It's . . . Wait a minute. It shouldn't be that wet. It's rotting on the other side, isn't it?"

"Exactly." His father eyed him with satisfaction, and Jeriah felt a flicker of pride. It was the first question he'd answered right.

"It's not just the gate," his father went on. "There's also seepage through the dike. See here?" He led Jeriah to a mud puddle twenty feet from the gate. To Jeriah it looked like all the other puddles he'd seen that morning. *If you can't make an intelligent comment, ask a question.*

"Is it dangerous, sir?" He gestured to a cluster of cottages in the midst of the low fields. As their campfire had burned low, Todder Yon had told Jeriah something of the sorceress' history—including the tale of how she'd flooded her own village.

"Of course it's dangerous," his father said. "Oh, not to people's lives or I'd evacuate the place. The houses are higher than they look—even if the whole dike gave way, there'd only be a few feet of water over the floors of the lowest buildings. And that's now, with the river at full flow. The higher buildings would be left on an island, but the tenants could wade ashore. The fields would be lost, though, along with the crops they're carrying."

"But why haven't you . . . ah, I thought winter was the best time to repair dikes."

"It is." An expression that held both pain and pride swept over his father's face. "And I'd have done it, except Master Averas has told us that we'll have to leave this land forever next spring. The spring after that at the latest. I am ordered to move all my people into the north."

He started back to the horses, with his son slogging behind. "Jeriah, I've been meaning to ask you . . ." The hesitation was so unlike his father that it captured Jeriah's attention.

"Sir?"

"The Hierarch is the Sunlord, chosen of the Seven Bright Gods, but the priests who serve him are only men. I've been wondering . . . You fought the desert barbarians yourself, last winter, and you've always had a mind of your own. Do *you* think this relocation is necessary?"

Jeriah had never actually fought the barbarians. He'd only patrolled with a troop for several months before the conspirators had recruited him. But he'd heard the stories of howling mobs, white as ghosts, swarming out of the flying sand. Of the gutted remains of Southland farms. Of human bones in the refuse heaps of barbarian camps. Some of those stories had come from his brother. "Yes, sir. It has to be."

"Ah." His father's shoulders slumped, then straightened again. "Well, that's the other reason I didn't repair the dike. Before we leave, I'm going to open all the gates and flood the land. They'll get nothing I can keep from them."

His father might be short on forgiveness, but he'd never lacked courage. This probably wasn't the best time, but Jeriah didn't have a lot of time.

"Master Lazur gave me leave for a month, but with the problems involved in the relocation, everyone is needed. I was wondering if I could return sooner."

His father frowned. "I think you should leave Master Lazur's service. You're my heir now—and through no fault of your own, you haven't been trained to run the estate. I should have taught you along with Tob— your brother, but you weren't interested in farming and . . . Well, you have a lot of catching up to do."

Not if I can help it. "There'll be time for me to learn all those things when we're resettled in the north. Besides, I think the woodland soil is different. Half of what you're teaching me might be useless there." He saw his father's lips tighten and continued hastily. "Serving the Hierarch and the Realm is what I *am* trained for. I'd like to do it, at least till this crisis is past."

His father sighed. "I'll think about it."

Jeriah knew better than to press, and they mounted the horses and rode on in silence. His father noticed every bug, on every leaf, in every field. Jeriah could barely tell the wheat sprouts from the potatoes. Demon's teeth! He hadn't been trained for this. It was Tobin who loved the land, who cared which worms ate the barley. Jeriah had dreamed of serving the Realm, of doing something brave and worthy. Now Tobin, who'd wanted to stay home and plant crops, was a hero, and Jeriah was stuck looking at muddy roots.

The brightness of raw lumber caught his eye. "Why did you fence off the east wood?" Jeriah was only mildly curious—the east wood was one of their best hunting grounds—but his father's face darkened.

"It's not our fence. I sold that land."

"Why? The amount of land we own now will determine how much we're granted in the north!"

"The money was needed. It's not your . . ." His father stopped and shook his head. "I'm sorry. As the heir it is your business. I sold the wood, several fields, and some of the land on the east bank to bribe the tribunal to spare your brother's life."

The silence echoed. He should tell him the truth. Jeriah owed it to Tobin, as well as his father, to tell the truth. But the angry grief in the old man's face froze Jeriah's tongue, and telling that particular truth required more courage than he possessed. Perhaps he wasn't cut out to be a true knight after all.

"How much did it cost Father to bribe the tribunal?"

His mother looked up from her embroidery, calm in spite of Jeriah's tempestuous entrance. "I don't know the exact sum. He sold a lot of land. But I gather you've discovered that."

"How could you let him do it? This place is like . . . like part of his own body! How could you let him hack off pieces, and not tell him that it was me and not Tobin?"

"It would have been more expensive to bribe them to release a second son. I did consider telling him privately, but he's such a bad liar, I don't think he could have pulled it off. He might not even have agreed to lie, and then we'd have had to pay a *lot* more."

Jeriah paced restlessly. "You could have let me face the consequences, instead of protecting me like a child."

Her smile grew. "Of course, dear one. Just like you're going to let Tobin take the consequences of *his* actions? Though I must say, your father took the whole affair ridiculously hard. There were several families in the area who had members involved in the conspiracy, but your father has become almost a *recluse* since we came back, and that's not like him."

"Who else from this area was involved?" Perhaps some of the priestly conspirators had escaped. If Jeriah could get one of them to cast the gate spell . . . No, he'd still need the goblins to help him locate the sorceress and his brother in the Otherworld.

"Don't you know?" his mother asked. "I'd have thought—"

"I hardly knew any of them." Jeriah stopped pacing and sank into a chair. "The conspirators only recruited me because . . ."

Jeriah had always known that some landholders abused their privileges. But Jeriah's father, for all his sternness, was fair both with his sons and with his tenants. It was only when Jeriah went to the Southlands, to join his older brother fighting the barbarians, that he learned that abuses he'd considered rare aberrations could be commonplace in other parts of the Realm. Some of the Southland lords were like his father, but there were others who imposed rents so high no farmer could pay them—and disputes were settled in favor of the man who paid the biggest bribe.

That was bad enough, but conditions in the army were even worse. Most of the officers were younger sons, whose troops frequently consisted of troublemaking tenants their fathers wanted to get rid of. And army discipline was harsher than any civilian community would tolerate.

When the conspirators had realized that the men Jeriah played "pranks" on were invariably officers who abused their men, they had cautiously approached him. The conspirators had considered him reliable. Had trusted him with serious matters.

The conspiracy was over.

"I was recruited because they needed a liaison between the military branch and their spies in the palace," Jeriah finished. "But I knew only a handful of men. They said they'd tell me more when I needed to know it."

"Very sensible," his mother approved. "It's a pity they were exposed. Do you think their goals . . . What were their goals—did you mention them?"

Jeriah recognized the signs. "Don't change the subject. We were talking about . . ." For a moment he couldn't remember. His mother often had that effect on people. Jeriah, through long practice, dealt with it better than most. "Who from this district was involved in the conspiracy?"

"Poor Kirlath Ivor, and that awful Lord Glovinscourt. You know, I thought worse of your conspiracy when I learned he was involved."

Lord Glovinscourt was one of the landholders Jeriah had thought was an unusual aberration.

"Your father was the only one in the area who dared stand up to him," his mother rambled on. "Do you remember the time that poor woman escaped, and he came after her with *forty* armed men! I was never more frightened!"

"It would be hard to forget." He'd been ten years old, trembling in a tower window with Tobin's arms around both him and Senna as they listened to their father. The old man had stood alone at the top of the steps, telling Lord Glovinscourt to take his filthy brigands and get off Rovanscourt land. Telling him quite a few other things, too. "You wouldn't have given her back to him either."

"Of course not. I'd have hidden her away, then smuggled her off to someplace out of his reach."

Jeriah grinned—and then realized he'd been distracted again. "Do you think Kirlath would help us? He was older than Tobin and me so I don't know him well, but . . ."

His mother's eyes shifted aside.

"Mother?"

"I'm sorry, but Kirlath and Lord Glovinscourt must have been more deeply involved than you. Lord Ivorscourt beggared himself with bribes, but . . . They were both executed. So I think, dear one, you'd better stay away from any survivors of your conspiracy."

"If there are any."

It could have been him. If Tobin and his mother hadn't intervened . . . Jeriah took a deep, calming breath. He was alive, and he was going to repay Tobin for everything. As for his mother . . .

"Mother, we need to have a talk about your sleeping drugs."

✧ ✧ ✧

That night when Jeriah went out to the garden shed, he brought his cloak and a saddlebag the bandits had cut up. He could have asked a groom to mend it, but he thought he'd be less likely to fall asleep if his hands were busy. Surely the goblins couldn't bespell him when he was awake and ready for them. He put out the milk bowl, took half a dozen stitches, and began to yawn.

When he awoke just before sunrise, there was a pillow under his head, and the saddlebag, neatly mended, lay beside him. He didn't even have to look to know the bowl was empty.

Three dawns later, Jeriah picked up the wild brillnuts they'd left beside him and stumbled to his feet. The goblins had mended his tunic, polished his boots, and returned a knife he'd lost two years ago. He rubbed his face, almost too weary to swear, and started back to the house. He'd been napping through the early hours of the night, but it wasn't enough. He was no longer certain if it was goblin spells or natural exhaustion that knocked him out each night.

And yawning his way through his father's lectures on oat blight and fertilizer wasn't doing either of them any good. The memory of his father's sarcastic comments roused a tired flash of resentment. He was bored, but he'd been going short on sleep all week, and he was *trying*. He was also losing time. Seventeen days had passed since

Tobin had entered the Otherworld.

It was his furious awareness of time slipping away that had led Jeriah to add a few drops of his mother's sedative to the milk the previous night. He'd wakened from the familiar sleep, cold, stiff, and missing every button and tie that held his clothing together. Thank the Bright Gods no one had caught him dumping the untouched milk and returning the bowl to its place with one hand holding up his pants! But the goblins seemed to have forgiven him; this last bowl of milk had vanished as usual, even if they hadn't returned his belt and buttons.

Jeriah rinsed the bowl in the horse trough, wrapped it in his cloak, closed the kitchen door quietly behind him . . . and almost walked into his father.

"Ah . . ." Slices of bread and cheese on the table explained his father's presence—he'd said something yesterday about an early start. But how could Jeriah explain himself? "Sir, I was just—"

"Jeriah." The old man's face was hard. "The position of heir doesn't give you the right to abuse your privileges."

Jeriah gaped at him. "Do you think I was . . . was . . . ?" Of course he did—what else could he think? The way the local girls sighed over Jeriah had given him something of a reputation in the district. He didn't believe he deserved it, and if it kept his father from looking for another reason he might have been out at night, he should be grateful. Even so . . .

"Sir, you can't believe I'd use my *position*"—his voice grated on the word—"to abuse anyone, man or woman!"

"I don't think you've been forcing girls." Anger stained his father's stubbled cheeks. "But I do think you haven't considered how your position as heir affects the people who will one day be under your hand. Sometimes just knowing your rank makes them do things they ordinarily wouldn't."

Deep inside Jeriah something began to crack. Was this his father's real opinion of him? That he had neither honor nor decency?

"Sir, I—"

"You weren't brought up to be the heir, so you might not understand this like Tob— like your brother did, but—"

Restraint shattered. "If he was so perfect, why can't you even say his name? If he was so perfect, why did you disinherit him, and send him off into danger, instead of bringing him home and keeping him safe? I'm sorry you don't have your *perfect* son anymore, but I'm . . . I'm . . ." Jeriah had the sense to stop there. His stomach was shaking. His hands were shaking.

His father's face was scarlet. "I knew you were jealous, but I never knew how much. Perhaps it's not surprising that he went off with you and—" He stopped himself, but it was too late.

"Finish it," Jeriah whispered. "Go ahead, say what you're thinking. He went off with me and he *didn't come back.* You think I killed him."

"You could have stopped him." The old man's voice was

shaking too, his face twisted. "By your own account, all you had to do was make some noise in that priest's tent, and Tobin and that sorceress would have been caught, and he'd still be here!"

"If they didn't execute him as her accomplice, maybe he would! But I couldn't be sure of that. I tried to stop him and it wasn't good enough, just like I've never been good enough. But clear your mind of one delusion—if I was jealous, it wasn't because I wanted Rovanscourt. I didn't and I don't."

He couldn't endure this. He couldn't stop talking. Jeriah backed toward the door, away from his father, away from rage and pain.

"I don't want this place, do you hear me? I never wanted it. I hate . . ."

He stopped. "May the Dark One take the lot of you!" He turned and ran.

Jeriah threw a saddle onto Glory's back, fumbling with the cinch. He set off at a gallop for the east wood before he remembered it had been sold. Sold, to buy his brother free of *his* crime. Cursing, he turned Glory toward the north road and galloped until her heaving sides forced him to slow.

"How could Father think such . . . such vile things?"

Glory's ears swiveled. His mother's voice echoed in his memory: . . . . *unreasonable to expect him to understand, when you and I and Tobin have all been lying to him from the very start.*

She was right. His father had no idea what was going on—no wonder he was drawing false conclusions. He must have noticed that Jeriah wasn't grieving for Tobin as the others were. As he would have been, if he still thought his brother was going to die. That was the source of his father's . . . disgusting conclusions.

I should tell him the truth. Even as Jeriah thought it, anger swamped him. After what he'd said this morning, the old man could whistle for the truth!

He thought of going south and rejoining his old commander. Of finding some way to repel the barbarians and covering himself with glory and honor.

He thought of going north, of becoming one of the explorers who were mapping the vast woodlands, and never setting eyes on his family again.

He thought of rescuing Tobin and bringing him back, of his father praising Jeriah's courage with tears of joy streaming down his face.

But even as he thought about it, Jeriah knew that all of those plans were . . . lightweight. In order to rescue Tobin Jeriah had to get the spell notes from Master Lazur, which meant he had to have his father's permission to return to the priest's service, and that meant he had to go home. He swore softly and turned Glory around.

It was midmorning when Jeriah rode into the stable yard and dismounted. His father would be out on the land now—he'd planned to spend the day on the other side of the river.

So with luck, Jeriah thought, he might avoid his whole family till dinner. He unsaddled Glory, rubbed her down, and led her back to her stall . . . where he found Sennahra waiting for him.

"I saved you some breakfast." She put down her book and gestured at the covered basket by her side.

"How did you know . . . ?"

"Everyone with a room on that side of the house knows. You were both yelling."

She stood and brushed the straw from her skirt, waiting while he fetched water and oats for Glory. Then she led the way up the ladder to the loft, which had always been their place for secret councils. It smelled of hay, dust, and peaceful memories, and Jeriah's stomach rumbled.

Senna snagged an apple from the basket, and it occurred to Jeriah that neither of the girls seemed to be grieving much. He'd noticed his mother spending a lot of time with them. What lies was she telling now? He didn't have the nerve to ask.

"Father didn't mean it," Sennahra said. "You must know that. He's hurting, so he was looking for someone to hurt back. I've been tiptoeing around him for days."

"I know, but he was so . . . so . . ." Rummaging through the basket was a good excuse to conceal his expression. Only when he found half a cold meat pie did Jeriah realize he was hungry. "You don't believe I got Tobin lost deliberately, do you?"

"That," said his sister judicially, "is probably the stupidest thing I've ever heard you say. And you say a lot of stupid things."

"Thanks."

"Don't mention it."

They grinned at each other; then she sobered. "Jeri, there's something I have to know. If we hadn't locked you up like mother wanted would . . . would it have turned out differently for Tobin?"

Jeriah's mind filled with soothing words; but even though Senna was a horrible liar herself, she could frequently tell when he was lying.

"I don't know. There's no way to know what might have happened."

Tears rose in Senna's eyes, but she blinked them back. Her courage was more moving than if she'd let them fall, and the need to tell her the truth welled up in Jeriah's heart. But Senna would insist on trying to help him. Besides, to give her hope and then have Tobin die after all would be horrible. For himself, Jeriah had no fear of failure—if he couldn't bring his brother home, he wouldn't be coming back from the Otherworld either.

"All right." Senna sighed. "You can keep your secrets. Just like Moth— Oh, that reminds me; I'm supposed to tell you that Mother needs you to go back to being Master Lazur's assistant as soon as you can, and if you can't manage it yourself, she'll have to—"

Jeriah choked on a mouthful of pie. "Stop her! Whatever she's doing, I . . . ah . . . Tell her I can manage that myself. What's Mother up to? Do you know?"

"Not very much. She says she may have to use leverage, and that she'll tell me all I need to know when my part comes."

"Wonderful." At least his mother didn't consider him a complete incompetent. Still . . . "I'm counting on you to stop her from doing anything stupid," Jeriah said firmly.

"I'm more worried about stopping you." Senna put her apple core back in the basket. "Where are you going every night? And don't spin me tales about a girl—you haven't been home for a week, and Father's taking up all your time."

"If you can see that, why doesn't he?" Jeriah asked bitterly.

"Mostly," said Senna, "it's because plain men are always suspicious of the handsome ones. Haven't you noticed that?"

Jeriah chewed and swallowed as he thought about it. "Maybe. Sometimes. But I'm his son."

Senna shrugged. "You're both men."

"Humph. Aren't women suspicious of beautiful women?"

"No. Jealous, catty, and shrewish, but not suspicious. And you're not going to distract me. If . . . if you're meeting the conspirators . . . Please, it's so dangerous." Her voice quivered. "If the authorities get even a hint that you were involved, they'll—"

"It's not the conspiracy. I haven't heard a word, not a whisper, from any of them since they were exposed. I think most of them are dead. By St. Spiratu's voice, I'm not involved anymore."

"Then what are you doing?"

He hesitated, but why not? "I'm trying to meet someone, but they . . . they aren't coming to the rendezvous. It's not conspirators, truly. But I have to keep showing up till they arrive."

Senna waited until it was clear that he wouldn't say more. "Why don't you write them a note and leave it at your rendezvous? Then you could get some sleep."

She packed the remains of their breakfast and prepared to descend. Jeriah stared at her with his mouth open.

He didn't even know if they could read. But he didn't know that they couldn't, either!

I need to speak to someone who knew Makenna of the Goblin Wood. Please have them contact me.

Jeriah smiled grimly and laid stones on the corners of the paper to hold it flat beside the bowl. Short and sweet. He had no idea who to address it to, but the goblins certainly knew who he was. He'd pushed the bowl deeper into the bushes, where they'd be able to find it but the gardeners wouldn't. Jeriah intended to sleep late tomorrow morning.

✧ ✧ ✧

His father was carefully polite over the next few days. Neither of them mentioned the argument, which suited Jeriah fine, but the tension was still there. So Jeriah wasn't surprised to find himself dreaming that his father was tying down his blankets, holding him to the bed.

"What are you doing?" If he hadn't known he was dreaming it might have been frightening, but since he was almost awake anyway, Jeriah decided to let the dream run its course.

"We have to tie you down," his father said sadly. "I'm sorry, son, but they found out about the girl. Now they're going to drown you."

"What girl?" Jeriah demanded, trying to free his arms. But there was a girl, he dimly remembered, a beautiful blond girl and he was in love with her. She smiled gloriously at him and he smiled back. Why was she helping his father with the blankets?

Jeriah's mind struggled for wakefulness and finally broke through.

"Ugh." His skin was sticky with sweat. He started to sit up, but his blankets were stretched tight across the bed, holding him down. Something . . . someone was perched on the footboard.

For an instant Jeriah thought he was still dreaming. The creature was a man, only two feet high. His nose, all the lines of his face, were long and sharp. His clothes were well made but worn. He eyed Jeriah shrewdly, up and down, as if he could see his body through the blankets. He was visibly unimpressed.

"I hear you want to talk to someone who knew the gen'ral."

The goblins had made contact! But who was . . . ?

"The general? I need to speak with the sorceress, Makenna. The sorceress of the Goblin Wood."

"That's the gen'ral, near enough. What do you want with her?"

"With her, nothing. But she's got my brother and I've—"

"You're the soldier's brother? You don't look like him."

Did he mean Tobin? His brother had been a soldier, but Jeriah wished the creature would use people's names. "If you're talking about Tobin, he looks like our father and I take after our mother. And there's something important we have to discuss. Would you mind untying the blankets so I can sit up? I'm hot, and I feel silly looking up at you."

"But I feel just fine looking down at you. You can wiggle out when I'm gone." The creature's eyes glinted. Was he laughing? If Jeriah tried to free himself, the goblin would be gone in an instant, and who knew how long it might take him to contact a more reasonable goblin. If any of them were reasonable. Tobin had been in the Otherworld for over three weeks. A true knight would ignore the fact that he was sweating like a pig.

"All right. I asked you to come because I need your

help. There are things about the Otherworld you may not know . . ."

He told the creature the details of the Otherworld's nature quite concisely—he'd practiced so often, he could have recited them in his sleep. "So you see," Jeriah finished, "I have to get into the Otherworld. Todder Yon said—"

"That tinker fellow? He *talked* about us?" The goblin's voice was low, but the threat was clear. How could such a small creature sound so menacing?

"He meant no harm," Jeriah said swiftly. "He only talked to me because he knew that *I* mean no harm. To you or her. I just need your help to find Tobin and the sorceress in the Otherworld. If . . . ah . . . if you'll help me?"

He hated having to plead with them, but he didn't see any other choice.

"I'm inclined to agree with your priest. The gen'ral and our folk, they're safe in the Otherworld."

"*They're* safe? Why you . . . Tobin risked his life, gave up everything, to help your kind!" Jeriah struggled against the blankets and heard something rip. The goblin shifted uneasily.

"Don't get flustered. I liked the soldier well enough, and I'll be sorry for his death. But if your priest discovers there's a chance of the gen'ral getting out, he might send hunters in."

"A lot of good your 'sorry' will do my brother!" But Jeriah stopped struggling. "You don't need to worry about your own precious skin, or your friends'. If Master Lazur ever finds out what we're doing, he'll just arrest me and put a stop to it."

"Hmm." The creature didn't even have the grace to look ashamed. "I admit, I'd like to see the gen'ral again."

A burst of hope overcame Jeriah's disgust. "So if I can get the spell from Master Lazur's books, could you or one of your people cast the gate? And then help me find them? And get Tobin—"

"The finding is no problem," the goblin replied. "If you take a few of us in with you, and those spells you're talking about can protect our magic, there are several ways we can locate them. But not one of us can work the gate spell; that'll take human magic. The folk you need for that"—the creature's eyes gleamed in the darkness—"are the Lesser Ones."

"The Lesser Ones?"

"Humans like the gen'ral, who wield the small magics. They've been concealing their abilities since that cursed law passed, but there's a lot of 'em and they keep in touch with each other. Proper organized, they are."

"Can you put me in touch with them?" Jeriah tried to sit up again, but the blankets foiled him.

The little goblin grinned. "I *could*. But what for?"

"What do you mean, what for? To save Tobin!"

"Ah, I meant what'll you give *me* for doing it? We goblins, we don't care for indebtedness," he finished smugly.

"Indebtedness? After all Tobin did for your people, you don't think you owe him?"

The goblin's expression seemed to change, but in the dim moonlight that shone through his window it was hard to be certain. "That's between the soldier and us. What we're talking about now is the favor *you're* asking for. And its price."

That the goblins were ungrateful vermin shouldn't surprise him. "Very well. What's the price for your services?"

"What I'd really like," the goblin replied, "is for you to get the Decree of Bright Magic revoked so we wouldn't have to worry about being hunted and burned out."

Jeriah's jaw dropped. "That's impossible! I'd be willing to do it if I could—it's a bad law for humans as well—but it's not within my power. And it never will be!"

"Aye, I figured that, but I thought I'd ask. There is something else we need."

"What?"

"A place of safety where we can live. Quite a few of us were forced to leave the wood. It's spring now, and summer won't be a problem, but come winter we'll need a place."

At least this request wasn't completely impossible. "What kind of place?"

The goblin shrugged. "Anything that'll shelter a few hundred. A big cave would do, though most of us don't care for living underground. A ruined castle or deserted village would be better, but there's none about that we've been able to find. We could even build for ourselves, in a deserted field or wood, but only if it's somewhere humans never go."

"I don't know anyplace people never go. With so many Southland refugees, anything that can be inhabited is." All the villages would be abandoned when the relocation moved everyone north of the great wall, but for now . . . "That's impossible too. What else?"

"That's all I want, human."

"But . . ." How long would it take him to find these lesser magic wielders without the goblins' help? Jeriah didn't have any time to spare, but it went against the grain to give such greedy, ungrateful creatures what they wanted. *The heroes of legend didn't have to bargain with vermin.*

The goblin snickered. Jeriah realized he'd muttered the thought aloud, and ground his teeth.

"Well, young hero, are you going to find us a place? Or shall I be on my way?"

"Wait!" Someone had to cast the gate spell. Priests wouldn't. Goblins couldn't. Jeriah's only chance was this magical underground. But how in the Bright Gods' name was he to find a deserted village or ruin where there weren't any? Find . . . or make one? His breath caught. He couldn't do that. He *couldn't*! Jeriah squirmed half out of the blankets, then froze as the goblin tensed to flee. "Wait! I . . . I can do it, I think. I might . . . No. You ask too much."

The creature folded his arms. "That or nothing, human." His face was inscrutable, but there was no yielding in pose or voice. Jeriah *had* to get Tobin back. He had no choice.

"All right, I'll try. But I'm going to need your help to bring it off. Meet me tomorrow night, in the grove of brill trees by the river. Do you know where that is?"

"I can find it." The creature moved toward the door, silent as a shadow.

"If I find you a safe place to live, then you'll put me in touch with these Lesser Ones?"

"Aye." The goblin stopped at the door, his voice so soft Jeriah could barely hear it. "We pay our debts, for good or ill. Remember it, hero." And he was gone.

Tobin

THEY WERE CUTTING THE FIRST trees today, to begin drying the timber for use in the first houses, in the first village, in their new world. Growing up on a lowland farm, Tobin had never felled timber before. He'd thought it would be a task in which his greater size and strength would be useful, but now, bringing down the third tree of the morning, he was beginning to suspect that the goblins didn't need him at all.

They'd spent the years building in the great northern woods. Their small axes cut the initial wedge into the trunk like a brigade of beavers. Now most of them had joined Tobin on the rope—a rope they had climbed up the branches to tie off—while the two best woodsmen cut a wedge into the tree's opposite side.

Tobin's strength was valuable in dragging the fallen tree to the open meadow, where Makenna, along with several goblin helpers, had set runes that would make the timber dry swiftly and without warping.

Tobin knew it worried her, that she'd needed the goblins' help to cast a simple drying spell. But even tapping into the power of the ancient wall, she'd used so much of her own magic to cast the gate that it wasn't surprising it took her a while to recover. Maybe magic came from nature, as she said, or it still might be a gift from the Bright Gods. It might even be both, as he'd once pointed out to her. But either way, it made sense that if you used it all up, it might take some time to—

The tree creaked, and Tobin didn't wait for the wood-cutters' shouts, throwing his weight against the rope, digging his feet into the soft loam of the forest floor. For a long moment the green wood resisted; then a sharper crack sounded and the tree toppled slowly toward them. Tobin and his goblin assistants were well outside its reach, but they scrambled back a few more yards to be sure.

The rustling crash echoed through the woods, and when the branches stopped thrashing, the silence was broken only by goblin shouts.

The quiet bothered Tobin, although birds always fell silent after a noisy disturbance. There were plenty of birds in this world, though their songs were unfamiliar.

Still, there was something about this world, a waiting quality, that he sensed more clearly in the hushed quiet after a tree fell. Even more clearly than he did when he woke in the middle of the night, his heart pounding with dread for no reason at all.

He was getting fanciful. Too much stress, too much strangeness, in too short a time.

That might be part of what was giving Makenna so much trouble. As Tobin strode forward to help trim the branches, he knew he was wearier than he should be. Makenna wasn't the only one who'd overexerted herself in the calamitous days before they'd escaped. They'd all recover in time. This world was as beautiful as anyplace he'd ever seen.

He still wished the birds would sing.

CHAPTER 5

Jeriah

JERIAH WIGGLED OUT OF HIS bed and sat a moment, enjoying the cool air. By the time he finished untying his blankets, his brain was whirling with plans and problems. He didn't like the only idea he had, but the goblin had given him no choice. He had to think with his head, not his heart.

The major points were straightforward; it was the details that would be difficult. The first thing he needed was an excuse to ride out at night. If his father suspected what he was going to do . . . Jeriah shivered and pushed the thought away. No, his father had to ask . . . Ah, that would do it. All he had to do was kill a chicken.

Grimacing in distaste, Jeriah pulled on his tunic and crept out to the chicken coop. He chose an old hen, one that would have been slaughtered for dinner within a few months, and carried her out to the yard so as not to disturb the sleeping birds. With a murmur of apology and a sharp merciful twist, he wrung her neck. With a shudder of revulsion—knights killed men in battle and he was flinching over a chicken?—he dropped the twitching body and went to the smithy for a nail and the rake the smith used to pull clinker out of his coals. By the time Jeriah returned to the henhouse, the body was still. A few bloodstained feathers set the stage. He'd have to bury the chicken's body, since a predator would carry it off. But first he took the rake and dug under a corner of the fence, so it looked like it had been done by an animal's claws. Then Jeriah found a patch of damp earth. Using his thumb and the nail, he carefully shaped two distinctive footprints.

His father came late to breakfast. "A nightstoat got one of the hens last night," he announced, taking his place at the head of the table.

Jeriah's mother murmured something.

"Can I see it?" Tami asked.

"The stoat will have carried it off to his den. And eaten it by now. Why do you want to see a dead chicken?"

"Because nightstoats are the worst! They have magic, so no one can catch them, not even dogs. They can kill everything on a farm in one night!" Her eyes sparkled with gruesome excitement.

Senna began to giggle.

"Where do you hear these things?" her father asked. "Almost none of that's true, Tamilee. They have no magic. The reason dogs can't track them is because they're almost scentless. And their ability to see in the dark is natural—their eyes are larger than day creatures, which is why they only leave their dens at night. Any light brighter than moonlight blinds them; they can be stopped simply by putting torches around the livestock pens." He paused a moment, then grimaced. "Unfortunately, torches burn out, and enough to surround all the pens would cost more than a few chickens. They take livestock only one or two at a time, but they are indeed 'the worst.' We'll have to hunt it down, but with the late planting I hardly have a man to spare. We've got to get the wheat in before the last of the rains."

"I'm sure you'll manage, dear," said Jeriah's mother, her thoughts clearly elsewhere.

"And just how, madam, do you think—"

"Could I hunt it, sir?" Jeriah's palms were damp. "I'm not much use with planting, but I'm a fair tracker."

Hunting the dangerous vermin that preyed on livestock was the only heir's duty at which Jeriah had been better than his brother. His father, he noted bitterly, obviously hadn't remembered that—the old man's face lit with relief.

"Thank you, that's an excellent idea. You can try tracking it this morning, get some sleep this afternoon, and start hunting tonight."

Jeriah looked away from Senna's startled, knowing eyes.

"I'll do that, sir."

A light breeze set the brill trees whispering. The moon was half full and the sky clear—a perfect night to hunt. Jeriah wished a simple hunt were all he was engaged in.

"Well, young hero." The voice made him jump. "You've got some idea?"

Too late. When had he passed the point of no return? When Tobin leapt into the light? Sometime after that? Jeriah didn't know, but he had no choice now.

He looked around till he spotted the goblin seated on a branch. Above his reach.

"Yes, I have an idea. I'm pretty sure I can get a place for you, but . . . Can your people swim?"

"If we must." The goblin cocked his head curiously.

"Then follow me. Or would you like to ride?" Jeriah maneuvered Glory over to the goblin's tree, but he was astonished when, after a brief hesitation, the small creature scrambled down the branches and dropped lightly behind the saddle.

He didn't much care for the company, but it would get them there more quickly. The faster this was over, the better, as far as Jeriah was concerned.

When they reached the rotten dike, Jeriah dismounted and watched as the goblin gave Glory a reassuring pat, climbed down the stirrup, and dropped to the ground. How did a goblin become accustomed to horses?

"So what are we doing here?"

"That gate is waterlogged," Jeriah told the goblin. "If I open it—or better yet, break through the rotten wood—the river will flood these fields. That village will be deserted as soon as the tenants can move their things out. Would that serve your needs?"

"Hmm." The goblin scrambled up the dike and walked along it, surveying the land and the sleeping homes. Jeriah tried not to look in that direction. They'd be forced to move in a year anyway, he told himself fiercely. They all knew the dike would soon give way. He was doing no harm. Very little harm. Almost—

"Not a bad plan, human. Nearly worthy of the gen'ral. There's a few problems, but I think we can handle them."

"I got the idea from something she did. What problems? The water won't be more than a few feet deep, especially when the river goes down, and you said you could swim."

"No problem there. But what's to stop your fa from rebuilding the gate, draining the land, and replanting?"

"I don't think he could, this year. We're going to start moving our people north next year, so I don't think he'll bother."

"I'm not inclined to take chances on what you think. Suppose we dig a series of tunnels under this dike, so when you let the water in, it'll flow through 'em and bring the whole thing down? Hard for anyone to be repairing that. And we can rig it so the gate'll be washed away. Because standing down below and chopping through that wood is like to drown the chopper!"

"You can collapse the whole dike?"

"I think so. It'll take time, and care, so's not to bring it down on our heads while we're digging. And we'd need your help for some of the heavy work, but I think we can manage."

Jeriah eyed the goblin suspiciously. "That would take months! Tobin will be dead by then. You know we don't have that much time."

"It won't take months." The creature raised his fingers to his lips, seeming to whistle though Jeriah heard nothing.

"What—"

A swarm of shadows erupted around him, from the bushes, from the young corn—they seemed to spring from the earth itself. Within moments, Jeriah was surrounded by goblins.

"Two or three nights," said the creature. "Four at most."

Tobin had been in the Otherworld for almost a month now.

"Make it two nights," he said curtly, "and you've got a deal. As long as you're sure no one will drown. They'll lose their homes in a year or two no matter what we do, but I won't let anyone be killed."

"If most of the village wasn't on higher ground, there'd be no point to the whole thing, would there?"

Jeriah waited.

"Ah! They'll suffer nothing worse than wet feet. My word on it."

Could he trust the goblin's word? And what could he do

about it if he couldn't? If he was going to save Tobin, he had no choice.

"Then do it."

In the morning his father asked if he'd made any progress. Jeriah said not much. His father said tolerantly that it was early yet, and changed the subject. Jeriah wished that he could find a nightstoat, so he wouldn't look completely incompetent, but they were rare. Perhaps when no more chickens died, his father would assume the nightstoat was just passing by. Compared to the shock of losing a dozen prime fields along the west bank, the chickens would no longer matter. And perhaps his father would think Jeriah's inability to meet his eyes was because of their fight. Perhaps.

When he brought Tobin home, none of it would matter. When he brought Tobin home, he could tell the truth and his father would forgive everything.

At night Jeriah helped the goblins, hauling away the earth they dug, scattering it in plowed fields where it wouldn't be noticed. Sometimes he had to crawl into one of the tunnels that were eating away the underside of the dike, and pry loose a rock that was too big for them. Trapped in the narrow tunnel, Jeriah could almost feel the river pushing against the increasingly fragile barrier of stone and earth that was all that stood between him and drowning.

He was almost too ashamed to feel the terror of those underground tasks, but before he returned home in the dawn, Jeriah washed the dirt from his hands and arms as if it were blood.

It rained that afternoon, in wind-driven showers. About an hour before dark it settled to a steady downpour, the kind of rain that sent the swollen river surging.

The goblin's original estimate had been right—it had taken three nights to dig the tunnels, but they'd done a thorough job. Jeriah half expected to find the dikes crumbling under the weight of the rising water when he arrived. He tethered Glory in the high brill grove, where he was sure no flood would reach, and peered through the curtains of rain. He could see only about ten feet; then everything faded into night and rain. There could be goblins all around him and he wouldn't know it. The swelling river might already have consumed— A flash of lightning painted the scene with livid light. The dikes were still standing, the fields beyond them glimmering with muddy water, but that was all.

"It's a good night for a flooding, hero, I'll grant you that."

Jeriah jumped. "Don't sneak up on me," he snapped in a whisper. The ironic nickname stung.

The goblin's grin was barely visible in the wind-whipped darkness. "You can yell if you want—the closest humans are in those houses." He gestured toward the doomed village.

The sickening guilt was so familiar by now that Jeriah ignored it, like the rain soaking through the shoulders of his cloak. "Are you ready?"

"Aye. All you have to do is open the gate, and your end of the bargain's done."

"You're not coming with me?"

"Not a chance. We're a bit small to go swimming, if that dike gives way faster than we think it will. You'd best get off it in a hurry . . . young hero."

Jeriah turned his back on the goblin's smirk and scrambled onto the dike. He could just see the surface of the river, almost halfway up the other side by now. Surely he was imagining that the dike vibrated, just a little, under his feet.

The sluice gate loomed out of the darkness. For a moment Jeriah ignored the wheel that lifted the screw, looking through the rain toward the homes he was about to destroy. He couldn't see them but they were there, their owners sleeping safely as rain drummed on the roofs.

This was the kind of thing that knights in legends were supposed to prevent! One should leap out right now, and threaten to chop off Jeriah's hands if he dared to lay them on that wheel.

"No one is going to die," he muttered savagely. "Nothing is going to happen that wouldn't happen in a year, anyway. No one will get hurt."

Jeriah grabbed the rain-wet wheel, twisted, and felt the shuddering race of water beneath his feet. He turned it again. No one leapt out to chop off his hands.

True knights ended up with dead brothers.

The wheel was level with his head when it finally

jammed—the gate wide open. Jeriah looked down at the torrent of murky water pouring through. It wasn't his imagination; the dike was quivering. He jogged along it, moving as fast as he dared, till another flash of lightning revealed that the muddy furrows below were still free of the flood. He gave it another hundred feet, climbed down, and fumbled his way back to the grove where the goblins were concealed. Only then did Jeriah look back.

Darkness spread before him. "Can you see what's—"

He was interrupted by a flicker of lightning, bright enough to let them see a stream of water arcing down into the spreading shimmer of a rising pond—such quiet deadliness. Thunder grumbled, and Jeriah felt a tug on the leg of his britches.

It was the smallest goblin Jeriah had seen—only half as tall as most of the others.

"Don't be so sad," the creature said. "They'll be all right. And now you'll be able to open a gate and save Tobin."

The voice sounded like a child's. Jeriah supposed they must have young.

"You know my brother?"

"Of course. We were all friends with him, Regg and Onny and Nuffet and me. I'm glad you're—"

The goblin broke off and cocked his head, listening. The sound was deeper than the thunder, vibrating through the soles of Jeriah's feet as much as in his ears.

A gasp rippled through the crowd, and Jeriah strained his eyes against the darkness. He could just make out the dark silhouette of the dike as a whole section of it leaned forward, like a giant turning in its sleep. Lightning flashed again as the river poured through a dozen fissures. The surface of the rising water churned around the gaps. Jeriah heard another section groan and fall.

"What's happening?" he demanded.

"The water's going up fast." The young goblin's voice quivered. "It's reached the houses now."

"You can see—"

In the direction of the distant village, a child screamed.

Jeriah was running back to Glory before he thought, leaping into the saddle. He smashed through the wet branches and galloped down the track into the water. Only then did he realize that he was shouting; in warning, for help. He fell silent to listen as the mare waded deeper, stumbling over the rough ground below the swirling currents, snorting in dismay.

If she'd trusted her rider less, she'd have balked.

Jeriah knew he should go back—he could see for only a few yards in any direction. But he turned Glory toward the sound of shouting voices and she pressed on.

The next flash of lightning showed the village off to his left—he'd been about to pass it. But Glory saw it too and increased her cautious pace, nostrils wide. Soon the dark shadow of a building loomed before him.

A toddler in a nightshirt perched on the steps, shrieking, unable to go farther without stepping into the water. Jeriah bent and hoisted the boy onto his saddlebow.

The rest of the night passed in a mosaic of action that gave him no time for any thought beyond the needs of the moment. Soon lamps lit the windows of the flooding houses, so Jeriah could at least see where he was going as he crossed and recrossed the treacherous fields.

Adults waded through the swirling currents, as the river fought to establish its new bed. Jeriah and Glory carried children, elders, and household goods, seed grain, and livestock. Glory almost went down once, setting pans clanging, and the piglet on Jeriah's lap squealed. But there was little danger, just the grim, wet work of saving what could be saved.

The rain had stopped without Jeriah noticing, and moonlight slid through the scattering clouds. His father and the men of the estate began to help without him noticing their arrival. He didn't realize it was over until he found himself sitting on his exhausted horse, staring at the swamped village in the cold light of early dawn with a perfectly blank mind.

The first wave had sent a foot of water through even the highest houses. All the cellars were flooded, the food stored in them ruined. But no lives had been lost. Even the penned animals had been saved, soaked and indignant but alive. Just as Jeriah had hoped.

The water had receded from the higher ground, leaving most of the houses on an island with almost a quarter mile of shallow water between them and the shore. It would be perfect for the goblins, but the families who had owned those homes . . .

When he got Tobin back, Jeriah would tell him about this. As the heir, Tobin could help him make it up to these people. In the northern woods they could have better houses than the ones they'd lost, the most fertile land. But for now . . .

Jeriah roused enough to listen to the comments around him. A few children sobbed. The adults were quiet, except for a group of men farther down the bank who were dragging something heavy from the water. His father came to stand beside him.

"It could have been worse." He sounded drained, but his hand fell warmly on Jeriah's shoulder. "Good thing you were there! No one was killed—that's the important thing. There's not a village on the estate that doesn't need workers. They'll be taken in. Right before the relocation is a bad time to lose seed, but it could have been far worse. You did well, son."

Jeriah said nothing. He refused to tell more lies.

"M'lord." A man from the group downriver came panting up to them. "You ought to see this."

Jeriah's father signaled him to follow, along with old Woder, who was their steward, and the village headman. Jeriah was, after all, the heir, responsible for the safety of the estate. He bit his lip to silence bitter laughter. Then he saw what they'd pulled from the flood and the laughter froze.

It was the gate. Most of the door had been smashed away,

only part of the heavy frame still clinging to it, but the screw and wheel were clearly visible, locked open.

He should have taken an ax and broken it—let the water pour through and drown him. It would have been cleaner than this.

"Woder," said his father gently. "You were supposed to close the west bank gates this afternoon. Did you?"

"Aye, m'lord. I closed this gate."

"You might have gotten confused in the storm. Not . . . not your fault, old friend."

"M'lord!" the old man cried. "I closed all the gates! I know the danger, and even if I somehow forgot one, I'd never raise any gate to the top like that!"

"How else could it have happened?" a villager asked.

The lord of Rovanscourt shrugged. "We'll probably never know. The gate was rotten—the flood alone could have brought it down. No blame will be attached to this accident." His tone made it an order and the men around him nodded. But they looked at the elderly steward with doubt and pity in their eyes.

Woder was staring at the gate, and Jeriah saw the same doubt in his wrinkled face. He was questioning himself, wondering if he had somehow—

"I did it," said Jeriah abruptly. Something inside him ached at the sound of his own voice, but it was a clean pain, like lancing an infected wound. "I . . . There was a night-stoat. It darted into a burrow in the dike. I thought I could flood it out, so I opened the gate and ran to catch it when . . . when . . ." His voice faltered at the fury and disgust in every face. "By the time I realized the danger, the dike was collapsing—it was too late to do anything but get people out. I'm . . ."

The word stuck on his tongue. Irresponsible. Lightweight. His apology was worthless to men who'd lost their homes. Their anger seared him. He deserved it. More than they would ever know. Jeriah turned to face his father.

"Didn't you remember that gate was dangerous?" His father sounded as if he were being strangled. His hands worked.

I got confused in the dark. I didn't realize it would rise so fast. I was caught up in the hunt. . . .

Jeriah gritted his teeth and said nothing.

His father drew a shuddering breath. "You've convinced me, Jeriah. You really don't care about Rovanscourt. You never have. You never . . . Go. I . . . I banish you from this land."

The men around them gasped as the ritual words were spoken. Jeriah had expected it and didn't flinch.

"I reject you, the land rejects you, its people reject you. You will go forth, never . . ."

Jeriah watched his father remember that Jeriah was now his only son—the only heir. He couldn't banish him forever.

"You will not return until I give permission." Rage shook

his father's voice, as he was forced to abandon the formal words. "Go home. I'll give you a letter for that priest you're so anxious to get back to. You'll leave at first light."

He spun away. Jeriah turned Glory and kicked her into a weary walk, fighting to keep his back straight under the pressure of angry eyes.

It was still early morning when Jeriah finished buckling his saddlebags and pulled his cloak over his face. He closed his bedroom door quietly—he'd managed to avoid his mother and sisters so far, and he intended to go right on doing it. He couldn't endure any more "confessions." He would saddle Glory, get that cursed letter from his father, and go. If he weren't the only remaining son, he'd be leaving for good.

It was easy to avoid notice. The hall and most of the lower rooms were full of milling refugees and people who'd come to help. Children were bedded down on the floor, and food arrived from the kitchen as fast as the cooks could produce it.

Jeriah twisted through the crowd and out to the court-yard, which was even more chaotic, crowded with the goods and livestock people had saved. He sighed with relief as the stable door closed behind him, cutting off the noise. But he wasn't alone.

Fiddle, already saddled, huffed curiously. His father finished fastening a halter on Glory before turning to look at his son. His gaze was flat, unreadable, but his voice was bleak.

"She's too tired to ride far. You'd best take it easy today."
He tied the lead rope to Fiddle's saddle and swung a traveling
pack onto Glory's back. "I put your letter in here."

It would do no good to argue, not when he'd lost his
father's trust so completely. *Would he have trusted Tobin?*
Jeriah pushed the ugly thought aside. "Shall I send Fiddle
back when I reach the city?"

"No, keep him. You're the heir. You should have good
horses. Tobin has . . ."

Tobin has no need of a charger now.

The unspoken words hung in the stillness between them,
raw with grief. Jeriah's bitterness dissolved. "Father, there's
something . . ."

His father looked up, and Jeriah's courage failed under the
hard gaze.

"Yes?"

"Nothing." He mounted Fiddle and rode out. There was
no way to conceal his identity from the crowd now, so he
shook back his hood and lifted his head.

Their hatred struck like stones. They fell silent as he
passed; the horses' hoofbeats were the only sound. Jeriah's
palms were damp when he finally rode through the gate, but
his back was straight, his head high.

He waited in the brill grove for ten minutes, but the goblins
didn't come. Or if they did, they didn't show themselves.
Jeriah smiled grimly. He knew where to find them. He rode

down the bank and urged Fiddle, splashing, into the shallow, turbulent water. The price was paid. His father would never trust him again, but at least Jeriah was free to start the process of getting Tobin back.

The village had already acquired the tattered, empty feeling of a deserted place. Jeriah pulled Fiddle to a stop in the center of the square, where several houses concealed him from the shore. He was prepared to wait for hours if need be, but the goblin came around one of the buildings almost at once.

Jeriah had never seen that expression on the dour little face before—it took him several moments to identify it as happiness.

"Hero, you've done it! This place will serve us just fine."

Anger snapped through him. Fiddle felt it and shifted restlessly.

"My name is Jeriah Rovan," he told the goblin icily.

"And mine's Cogswhallop . . . young hero." The creature's eyes glinted mockingly, but Jeriah was too startled to care.

"Cogswhallop? The sorceress' second-in-command?"

"Tinker mentioned me, did he?"

"Yes, but he thought you'd gone with her."

"I would have." Some of the pleasure drained from the goblin's face. "It didn't work out."

Possibilities stirred in Jeriah's mind.

"Then you must want to get back to her. Very badly."

"I don't know about 'very badly,' but I'd like to see the

gen'ral again. Enough that if you open a gate, I'll guide you to the soldier myself."

"What if I need your help to get the gate cast?"

"Ah, that's another bargain."

"Haven't I done enough already?"

The creature's silence answered.

"Very well," said Jeriah bitterly. "What else do you want?"

"You know what I want, human. Get the Decree of Bright Magic revoked, and I'll do whatever I can to save your brother."

"That's impossible and you know it."

The goblin's face was inscrutable. "That's all I want."

When a true knight faced an impossible quest, he always managed. But slaying monsters and rescuing prisoners were straightforward tasks, no matter how dangerous. No one asked a knight to get a law repealed. He'd have to manage the rest of it on his own. And pray that this worked out better than the last plot he'd gotten involved in!

"You'll tell me how to contact the Lesser Ones?"

"Aye, that you've earned. The man you want is Todder Yon. He's got no magic himself, mind, but he carries messages between the Lesser Ones all through the north."

"Todder Yon!" Fiddle shied into Glory, snorting. Ghostly snickers came from the buildings around him. "That filthy, demon-cursed . . . Why didn't he tell me?"

Jeriah didn't expect an answer, but the goblin said, "Likely the same reason I didn't give you my name."

"And just what reason is that?"

"You didn't ask me."

There was a long silence. Only a month left before Tobin became ill. Would Jeriah have time to track down the elusive tinker? Again. "I don't suppose you know where I can find him. Or do you need payment for that, too? All the gold in the world? My life's blood?"

"No, I'll see that he gets your message."

"That's it? I did all this, and all you're going to do is deliver a cursed *letter*?"

"And we'll make sure he passes it on. You gave us a place to live, so we'll see that your message reaches the Lesser Ones. That was the bargain, and we pay our debts."

"What about your debt to Tobin?"

"Ah, as I said, that's between him and us. Another bargain entirely. Write up a letter. I'll see the tinker gets it into the right hands. And then you're paid. Agreed?"

It was the best bargain Jeriah was likely to get.

"Agreed."

Makenna

"WHAT'S GOING ON HERE?"

The sound of angry voices had drawn her from her tent just after dawn, and over to the site where the first of the goblins' small houses was under construction. Or not under construction, given how much timber had to be taken out because it had warped after being pegged into place. But the goblin homeowner confronting the Stoners who'd laid the foundations was gesturing at the stonework, not the walls, and as Makenna drew nearer, she saw why. Cracks, like jagged lightning, ran through the thick stones of the small home's foundation, leaping from one block to another.

"What in the Dark One's name could do that? These stones were laid only a few days ago!"

"Not solid." Harcu picked up a piece of what looked like gray granite. When he closed his fist, it crumbled like cornbread.

"We had a bargain!" Dannut, the homeowner, snarled. "And they used shoddy materials—"

"The stones were fine when we started building the walls," another goblin protested. "They were fine yesterday."

"Just like that flax fiber we had such hopes for," Thadda the Weaver said grimly. "It seemed perfect for thread until you got a spindle full of it. Then it withered into a handful of cobwebs. I'm beginning to think this world's accursed!"

Makenna suddenly remembered a conversation she hadn't thought important at the time. "Harcu, when you first started working this stone, you told me it was 'funny' and 'not right.' What was wrong with it?"

Most humans found the Stoners' faces unreadable. Makenna had dealt with them enough to see his baffled frustration. Stoners were the least articulate of all the goblin kindred. The Bookeries, the Charmers, the Makers, and even the scatterbrained Flichters considered them stupid, but Makenna had long since realized that a slow tongue didn't necessarily mean slow wits. She waited patiently as the Stoner tried to fit complex knowledge into his limited vocabulary. Finally, his thick shoulders rose in a shrug. "Not solid."

"We know it's not solid," said Dannut, almost dancing with fury. "That's why it's crumbling to bits! That's why—"

Tobin, who had joined the group so quietly she hadn't noticed him, laid a gentle hand on Dannut's shoulder and the goblin stopped yelling—though his scowl made words unnecessary.

Harcu turned away.

"Wait," Makenna said urgently. "If you can't fulfill your bargain, the least you can do is try to tell us why."

Not fulfilling a bargain was serious insult among goblins. Harcu stopped.

"Underwalls built. Bargain full."

"Well, they're not built now." Makenna glanced at the collapsing stones. "But I don't believe that's your fault. You tried to tell me, didn't you? To tell me there was something wrong with the stone."

Harcu nodded. Makenna didn't recognize the expression in his flat eyes.

"What was wrong with it?" she asked. "I wasn't paying attention then, but, I promise you, I'm listening now."

Harcu shrugged again. It was the usual response of a Stoner who couldn't put something into words, but Makenna persisted. "Harcu, try. I think this is important. What was wrong with the stone?"

"Not solid," Harcu repeated. "Not solid solid. Not stone solid. Not stone."

"Well, if you knew it was shoddy materials," said Dannut, "then you owe—"

Tobin must have suppressed him, but this time Harcu didn't turn away. And now Makenna recognized the look in his eyes, for the same fear rose in her own heart.

"Are you telling me that it's not that it wasn't sound," she said slowly, "but that it wasn't real stone?"

Harcu nodded.

"But that's ridiculous!" Thadda said. "Of course the stone's real."

"As real as the plant fiber you spun," said Makenna. "Which made a fine strong thread for almost three days and then broke when you blew on it. As real as timber that dried straight and true, then warped into pretzels as soon as we tried to build."

Erebus, who'd been watching curiously, spoke for the first time. "What are you saying, mistress? If this world wasn't real, we'd all have starved by now."

"I don't know what's going on," Makenna admitted. "But we need to find out. And someone besides me is going to have to power the spells," she added. "My magic still hasn't recovered from casting the gate."

In truth, she felt like her magic was weaker now than when she'd arrived, but that had to be nonsense.

"Thadda, you're a strong Maker. If I laid out the runes, do you think you could feed them power?"

Makenna was already reaching for one of the buttons on her vest, but the little woman's uneasy frown stopped her.

"Mistress, I'd be willing to try, but you'd be better asking someone else. My magic . . . I don't know where it's going, these last weeks, but it's as feeble as an infant's. I'd say I was overusing it, if I'd been able to do anything. Maybe someone else?"

No one volunteered. The dread on the faces around her grew.

"What?" Tobin asked. "What is it?"

Someone had to say it aloud. "All of us?" Makenna asked. "Are you telling me that the magic of everyone in this camp is gone?"

The silence that fell then felt like a drought wind blowing through her bones. One by one they turned to Tobin.

"Don't look at me! I don't have any magic to lose. If there's something suppressing all your magic, we'll find out what it is and put a stop to it."

He tried to sound calm and confident, but Makenna thought that he'd known something was wrong before any of them. His ordinary face was thinner now, and he'd been jumping at shadows for several weeks.

If their magic was being stolen away, "something wrong" wasn't the half of it. Magic was the only way in or out of this world, and right now "out" looked like a really good idea. Making flax rot, wood warp, even solid stone crumble—that was one thing—what could possibly reach into their own bodies and steal the magic out of blood and bone?

"What in the Dark One's name is going on here?"

CHAPTER 6

Jeriah

THE CITY OF STEPS WAS a three-day ride from his home. If he changed horses frequently enough, Jeriah decided, he could arrive in two.

Soon Todder Yon would receive his letter, and surely the tinker would at least ask the Lesser Ones to contact him. And if the Lesser Ones would open the gate, he had Cogswhallop's promise to lead him to Tobin in the Otherworld for free! This was progress! If shame and disgrace were the price, then so be it.

Jeriah set a sufficiently brisk pace that Fiddle had tired by midmorning, but Glory was still tired from the long night, so he was forced go on more slowly. He bought bread and cheese at a farm he passed, spending several of the coppers he'd gotten from the tinker, and then found a sunny meadow with a stream where the horses could drink and rest for a while. After midmeal he planned to investigate the traveling pack his father had given him—he hoped there'd be some money in it. Banished or not, he had to eat.

Jeriah dismounted, pulled off Fiddle's saddlebags, and tossed them to the ground.

"Ow!"

Jeriah spun. He saw nothing that could cry out, but as he stared, the clasp on one of the bags slid open. Jeriah drew his sword and stepped back. The flap lifted and a tiny face appeared. The goblin boy who'd spoken to him by the river eyed him warily.

Jeriah shoved his sword back into the sheath.

"What are you doing here?"

"Following you." The child scrambled out, rubbing his elbow. "You didn't have to be so rough."

"I'm sorry," said Jeriah with deceptive mildness. "But I didn't know you were there. If I had known . . . I'd have pitched you off a cliff! Your kin are going to think I've kidnapped you! Get out of here! Now!"

He reached down and picked up a rock to enforce the order, and the child scrambled back.

"Wait! They know where I am. Fa's the one who . . . ah . . ." The tips of his pointed ears turned pink.

Arm cocked to throw, Jeriah hesitated. "Your father was the one who what?"

The child stopped, eyeing him warily. "I told Fa that Tobin was my friend, and if he died because of helping us and I'd done nothing to help him, it'd leave me indebted. He saw that right enough, so he said I could as long as I didn't do anything dangerous. I had to promise, but I'll do all I can to help you." When he'd first seen the boy, Jeriah had assumed he was very young because of his size. In the daylight he appeared to be . . . twelve? thirteen? Whatever his age, he wasn't old enough to lie well. The latter part of his speech had the ring of truth, but it wasn't what he'd started to say. He knew something. And Jeriah needed all the information he could get. He dropped the rock and folded his arms.

"Goblins never do anything for nothing. You expect me to believe that you're willing to leave your people and come with me, just because you like my brother? Try again."

"I do like Tobin," the boy said indignantly. "Though there's other things too. Onny and Regg and Miggy, all my friends went into the Otherworld with Mistress Makenna, and I want them back."

That made more sense, but the goblin's eyes had shifted aside. He still wasn't telling the whole truth. On the other hand . . . "Let me get this straight. Cogswhallop is your father?"

"Aye." The boy perched cautiously on a fallen log.

"And he gave you permission to come with me?"

"Aye. He really likes you. I can tell."

"He *likes* . . ." Jeriah snorted. "If he likes me, then the Bright Gods help his enemies!"

The boy grinned, and Jeriah regarded him thoughtfully.

"You're here to help me? Your father wasn't interested in that, last time I talked to him."

"Aye, but this is between you and me. I told you, Tobin is my friend."

It sounded convincing, but the small ears had turned pink again. Jeriah couldn't trust the creature. But if the goblins were going to guide him to his brother, he needed to learn more about them, and this boy was less guileful than Cogswhallop. He might even know something about those mysterious Lesser Ones.

So find out everything he knows, then send him packing.

Jeriah remembered a lesson Cogswhallop had taught him the hard way and asked, "What's your name?"

"Daroo."

"Well, Daroo, if you're here to help you can begin by undoing this pack." He pulled it off Glory's back and dropped it at the child's feet. "You can tell me what's in it while I unsaddle the horses."

"What for?"

"Because my father packed it, and I don't know what's there."

"No, I mean what'll you give me for doing it? You don't want to be indebted."

"Indebted? Because you unpacked a bag? I thought you wanted to help."

"That's about Tobin," said the child, with exaggerated patience. "Unpacking bags is different. Here, I'll talk you through it. See that pinecone over there?"

"Yes."

"Give it to me, and I'll help you unpack."

"Why?" Jeriah picked up the pinecone and handed it over. "It's worthless."

"That's my lookout." Daroo eyed the pinecone, nodded in satisfaction, and pitched it over his shoulder. "Now I'll unpack." He did so, leaving Jeriah shaking his head in bewilderment.

Jeriah kept an eye on the boy as he worked, but as far as he could tell the child played no tricks. The pack held the usual camping gear, food for a week, the letter for Master Lazur, and a bag of silver coins. Jeriah sighed, remembering his lost gold pieces, but he could hardly blame the old man for not trusting him with the same amount this time. Considering the circumstances, his father had been generous.

After their meal they took to the road once more. The afternoon was cool but clear, as if last night's storm had drained the sky. Soon the spring rains would end and the dry heat of summer set in.

As the day passed, Jeriah's decision to bring the boy along paid off. Daroo, riding behind Jeriah hidden under his cloak, was a well of information—assuming, of course, that what he said could be trusted. He made Jeriah pay for every bit of it, but payment could be a half-open flower or a pretty stone as easily as a bit of cheese or an apple.

Jeriah learned that although every goblin had a "gift," each could work only one type of magic. Daroo's gift, which he'd inherited from his father, was the ability to work with iron and steel—metals other goblins couldn't touch.

"That's why I could work the catch on your saddlebag from the inside. Because it was iron, see?"

"Sort of. How did you get into the bag in the first place?"

"I just crawled in, when you were talking to Fa."

"I didn't see you."

"You weren't looking."

Jeriah sighed.

The boy also explained the goblins' philosophy of trading for everything they gave or gained.

". . . or else you'll be indebted. If you're indebted or owed, then you can't be equals, and if you're not equal, you can't be friends. See?"

"Not exactly," Jeriah admitted. It still seemed like nonsense, especially since the payment involved was trivial.

The boy was also useful when he made camp at night. By the time darkness fell, both horses were tired and Jeriah was exhausted. Daroo helped him make camp for a share of his supper, gathering dry wood from the Gods knew where—though he almost drowned when he led the horses down to the stream to drink and a sudden tug on the lead rope pulled him in.

Swearing as he hauled the child out of the rushing water, Jeriah felt like he was dealing with Tamilee. Did all children insist on tackling jobs that were beyond their strength?

Jeriah pushed the pace as much as he could, but it wasn't till midmorning of his third day on the road that the City of Steps appeared on the horizon. For Daroo, this was the journey's end.

"But how can I help if I'm not with you?" Frustration tightened the goblin's voice.

"Look at that." Jeriah gestured to the distant hill, towering over the plain and marsh around it. "The City of Steps is the Hierarch's own city. The palace, where I'll be, is full of priests and the sunsguard, all of them sworn to destroy servants of the Dark One—which includes you, demon brat!"

"That's pigdung." The child folded his arms, looking so like his father that Jeriah bit back a grin.

"Maybe, maybe not. All right, it is pigdung—but the guards and priests don't think so. If they caught you, you'd be killed. You can't help your friends get back from the Otherworld if you're dead, and there won't be anything you can do in the city to help Tobin or me."

Daroo had been helpful, but smuggling a goblin into the Sunlord's own palace would be far too risky—particularly since Jeriah still hadn't learned what the boy was concealing.

"You've told me several times that you can take care of yourself," Jeriah finished. "So prove it. Go home to your parents. That's an order," he added, as Daroo opened his mouth to argue. "And I wouldn't take an ally who can't obey orders with me, anyway."

"Humph!" The child turned and stalked into the bushes, vanishing in seconds.

Smiling, Jeriah turned Glory and set off for the city

before Daroo changed his mind. That stubborn loyalty also reminded Jeriah of Tamilee. In truth, Daroo had begun to feel more and more like a younger brother over the last two days. All the more reason to leave him behind. Jeriah's last attempt at plotting and conspiracy had gotten Tobin flogged, and ultimately trapped in the Otherworld. Trying to smuggle Daroo into the palace would be madness—because if someone captured the tiny creature, Jeriah could never abandon him to die.

Riding through the farmed land surrounding the City of Steps took half a day. As morning passed into afternoon, Jeriah could make out the three walls that sculpted the hill, like an off-center layer cake. The top four levels of the City of Steps comprised the palace and temple—perfect circles, each wider than the one above it. The three lower tiers followed the shape of the hill forming irregular ovals, each one spreading farther toward the west.

Closer to the city the road was crowded with exhausted Southlanders, carrying all they owned in small carts and ragged packs. In the furor over his own banishment, Jeriah had forgotten that soon everyone in the Realm would have to leave their homes.

If he could get Tobin back, surely the old man would relent. Would understand that Jeriah had been forced to flood that village, would understand all the other choices he'd been forced to make.

For the refugees around him there was no going home. Ever. But Master Lazur and the Hierarch would see them relocated behind the wall, where they could build anew, and Jeriah had enough on his plate already. His job was to get Tobin back. The refugees would have to look out for themselves.

Jeriah reached the gate in the first wall by midafternoon. The low city was dirty, clamorous, exciting, and, well, low. It had always fascinated Jeriah, in a way his respectable brother had deplored.

At the third gate, where army guards were posted at night, the straight road to the palace began. But there Jeriah turned aside, riding past the gardens and into the woods that concealed the barracks where visiting knights and lesser nobles and priests were housed.

Past the barracks, he settled Glory and Fiddle in a stable and arranged for their care before going on to the palace.

The gate that lay beyond the Hall of Justice and the Hall of Plenty (which most people referred to as the treasury) was guarded at all times by the sunsguard itself.

Jeriah halted when challenged and told the guards his name and business. They looked bored, but Jeriah knew they'd remember his name, his face, and what he'd told them. The Hierarch's personal guard, in their sunred tunics, were the best in the Realm.

He climbed two flights of wide stone steps, which ran all the way up to the high temple, broken by a wide landing at each level. The numbering of palace levels started at the top; the temple was on level one, the Hierarch's rooms and highest government offices on level two, midlevel functionaries on level three, and the big public rooms on level four.

Jeriah turned off the stairs at the third-level landing. Flower beds and planters ringed the terrace, brimming with the brilliant blossoms of the Midland spring. Trees carried the vibrant sheen of new leaves, and fountains splashed soothingly. Jeriah circled around the terrace to Master Lazur's office.

Master Lazur had two rooms in corridor five, one an outer room with a window. That wasn't bad for a priest of his rank in this crowded place. What other fifth-circle priest had so much influence? Power without rank.

Jeriah's palms were damp as he knocked on the door. He had too much to hide.

"Come in."

He took a final breath and swung the door wide.

"Jeriah! I'm pleased to see you, but surely it hasn't been a month?" Master Lazur rose, smiling, from behind his desk. Bookshelves lined the walls around him.

"My father released me. I want to serve the Realm until the difficulties and dangers of the relocation are past."

"And he agreed?" The priest's brows rose.

Jeriah handed over his father's letter. He wished he knew what it said, but it had been sealed. Some people could remove and replace a seal without destroying it, but Jeriah wasn't one of them. Still, his father wasn't likely to reveal family quarrels to a stranger.

"Very well." Master Lazur set the letter aside. "I've received another message concerning you . . . from your mother."

"Oh." Jeriah had forgotten about his mother's plans. "She said she was going to write."

"Yes. She feels that I should mount some sort of expedition to rescue your brother, and that if I don't I'll . . . How did she phrase it? I will 'deeply regret' it."

"Ah . . ."

The priest swept on. "I do regret your brother's death."

He's not dead yet.

"But if you're to stay here, you must understand that it's the relocation, the safety, the survival of the Realm that matter. If you can't understand that, I'll have to reconsider allowing you to work in the palace. In truth I'd planned to assign you as a courier between the palace and the army, but your mother's service has earned you a palace post"—Master Lazur glanced down at the letter—"as she repeatedly reminds me."

A courier, on the road all the time, would never be able to search for spell notes.

"I do understand, master, but I'd rather be assigned in the palace. I've seen too many refugees in the last month not to understand how important the relocation is."

And that was true. He just wasn't prepared to sacrifice his brother's life for it.

"Surely I can do more for the Realm as your assistant than as a courier," Jeriah went on desperately. "Besides . . . ah . . . my mother has made it very plain what kind of career she expects of me."

As long as he could stay in the palace, Jeriah didn't care what job he did. Though he'd assumed— "I'm not to continue as your assistant?"

"I have a new assistant," said Master Lazur. "Not because you served me badly—you did well enough. I'm taking on young Nevin for political reasons."

"Political reasons?"

"His father is Lord Brallorscourt, who has more influence with the lesser landholders of the Realm than any other man on the council. He waited to be certain our faction would come out on top in the recent power struggle, and we did, so now he's bringing his influence to our support. We're going to need it. Those who favor the relocation have been struggling for years against . . . well, everyone." He rose and paced to the window, gazing out to the south. "So few understand the necessity for the relocation that it seems as if every vote has been balanced on a knife edge. With Lord Brallorscourt's support, I'll have a far better chance to get the votes I need."

"I thought the relocation was assured. Orders have gone out to all the towns and the landholders . . . haven't they?"

"Yes." The priest's voice held a weary triumph. "The orders are out. But there's still resistance to the idea in the council, as well as the Realm. It won't be a sure thing until the last household is settled on the other side of the Goblin Wall. So Lord Brallorscourt's son is my new assistant. Or he will be, as soon as we find a proper replacement for his current post. He's been serving as the Hierarch's squire, and replacing him is proving . . . But that's not your problem."

Fleetingly, passionately, Jeriah wished the conspirators had succeeded. This kind of influence peddling was one of the many things they'd hoped to reform. But they had failed, and as long as Jeriah was working somewhere in the palace, he could search for the spell notes.

"So what will I be doing?" Jeriah asked.

"I'm assigning you to Master Goserian, who runs the Hierarch's household," said Master Lazur. "He can always use someone to run errands and generally assist him—much the same work you were doing for me. If you do as well for him, I'm sure you'll soon rise to better things. If you prove troublesome . . ."

The priest shrugged. They both knew what kind of trouble he meant.

". . . troublesome people don't remain in the Hierarch's service."

"Don't worry, sir," said Jeriah. "I intend to be here for a long time."

"You'll need a room, as well as an introduction." The priest returned to his desk and scribbled a brief note. "Present this to Master Goserian. He'll find a room for you—only the

128

Bright Gods know where!—and instruct you in your duties. Clear?"

"Perfectly." Jeriah hoped that didn't sound as ironic as he thought it did. Master Lazur glanced at him searchingly, but he handed Jeriah the note and nodded dismissal.

Jeriah left. At least he'd still be in the palace. As long as those cursed notes were in the same city, he'd find them!

Within a month?

Yes, because he had to.

It might even be easier out from under the priest's sharp eye. And serving the Master of Household, nothing job that it was, would probably get Jeriah into more places than being Master Lazur's assistant would.

Enjoying the sweeping view over city and countryside and trying to calm his nerves, Jeriah walked back to the great staircase between the levels where more of the sunsguard were always posted.

The guard told him Master Goserian was in the housekeeping offices in the interior of the fourth level. "When he isn't hustling around checking for dust, the old . . . ah, he's very conscientious."

The flower beds that lined these steps were smaller than those on the third level, but no less lovely. This was a level where Jeriah had been before—it held the great dining hall where large ceremonies took place. There were many passages to the inner corridors; Jeriah spent some time wandering through the maze of hallways, and once into a steam-filled laundry, before he finally found the house-keeping offices.

Master Goserian wasn't there, but they thought he might be one level up in the library, or perhaps out on the second tier dealing with some problem with the produce that came from the palace farm.

Jeriah was very familiar with the grounds that surrounded the army barracks, but he'd spent almost as little time in the palace's gardens and grounds as he had in its inner corridors. Soon he would probably know them as well as Rovan Manor. He followed a clerk's directions to a narrow servants' staircase and came out in the library.

"I haven't seen him today," an ink-stained librarian said. "But Koryn might know. I think she's in the scroll cupboard, under the stairs there."

The corner to which she gestured held not a staircase, but a recessed wedge in one corner of the back wall. The stairs were clearly on the other side of the wall, but for some reason the palace architects had opened the space beneath it into this room. The taller part of the wedge was filled with bookcases, like every other wall in the library, but as he approached, Jeriah saw that the narrow end had been partitioned off into a real cupboard, with a small access door. A pair of slender feet in well-worn shoes stuck out of it, twitching when their owner moved.

Jeriah knelt beside the hatch and called softly. "Mistress Koryn? I'm—"

A muffled thump, followed by a not so muffled curse, interrupted him. Jeriah hadn't intended to startle her, but he had to suppress a laugh before he went on. "I'm looking for Master Goserian, and one of the librarians thought you might know where I could find him."

She emerged as he spoke. Rump first, clad in a drab green gown. The gown was dusty. Jeriah, who'd expected the gray robe of an underpriest, was mildly surprised. The rump was followed by slender arms and shoulders, also dusty, and then Mistress Koryn was sitting on the floor beside him. Her face was too thin, her eyes too big, and the dark curly hair of the Southlands was also covered with dust.

"I'm sorry to interrupt your work, but if you've any idea where Master Goserian might be . . . ?"

Jeriah wasn't really the flirt that gossip claimed he was, but when he smiled at girls, they usually smiled back. This one didn't.

"So you're him," she said. "I wondered."

His smile wilted under that cool gray stare. Most Southlanders had brown eyes. And manners. But there was no point in him being rude too.

"I'm Jeriah Rovan. The librarian thought you might be able to tell me where I can find—"

"I know who you are," she said. "And I know what you want. I'm the one you've been pretending to be for the last few months."

"I haven't pretended to be anyone," Jeriah said in some

confusion. He'd lied a lot, but that wasn't the same thing. "And all I want is to find Master Goserian. So if you'd kindly—"

"What, not to rescue your brother? Or to overthrow the government? Or even just pursue a political career?"

Her voice wasn't loud, but Jeriah flinched and looked around—no one near enough to overhear. "How in the Dark One's name do you know all that?"

"Because I'm Master Lazur's assistant," the girl said. "He's been working on your file lately, so I read—"

"He has a file on me?" Jeriah demanded, outraged. "And you read it?"

"He has files on everything and everyone in the Realm. At least, anyone who matters." Enthusiasm brightened her rain-colored eyes. "As his assistant, I have access to—"

"Wait a minute," Jeriah said. "He told me his assistant was Nevin something-or-other."

"Ah, your pardon," the girl said. "I'm just his clerk."

Jeriah rose to his feet, staring down at her. "You're his *real* assistant. The one who does the work."

If this girl—she couldn't be much older than he was, and she looked younger—but if she was Master Lazur's real assistant, she was Jeriah's enemy. On the other hand, if she was in the priest's confidence, and it sounded like she was, she could be a mine of useful information. If he could charm it out of her.

She looked remarkably charm-proof, gazing critically up

at him, but Jeriah reached down and extended a hand to help her up.

"Then when I was serving Master Lazur, I guess I was pretending to be you!" He tried another smile. "In my own defense, I did give him a fair day's work—and sometimes more! I did my job, Mistress . . . ? I only know your first name."

She eyed his extended hand for a moment, then grimaced and gripped it. Jeriah helped her to her feet. She didn't weigh much, which was good, because she needed more help than he'd expected. She staggered a bit on standing, and released Jeriah to clutch one of the shelves. She might have been stiff from kneeling so long, but something in the hip-shot way she stood . . .

"I'm sorry," Jeriah said gently. "Are you lame? I wouldn't have hauled you up so quickly if I'd—"

"That doesn't matter," she said. "Except to me. Which means it doesn't matter."

That cool, steady gaze was beginning to get on Jeriah's nerves. "Well, I'm sorry. If you can tell me where I might find Master Goserian, I'll stop disrupting your work, Mistress . . . ?"

"Goserian. I'm Master Goserian's niece, which is why they thought I might be able to tell you where he is."

Goserian hadn't looked or sounded like a Southlander, and only a bit of the accent clung to this girl's words. Had Master Goserian's brother wed a Southland bride, perhaps?

It was none of Jeriah's business.

"So where is your uncle?"

"I have no idea," Koryn Goserian said. "Try his office."

"I just came from there."

She shrugged. "Then you might check the kitchen. That's what gives him the most trouble on any given day, so it's worth a try."

"Thank you." Jeriah turned away, unable to summon up another smile—and he usually found it easy to smile at women. This Koryn seemed to be not only uncharmable but charmless. He pitied her crippled leg, but . . . Oh well, she was only Lazur's clerk. He probably wouldn't see much of her.

The kitchen occupied the center of the fourth level, with circular walls filled with fireplaces and a high ceiling blackened with smoke. The scent of cooking reminded Jeriah that he'd missed midmeal. Perhaps he could beg something from the cooks later, but not now. The tall man haranguing a plump man in an apron had to be Master Goserian.

He was about Jeriah's father's age, and he held his back so straight and his balding head so high that the small potbelly only added to his dignity.

Jeriah approached, then waited until Master Goserian finished scolding the red-faced cook about improperly peeled vegetables. Then he turned to Jeriah.

"You require something"—his eyes ran over Jeriah's dusty

travel-stained form, placing his rank to the last degree—"young sir?"

"I'm Jeriah Rovan. Master Lazur has assigned me to your service." He held out the priest's note, but Master Goserian didn't read it immediately.

"If you're the brother of Sir Tobin Rovan of Rovanscourt, who recently gave his life in the service of the Realm, then you are now Jeriah Rovan of Rovanscourt. Or is there another brother, older than you?"

"Uh, no." Jeriah felt a pang of guilt, as if he'd stolen the heir's title from his brother. He was going to get Tobin back. And he suspected everyone who talked to the Master of Household felt guilty. If the housekeeper was this intimidating, what would the Hierarch be like? Working for the Master of Household, Jeriah would be bound to meet the Sunlord eventually. Or did glorified menservants ever rise that high? No matter. Jeriah was there to find spell notes, not to carve out a career.

Master Goserian finished reading. "I see. Come with me, Rovan of Rovanscourt." He must have seen something in Jeriah's expression, for he added, "I don't know whether formalities were observed in your home"—his tone relegated it to some backward corner of the Realm—"but this is the palace of the Chosen of the Seven Bright Gods. You will use your full title when introducing yourself, and others' titles when addressing them."

He led Jeriah through the dining hall as he spoke, their

steps echoing from the pillared vault of the ceiling. The servants were setting up tables for dinner, and Jeriah wondered when it would be served. He was famished.

"Dinner is served at the sixth hour past noon." Jeriah jumped guiltily. "Midmeal is at noon and breakfast six hours before that. The palace chimes sound hourly, and ten minutes before each meal a warning chime will sound. Food service ends one hour after it commences, and the tables are generally cleared an hour after serving ends. This time of year, however, the sun gong summons us to Sunset Prayer less than half an hour after the end of food service, so we must accommodate ourselves."

Jeriah suppressed a grin. The irregularity of the sun appeared to be a considerable annoyance to Master Goserian.

The dining hall exited onto the fourth level's outer terrace, which held public offices where the Realm's business was conducted. The circular central rings contained the private quarters of the priests and nobles who made up the court. An inner ring around the kitchen, laundry, and bathing rooms held the servants' rooms, chambers for food storage, and "other household matters."

Master Goserian turned abruptly and led Jeriah into one of the rooms in the middle ring. No window for a Master of Household's assistant. Master Goserian pulled out a striker and lit the lamp. The stone-walled chamber would have been reasonably spacious if it hadn't held two beds, two chests, and one large desk. Probably only one desk because there wasn't room for another. Jeriah eyed the books on it warily.

"Who am I rooming with?"

"Seber Merro, one of Master Zachiros' assistants. I believe his function has to do with estimating future taxes; he's often traveling. He's not in residence now, though he's expected back by midsummer."

Thank you, Bright Ones. "Won't he be surprised to find me in his room?"

"I doubt it." Master Goserian opened the empty chest for Jeriah. The bed behind it must be his too. "Most who have rooms on this level share. The palace is always crowded."

"How many people live here?"

"Currently there are four hundred and eighty"—he eyed Jeriah consideringly—"seven. Half-hour prayer services are held at dawn and sunset; everyone in the palace is required to attend. Tomorrow, after Dawn Prayer, you'll report to me to begin your duties. I trust you'll find time to bathe and change your clothing before dinner. As I told you, the Sunset Prayer follows immediately."

He smiled firmly and left. Jeriah stared after him, unseeing. *Everyone is required to attend.* Master Lazur would be out of his quarters for over half an hour, and in a crowd of nearly five hundred, who could tell if Jeriah was present or not? It would be a perfect time to search Master Lazur's rooms.

✧ ✧ ✧

Jeriah took Master Goserian's not-so-gentle hint and next went to the bathing room, an echoing chamber that held more steam than the laundry. Buckets of warm water were available to remove the dirt, and a deep soaking pool, but Jeriah had no time to try it out. The warning chime for dinner rang as he was rinsing off the soap.

He toweled dry, dressed, and reached the dining hall not long after dinner began, though his hair was still wet. The selection was good for this time of year—each table held four different roasts, bread, and several dishes of late-lasting vegetables and fruits. Jeriah noticed a bowl of early greens on the table reserved for the high-ranking lords and priests.

He looked around for an empty place and a familiar face caught his eye—a squire he'd met last winter, when he and Tobin were fighting on the southern border. Soon he was seated at a table full of young men, several already known to him.

They talked about the barbarians, the surprise attack that had taken most of the Southlands, and the plans to hold the border while the Realm relocated. Only a few months ago it would have fascinated Jeriah, but now his thoughts were focused on Master Lazur's rooms.

What if the priest suspected his intention and was waiting for him? What if he locked the door? With so many assistants coming and going, and palace security so good, most of the offices weren't locked during the day. But Master Lazur might do it. Or worse, what if he decided to destroy the notes—a sure way to keep them from Jeriah!

But he had to try—Tobin's life was at stake.

When the sun gong rang, his plate was still half full, his appetite gone.

Jeriah's room was on the opposite side of the terrace from Master Lazur's, but it was the safest place for him to hide as the rest of the palace streamed up the central stairs to the temple at the top.

When no one had passed for several minutes, Jeriah hurried around the terrace, keeping close to the wall so he couldn't be seen from above.

Eight, seven, six, five. He hesitated at the entrance to Master Lazur's rooms. What if the priest was still inside? Should he knock? What if—

"He's gone."

Jeriah jumped and spun toward the familiar voice.

"What are you doing here?" He barely managed to keep his voice to a whisper. "I told you to go home!"

"Aye, and I still don't understand why you thought I'd do it. Since you're not my fa or anything." Daroo crouched among the flowers that rimmed the terrace, his face painted gold by the dying light, his eyes glinting with defiance and . . . laughter?

"I told you, I don't want an ally who can't obey orders."

And even less, an ally who was still keeping secrets from him.

"*Allies* don't have to take orders. And Mistress Makenna

is the only one who commands us goblins." Curse the little demon, he was laughing. "That priest left about five minutes ago. I heard someone say this sunset thing only lasts half an hour, so you should hurry."

The goblin had been helpful on the journey—but could Jeriah trust him now?

"I'm surprised you're not in there already," said Jeriah, stalling for time to think.

"I tried it." Daroo grimaced. "He's got charmed iron across the door and the windowsill."

"I thought iron was your gift."

"It's not the iron, it's the charm. It's bespelled so goblins can't get near it. Not even Fa could. So you'd best get in there."

"I don't need your advice." Jeriah kept his voice low. Not only had Daroo disobeyed him, but the goblin had secrets. He didn't dare trust him. Not when it mattered so much. "I don't want your help. I'll deal with you later, but for now get out of here before you get caught!"

"You're the one who'll be caught if you wait much longer. I'd stand watch for a button."

"I won't pay . . ." Daroo vanished into the flowers before Jeriah could finish. Even knowing he was there, Jeriah couldn't see him, and further argument would endanger both of them. Curse the stubborn brat. Gritting his teeth, Jeriah eased the office door open.

Not locked. Because Master Lazur knew that clerks and

assistants might need access? Or because the notes weren't there? There was only one way to find out.

During his interview Jeriah had barely noticed the furnishings. The desk was plain, made of a beautiful fine-grained wood. Bookshelves lined most of the walls, but against one wall stood a row of cabinets made of the same wood as the desk. In the wall opposite the window, a door giving access to the priest's bedchamber had been cut. Master Lazur must virtually own these rooms if they were willing to cut doors for him. He'd left the connecting door open, with a lamp lit in the room beyond. Much easier than fumbling in the dark when he returned from the evening prayers. The light that spilled through the door was almost lost in the coppery glow from the window. When the lamp-light grew stronger than the sunlight, it would be time to leave—better start now.

First the desk. The drawers were locked, but that didn't mean the notes would be there—it might just be documents Master Lazur didn't want disturbed. On the other hand . . . Why hadn't he learned to pick locks? The demon brat's gift was iron, but even if Daroo could open them, Jeriah couldn't bring him past the charm.

Maybe he'd find the keys elsewhere and could come back to the desk.

The bookshelves held a set of spell books, just like the ones the sorceress had stolen. The gate spell would be there, but Jeriah already knew that the spells that might keep his brother alive in the Otherworld weren't. Would any of those neatly bound volumes hold experimental notes? Probably not. Probably not where the keys were kept, either.

Jeriah stepped softly across to one of the tall cabinets and opened the door, and a moan of dismay escaped him. It was filled with papers; single sheets and sheets stitched together, ragged-looking scrolls and irregular scraps. A glint of copper caught Jeriah's eye, and he fished out one of the blood amulets they found on the barbarians' dead bodies. What a strange faith that must be, that the people required shamans to protect them from their own gods. Master Lazur had told Jeriah that if the church's spies wore these amulets, the barbarians wouldn't harm them, even if they'd been captured. Though if the spy took it off . . . No spy who'd taken off an amulet had ever returned to report, but the rumors in the army were gruesome. Because they were made with human sacrifice, the Hierarch had declared these amulets unholy and forbidden their possession. That Jeriah found it here revealed the strength of Master Lazur's obsession with the barbarians.

Jeriah replaced the amulet. The top paper on the stack beside it was a technical report on clearing timberlands. The top paper on the stack below that was a Southland ballad. Jeriah glanced down the row of cabinets; there were seven of them.

Well, as his father said, staring at it wouldn't make it smaller. He lifted down the papers on the highest shelf. An astronomical table. He sighed.

"I'll spare you the trouble," said a cool voice behind him. "It isn't there."

Jeriah spun, his dagger half drawn before he thought. A young man leaned against the bedroom door, lamplight glinting on straw-straight hair.

"Who are you?"

"I could ask you the same question. And what you're doing here." The stranger strolled forward, stretched out one finger, and pushed Jeriah's dagger back into its sheath. "But I don't have to ask. I'm Sir Nevin Brallor of Brallorscourt, Timeon Lazur's new assistant. And you're Jeriah Rovan of Rovanscourt, brother to the traitor."

He was enjoying this, curse him.

"Most people consider my brother a hero. His . . . transgressions have been forgiven."

"By most people. But we know better, don't we?" Sir Nevin—how had he gotten knighted? He was no older than Jeriah—cocked his head curiously. "I must admit, I didn't believe Master Lazur when he told me you'd come. Wouldn't you rather have a dead hero for a brother than a live traitor?"

"No," said Jeriah. "Master Lazur *told* you I'd be here?"

"Evidently"—Nevin perched on the edge of the desk—"you aren't that hard to anticipate. He asked me to deliver a message for him."

"I thought everyone was supposed to attend the Sunset Prayer."

"*You* are supposed to be at prayer. *I* was excused to run an urgent errand for Master Lazur. Aren't you curious about the message?"

"I can guess most of it."

"I doubt that. I'm supposed to tell you that he regrets the necessity for your brother's death. Though I don't know why, as your brother sounds pretty unreliable to me." He regarded Jeriah with malicious brightness.

He's only trying to provoke me. He was succeeding, too. Jeriah folded his arms and waited.

"He doesn't mind you trying to get the spell notes, but he can't permit you to succeed. Now that he knows you haven't given up, you'll be watched. And you'll never know who's assigned to watch you, so you can't trust anyone, now can you? It was stupid to try for them so soon—you should have lulled us for a while!"

Jeriah tried to keep his face blank, but his tormentor's grin told him he hadn't succeeded.

"But that's not part of the message, so . . . The notes you want have been hidden where you can't reach them, so you might as well resign yourself and concentrate on your new duties. He's got a point. Your brother made his own decision—and even if he made it for the wrong reasons, it was a gallant one. I don't think it's any of your business to meddle."

"You know nothing about it." Jeriah's voice shook with rage. "Do you really expect me to take your word, or his, that the notes aren't here?"

"It doesn't matter whether you believe us." Nevin rose and went to the door. "You can search these papers till you've memorized them, as long as you put them back in the same place. The notes you want are hidden where you'll never find them. And even if you did, you couldn't . . . Never mind."

Nevin knew where they were! Could he be tricked into revealing the location? Not likely, curse it. Why couldn't he have been stupid, as well as arrogant and malicious?

"It doesn't matter. You won't find them." Nevin held the door open; the sunlight was almost gone. Jeriah heard the distant murmur of the worshipers' "Praise and farewell."

"Unless you want to do penance for missing the service, you'd better go," Nevin told him. "Eventually we'll meet for the first time and pretend this conversation never took place. I won't even mention it if you don't."

"How magnanimous." Jeriah stalked past him, searching desperately for some cutting last word that would wipe the smug grin from Nevin's face.

"You're welcome." Nevin shut the door before he could respond.

Jeriah swore, and hurried off in the dusk.

Tobin

"HE'S ASLEEP." THE GOBLIN GIRL'S whisper was so loud that if Tobin had been asleep, it might have wakened him. "You shouldn't bother him with stupid stuff."

"I'm just resting." Tobin opened his eyes and smiled at Onny. As usual, Regg accompanied her. If anything, they'd grown even closer in Daroo's absence, but Tobin thought the small band was . . . unbalanced without the boy. "I didn't sleep very well last night," he added. "Is there a problem?"

There was always a problem, these days.

"No," said Onny. "Root's just imagining things, and he's got Regg doing it too. We shouldn't even be bothering you, much less the mistress."

Tobin looked more closely and saw a pair of stubby legs lurking behind Regg. Root was Regg's youngest brother . . . and Regg usually ignored him.

"What's the problem?" Tobin spoke to Regg, but to his surprise the boy pulled his little brother forward.

The child eyed Tobin thoughtfully, then stuck his thumb into his mouth.

Regg sighed. "Tell him about your friend, Root."

The boy nodded so firmly, his hair flopped on his forehead, but he didn't remove the thumb. Regg grabbed his brother's wrist and tugged, and the thumb came free with a small popping sound.

"Talk," Regg demanded. "You don't get it back till you do."

Root screwed up his small face and sighed. "I got a new friend."

"A *new* friend?" Root had known most of the goblins in their camp for the whole of his short life. How could he have a new—

"A rock friend." Root nodded. "He plays with me."

Tobin frowned. "You made friends with one of the Stoners?"

"It's stupider than that," said Onny. "He's made friends with a rock."

"Well, my sister Senna once got very attached to a tree. She was about your age, Onny, and she'd climb up into a fork and read for—"

"He plays with me," Root said calmly. "I like him."

Even at her worst, Senna hadn't given her tree friend a gender.

"He was about a mile from camp when we found him," Regg told Tobin. "He doesn't stray that far on his own. And when we first came in sight of him, I thought . . . It must have been a trick of the shadows."

"You thought . . . ?"

Regg shrugged, a flush creeping into his brown cheeks.

"He thinks the rock Root was sitting on moved," said Onny. "So it's got to be nonsense, doesn't it?"

Her voice was as firm as ever, but Tobin saw a shadow of worry in her eyes.

Keeping things like this from troubling Makenna was one of the reasons he'd come to this world. Tobin rose to his feet and boosted Root up onto his shoulder. "Show me this rock of yours."

Tobin thought they were more than a mile from the camp when they went down into a shallow dip and came in sight of a small pile of reddish rock. Root began to squirm, and he set the boy down.

"He shouldn't be wandering this far off. We haven't seen any dangerous predators . . ." They hadn't seen any predators at all, which still struck Tobin as odd. " . . . but a child can die just from getting lost."

Or drown. Or fall off a cliff and break his thin bones.

"I know that," said Regg. "And he knows better than to go off alone. Our mam will have a fit when we tell her."

"And probably blame us," Onny added gloomily.

Thumb firmly in place, Root squatted in front of the rock pile and patted it, as if he were trying to wake it.

Tobin frowned and knelt to inspect the rocks. The surfaces were a bit more weathered than some of the stone around them, but no different otherwise. He laid a hand on the rock and found it rough, cold, and solid. A fanciful child might have seen something like a face on the craggy surface, but there was nothing extraordinary about it.

The thumb popped out, and Root poked at one of the places Tobin had seen as a crooked eye. "He's asleep."

The gesture made the hair on the back of Tobin's neck lift, but the rock didn't budge.

"It was just a trick of the shadows," said Regg. "Couldn't be anything else."

It couldn't. Still . . .

"I want you two to keep a close watch on Root," Tobin said. "On all the little ones. I don't want any of them wandering out of camp again."

CHAPTER 7

Jeriah

BUT EVEN IF JERIAH FOUND them he couldn't . . . what? Couldn't get someone to open a gate? Couldn't read it? Couldn't . . . The arrogant toad might have meant anything!

The question had kept Jeriah awake, and it started bothering him the moment the page's tap on his door roused him next morning. Jeriah hauled his last clean tunic over his head—better get some laundry done—and searched sleepily for his boots. He'd always hated rising before dawn, dressing by lamplight—it had taken him five minutes' fumbling to light the cursed thing. He'd already lost too much time lying in bed as he tried to drag his eyes open, listening to the page working his way down the corridor and trying to figure out what the priest had meant.

Jeriah pulled on his boots and opened the door. By the time he emerged onto the terrace, the sky was bright with the approach of dawn—the stones, the flowers, even the cold air that crept beneath his tunic seemed to be coming alive. If he was supposed to arrive for prayers by sunrise he was going to be late.

Jeriah hurried around the empty terrace—everyone else must already be at the temple—but when he reached the central stairs, a slight, elderly priest in floppy slippers was hobbling up the steps.

"I'm late again! No need to tell me; I already know." He smiled at Jeriah and pushed up the spectacles that had slipped down his nose. "I believe I know you. You're Master Goserian's new assistant, ah . . . No, don't tell me, I'll remember in a moment. I'm sure I've heard your name."

"Jeriah Rovan," Jeriah supplied.

"Yes, of course! I've seen you somewhere. I don't at once remember where, but it'll come to me. Oh dear! We're both going to be late!"

As the stranger continued up the steps, Jeriah slowed his own pace. If he was going to walk in late, he'd rather have company. "Forgive me, master—you seem to remember me but I'm afraid I don't know you at all."

"We didn't meet. You were pointed out to me at some court function . . . or was it at . . . well, it was almost a year ago. I'm Master Zachiros, the Hierarch's secretary. The formal title is Pen and Memory, Scribe of the Chosen of the Bright Gods, but secretary is the truth."

"I'm pleased to meet you." Jeriah meant it—it was nice to see that not everyone here shared Master Goserian's taste for pomp. Although those slippers . . .

"Excuse me, but may I ask why . . . ?" Jeriah gestured to

the man's feet. Was the secretary absentminded enough to have forgotten his shoes?

Master Zachiros shrugged. "Sore feet. The curse of old age, lad. Luckily, one of the graces of old age is sufficient rank to wear shoes that accommodate them!"

Jeriah slowed even more, but in just a few more steps they had arrived at the temple, which stood at the very top of the palace open to the Bright Gods' sky.

A crowd of courtiers stood in front of the dais, shifting their feet and gossiping, but silence fell when the Sunlord emerged from a staircase at the west rim of the circle and walked slowly toward the great altar at the center. The chorus waited quietly, perched on steps that rose to the northern rim of the temple, cupping the altar like outspread wings. The Hierarch turned to the east just as the sun slipped over the edge of the horizon, bathing him with living light. He lifted his arms. "Praise and welcome."

The full Dawn Prayer was seldom used in the countryside, but the responses were simple enough that Jeriah was able to murmur through them without fumbling. The formal words had never brought him comfort before, but watching morning light wash over the land, he welcomed that half hour's peace. He was afraid he might need an extra bit of calmness before the day was over.

In fact, working as Master Goserian's assistant wasn't as frustrating as Jeriah had feared—under that stuffy manner, a sharp mind lurked. By the time Jeriah climbed the stairs for Sunset Prayer, he understood why the Master of Household needed it. In just one day he'd delivered messages to the palace farms, orders to the laundry, a reprimand to a spice merchant, queries, bills, complaints . . .

A few days later Master Goserian asked Jeriah to investigate a problem and report back on the cause. Was the meat in a certain storage locker rotting because of improper storage, or had the butcher sent stuff that was already going bad? It wasn't complex, but Jeriah's answer could cost the butcher his best client, or a cook's assistant his job. He wasn't offended when Master Goserian checked to be certain Jeriah's report was accurate before making his final judgment—and then canceled his order with the butcher.

All of this gave Jeriah a clearer view of the complexities of palace life than he'd ever had before, and also a clearer view of the immense difficulty of finding anything as small as a bunch of spell notes!

By now Jeriah's work had taken him to every public part of the palace, from the third level, which held not only Master Lazur's office but also the council chambers and the offices of the landholders who served there, to the subcellar two flights of stairs below the kitchen and laundry, where a great furnace roared day and night.

If Jeriah had been trying to hide those notes, he'd have chosen one of the dozens of overcrowded, paper-stuffed offices. The administration of the entire Realm moved through them, and finding one pile of papers among all those thousands would have been impossible. But there would be dangers in that as well; those piles of paper were being processed by hundreds of attentive clerks. If something came to light that shouldn't be there, Master Zachiros would certainly hear about it . . . and maybe Master Goserian, too. *Even if you found it, you couldn't . . .* Recognize it? Use it?

Whatever the answer was, it wasn't likely to be a problem—because as far as Jeriah could tell, finding the notes was going to require the direct intervention of at least three saints!

He needed to figure out where Master Lazur might have put those notes, without tipping off the priest or Nevin. And he knew just who to ask—the likeliest person to know where papers were stored was always the lowly clerk.

Jeriah hovered in a corner of the great hall, watching the crowd stream in for midmeal. Tracking the girl down in the library would be too obvious, and he'd have to interrupt her work—not the right way to start a casual conversation. It would be tricky to charm Mistress Koryn. He needed to catch her off guard, in a sociable mood.

If he hadn't been watching, he'd never have seen her come in—nothing she wore stood out among the drably garbed priests. The Sunlord seldom dined with his court, but when he did, the ambitious courtiers and priests scrambled to sit near him. The smarter of the ambitious realized that most people claimed an accustomed seat for meals, so tables near the dais were crowded.

The table in the corner where Mistress Koryn sat down was one of the farthest from the dais that held the Hierarch's throne. It was occupied by upper servants and low-ranked clerks. As he drew closer, Jeriah saw that she'd brought a book into the dining hall.

Jeriah seated himself beside her and waited for her to notice. And waited.

The book she was reading appeared to be handwritten—someone's journal, perhaps?

Koryn turned a page and went right on reading. Jeriah gave up on being noticed.

"What are you working on so diligently, Mistress Goserian? It looks a bit dry from here. Downright dusty."

She jumped slightly when he spoke. Widened with surprise, her pale eyes dominated her face like a full moon dominates the night.

"What are you doing here?"

"I wanted to thank you for helping me find your uncle the other day. I'm working for him now."

Once more, his easy smile had no visible effect.

"Is that something you're doing for Master Lazur?" Jeriah pressed on. "Clerking seems an odd job for a, ah, a lovely young—"

"For a girl," she said dryly. "You don't know anything about me, do you?"

The standard response, that he'd like to know more about her, rose to Jeriah's lips. He had better sense than to say it.

"I understand that women have brains," he said instead. "My mother is one of the smartest people I know. But you have to admit, it's an unusual job. Especially for someone who's not an apprentice priest."

Her eyes were still wary, but her expression softened a bit. "What do you want, Rovanscourt?"

"It's Rovan," Jeriah told her. "As long as my brother is alive. I'd appreciate it if you'd call me Jeriah."

"All right. What do you want, Jeriah?"

He wasn't accustomed to girls who were that direct. "I just wanted to get to know you better."

"Of course you do." She finally smiled, but it was thin with irony. Her gaze strayed back to the book—which she hadn't bothered to close.

"Why shouldn't I want to get to know you?" Jeriah demanded, nettled. "You're pretty, in a weird sort of way. And you're my boss's niece. I'd . . ."

Neither of those things, he realized, was exactly flattering.

"I just thought you might be interesting to talk to, that's all."

And she was interesting, curse it, so the sincerity in his voice should have helped. But her smile grew colder.

"Master Lazur is one of the most powerful men in the Realm."

Jeriah blinked at the change of topic. "I know that. Your

uncle is powerful, too, in a different way. So what?"

"So do you really think, Master Rovan, that you're the first person to sit down and oh-so-casually try to get to know me?"

Ouch.

"I hadn't thought about that," Jeriah admitted. And he'd been clumsy about it, too. "Well then . . . Well. I'll leave you to your book, Mistress Goserian."

He rose and fled to his accustomed seat, among his own friends. Thank goodness the servers hadn't brought out the meal, or his departure would have been even more awkward. He was sufficiently embarrassed as it was!

It was his own fault, anyway. He'd realized at their first meeting that this girl had a brain. He would have to go back to searching the palace the hard way. Charming Mistress Koryn would clearly be even harder.

Jeriah had worked at that search for four more days when, taking a few moments to try to figure out which third-level office belonged to whom, he walked briskly around a corner and almost ran into the Hierarch.

"Sunlord," Jeriah gasped, dropping to one knee. At least he hadn't run the man down.

"Stand up," said the Hierarch gently. "I want a cup of tea. I came to look for it."

Didn't the Hierarch's servants attend to that? Evidently not this time. Up close, the Hierarch's face showed lines that

Jeriah hadn't seen when he'd attended the Sun Prayers, and silver threaded through the pale hair.

"May I fetch it for you, my lord?" Jeriah asked.

"Yes, please!" The Hierarch's smile was so delighted that Jeriah couldn't help smiling back.

He rose and hurried down to the kitchen. The cook's assistant, whose job Jeriah's report on the butcher had saved, knew which tea the Hierarch preferred. He swiftly brewed a pot and put it on the proper tray with several gold-rimmed cups in case the Hierarch had company. Jeriah hurried up two flights of interior stairs, setting the tray down on the last step to straighten his tunic and smooth his hair. Master Goserian hadn't yet sent him to the second level, and the simplicity of the unadorned marble flooring and walls surprised him. But the stone was beautiful, and the Hierarch hadn't appeared to be a man who stood on ceremony. Perhaps he preferred these open, simpler surroundings.

A pair of guards stood beside the door to the Hierarch's suite, but they only watched as Jeriah took a deep breath and knocked.

Nevin opened the door. "What are you doing here?"

Jeriah held out the tray. "The Hierarch asked me to bring him some tea."

"You met him!" Nevin pulled Jeriah into the room so abruptly he almost dropped the tray.

"Hey!" Jeriah protested.

"Where did you meet him?" Nevin demanded. "When was this?"

"Just a few minutes ago," said Jeriah. "On the third level. Isn't he here now? He didn't say where I was to bring it, so I assumed . . ."

"Oh, he's back now," said Nevin. "No thanks to you. I want this tea tested."

Jeriah blinked. "Tested?"

"Rano!" Nevin strode toward a door on the other side of the antechamber and summoned the man Jeriah knew to be the Hierarch's Master of Wardrobe. "Go fetch the herb mistress. I want this tea checked."

"It came from the palace kitchen," Jeriah protested. "I'm sure it's fine."

He knew some people were fussy about how their tea was brewed, but—

"It's not that," said Nevin. "It's . . . the Hierarch has some stomach problems. We have to be careful with what he's served."

"It was prepared by the assistant chef," Jeriah told him. If the Hierarch had stomach problems, surely the kitchen staff knew how to deal with it.

Nevin ignored him.

Jeriah was fuming silently by the time the herb mistress arrived.

She was a priest of the fourth circle whom Jeriah hadn't yet encountered on his errands. Plump and comfortably middle-aged, with quiet brown eyes and graying hair. Although she didn't resemble Jeriah's grandmother, who was spare and sharp-tongued, somehow she looked like everybody's grandmother. She heard Nevin out with a serene expression.

". . . wandering around like that. Anything could have happened!" Nevin ranted.

"But nothing did," she said. "So you'd best ease up before you set folks to wondering."

Her soft country accent surprised Jeriah. And what should he be wondering about?

Nevin scowled. "I still want you to test the tea. Everything he eats is supposed to be checked. His doctors ordered it when . . . a long time ago."

The herb mistress snorted, but she went over to the cooling pot and poured tea into one of the cups. She sniffed it, then took a sip.

"It's fine."

Nevin looked as if he expected her to drop dead on the spot.

"Any idiot could have told you that." Jeriah was beginning to enjoy himself.

Nevin's scowl turned into a snarl, but the woman squeezed his arm in warning.

"I know you were worried, but you don't want to make more of the situation than it is. I'll see this lad back downstairs while you take the Hierarch his tea, shall I?"

Without waiting for an answer, she whisked Jeriah out of the room and down the corridor. They were descending the third-level servants' staircase before he'd gathered his wits enough to ask, "What was that about?"

"Young Nevin making a fool of himself? If you've met him, that shouldn't surprise you. I'm Mistress Chardane, by the by."

"No, I meant . . ." Jeriah wasn't sure what he meant. "Has the Hierarch been ill? I hadn't heard that he had stomach problems."

Severe ones, judging by Nevin's reaction. But if that was true, why conceal it?

"Stomach problems?" They'd reached the fourth level, and Mistress Chardane was already turning away. "Even being personally chosen by the Bright Gods doesn't grant a body perfect health, I suppose."

"No, but why—"

"Lad." The herb mistress turned back to him, her comfortable face inscrutable. "What happens on the second level is no business of yours or mine. If you want an old woman's advice—which no youngling ever does—leave it be."

Mistress Chardane departed. Was the Hierarch supposed to be so holy he was always in perfect health? Or was there some other reason to conceal the fact that he'd been ill? Chardane was probably right that it was none of Jeriah's business, but he still wondered.

✧ ✧ ✧

Two days after that Jeriah was checking out a discrepancy in the coal supply for the furnace—though furnace seemed too small a word for the thundering combination of water heater and pumps that not only supplied the laundry and bathing rooms, but also vented through all the floors and ceilings to heat the whole palace.

By midmorning Jeriah had determined that all the coal the merchant's invoice claimed had been delivered was indeed stored in the subcellar bins, so the error lay in the palace inventory. Jeriah was making a note that the merchant's payment should be expedited when Master Goserian came up to him, puffing from the long flights of stairs.

"Your presence has been requested in the Sunlord's chambers," he told Jeriah. "I wasn't aware you'd ever served there?"

"I took the Hierarch a cup of tea," Jeriah told him. "Which he requested! I don't know why Brallorscourt made such a fuss over it."

Master Goserian pursed his lips. "That would be Sir Nevin Brallor of Brallorscourt, not Lord Brallorscourt?"

Jeriah nodded.

"Then it probably isn't a problem." Relief brightened the Master of Household's face. "I must admit, Lord Brallorscourt is a man I'd hesitate to challenge."

"I've never even met Lord Brallorscourt," said Jeriah. "And if he's anything like his son, I don't want to."

Master Goserian cast him a disapproving look but said

nothing. After working for the man almost a week, Jeriah knew that meant that he agreed but didn't want to say so.

Jeriah's new-made resolve never to come to Lord Brallorscourt's attention was foiled the moment Master Goserian led him into the Hierarch's antechamber.

"So he's the one." The man who looked Jeriah over so critically had Nevin's straight, pale hair, and also his bony nose and chin. "He looks suitable to me."

Nevin scowled, but Master Zachiros, who was also present, nodded.

Master Lazur, the final person in the room, wore a particularly unreadable expression. "I never said he wasn't suitable. My reservations are because of the . . . delicacy of the situation."

Jeriah wished he knew what delicate situation they were talking about.

"He seems quite competent," said Master Zachiros. "And the Hierarch likes him, which matters. In fact, given how many have already failed, I think that consideration is paramount."

Who'd failed at what?

"It won't be paramount if he's out wandering the corridors unattended." Nevin cast Jeriah a scathing look.

"That wasn't young Rovan's fault," Master Zachiros pointed out. "And it wasn't yours either. You can't be in two places at once. Which is precisely the problem we need to solve."

Jeriah wished they weren't all staring at him. "What problem?"

"That's not the only consideration," said Master Lazur. "As the rest of you are well aware, because this is the third time I've said so!"

"But you've assured me the situation is under control," Lord Brallorscourt said coldly.

"It is!" Master Lazur flung up his hands. "Oh, very well. If you all think this is the solution, we'll try it."

"What situation?" Jeriah's voice was louder this time.

"Oh dear," said Master Zachiros. "I'm sorry, we shouldn't be ignoring you. But if Master Goserian gives you a good report . . . ?"

"I do," said Master Goserian. "Provisionally, because I don't know what matter is under discussion."

"We're talking about assigning Master Rovan here to a new post," said Master Zachiros. "As the Hierarch's body squire."

"What?" Jeriah's head spun. "But . . . isn't that Nevin's job?" No wonder Nevin looked so furious.

"It used to be," said Nevin's father. "But I want him in a post with more political exposure. And when I say 'in a post,' I mean actually doing it, not neglecting it to serve—"

"This is a high honor for you, Jeriah," Master Zachiros put in hastily. "The Sunlord himself requested your service. What do you say?"

What could he say? "It is an honor. Far higher than I deserve."

Being the Hierarch's squire would make it harder to look for the spell notes—had Master Lazur arranged it for that very reason? Tobin would probably start to sicken in just over two weeks. But it sounded like the priest had been arguing *against* giving Jeriah the job.

"It's not too high an honor," Master Lazur said, "for the brother of a hero who sacrificed himself for the good of the Realm."

Was that some sort of warning? Jeriah sought frantically for a clever reply, but his wits were numb. "I'm, ah, honored."

"Then it's settled," said Master Zachiros. "Before Dawn Prayer tomorrow, instead of reporting to Master Goserian you'll go to the Hierarch's rooms, and Nevin will begin instructing you in your duties. It's a more complex job than you might think."

Helping the Hierarch get dressed and serving him at meals? An honor, certainly, but complex?

Currents of hidden understanding seemed to flow between everyone present—except for Master Goserian, who looked almost as confused as Jeriah. Jeriah met Nevin's hostile gaze and shivered.

The page woke him an hour before dawn next morning. The sky was slate gray when Jeriah hurried around to the central stairs. He heard movement in some of the rooms he passed, and a distant bird call.

What would serving the Hierarch entail? No matter what else happened, Jeriah still had to make time to search for the spell notes—even if he had to do it in the middle of the night. He'd made some progress, at least in terms of finding a number of places where the notes weren't and marking many more places he needed to search. But it wasn't going fast enough. If this new position took even more of his time . . .

On the second-level landing a guard stopped Jeriah, and asked his name and business. He was still trying to explain when Master Zachiros emerged from an entrance and waved for the guard to let Jeriah pass.

"Sorry about that. The guards on this level are more strict than on the other levels because . . . well, the reason will be obvious shortly."

To Jeriah it already seemed obvious that the guards outside the Hierarch's rooms would be more strict, but Master Zachiros went on, "I was supposed to give you a lecture on your duties and schedule this morning, but I'm running late again so you'll just have to fake it." His expression became serious. "You'll soon see the way of things, I'm afraid." He led Jeriah around the terrace as he spoke. "Just do what Nevin tells you—and more importantly, watch how he does his job. He's very good at it."

The outer entrance to the Hierarch's quarters was a pair of guarded doors, embossed in gold with the emblem of the sun.

"Gentlemen," Master Zachiros addressed the guards. "This is Jeriah Rovan of Rovanscourt, the Hierarch's new body squire. He may be admitted at any hour on my authority." The guards nodded, memorizing Jeriah's face. Master Zachiros gave him an encouraging smile, opened the doors, and pushed him through.

Beyond the antechamber, which was even more richly decorated than the one Jeriah had already seen, was a beautifully appointed sitting room with comfortable benches and chairs. Warm woven rugs almost concealed the stone floor. The growing light from the windows told Jeriah he hadn't much time, so he followed the sound of murmuring voices to a half-open door and entered the Hierarch's bedroom.

There were three menservants present as well as Nevin, but Jeriah's attention centered on the man who stood by the bed being dressed in priest's robes that glittered with gold. Despite the creases age and responsibility had put on his face, the blue eyes held a deep serenity.

"You're late." But Nevin sounded more resigned than angry. "Come here. My lord," he said respectfully to the Hierarch, "this is Jeriah Rovan of Rovanscourt, who will serve as your squire and help you in all things."

Jeriah bowed. As he straightened, the Hierarch's hand fell on his shoulder, and the blue eyes peered at his face.

"Jeriah," said the Hierarch thoughtfully. "Good." The hand fell away. Jeriah stepped back, feeling as if he'd passed some sort of test.

He watched carefully as Nevin and the servants finished the Sunlord's robing. The garments weren't complicated, despite their elaborate embroidery, and the menservants knew the process. They would remember anything Jeriah forgot.

The Hierarch's gaze dwelled on the brightening windows. The sun awaited his welcome. What would it be like to have so much holiness, so much power?

Nevin glanced at the windows and murmured something, and the Hierarch rose and went to the door. Jeriah was about to follow him when Nevin hissed in annoyance and snatched a gold-trimmed tabard that matched his own out of a chest. He threw it at Jeriah, then dragged him after the Hierarch. Jeriah barely had time to pull it over his head as they climbed the temple stairs.

He'd been to enough dawn services by now that his mind had begun to stray during the prayer. This morning, knowing that he now served the man who welcomed the sun, its tranquility filled him once more. There were only three first-circle priests in the Realm, each of whom governed a separate district and held a seat on the Priests' Council. The Sunlord, divinely chosen from all the priests above the third circle, had no ranking.

Serving him really was an honor. It might even please his father, at least a little. If Jeriah hadn't had a brother to rescue, he'd have been thrilled by his new appointment.

After the ceremony the Hierarch disrobed. Jeriah put away

the gold-trimmed tabards, while Nevin chose the garments the Hierarch would wear that morning.

"A warm undertunic," he told Jeriah. "It's still chilly in the mornings. You have to pay attention to the weather when you do this, because after breakfast he hears public petitions— out of doors. The hearing room is that open area behind the Hierarch's quarters. They put a canopy over his chair when it rains, but it's never enough. So think when you choose his morning clothes."

"Why don't they do it inside?"

"'The Bright Ones' justice is to be administered under their sun, for all to see and hear,'" Nevin quoted. "It's been that way forever."

"What do they do if it snows?"

"Cancel the petitioning. We don't get much snow here, though in winter that damp cold is a beast."

The menservants brought breakfast, and Nevin lectured Jeriah as they ate. The Hierarch's jewelry was enchanted to protect him from evil magics, and it must be properly stowed in a locked chest as soon as it left his body. For the evening prayers he entered the temple by the east stairs, in the morning from the west. His clothing must be of sufficient richness to preserve his dignity, and on and on.

The Hierarch, whose gaze had strayed to the windows, said almost nothing. Perhaps the holiness of the ceremony was still upon him.

A corridor at the rear of the Hierarch's suite led out to a

crowded courtyard, where Master Zachiros sat at a writing desk on the dais that held the Hierarch's throne. The desk, Jeriah was amused to note, concealed a footstool to prop up the secretary's sore feet.

Nevin seated the Hierarch, then went down the dais steps to announce that petitions would be heard. "So, lad, how's it going?" Master Zachiros asked quietly.

"It's . . . confusing," said Jeriah.

The Hierarch was gazing into space, over the heads of the crowd.

"It soon won't be. Oh dear, where's my pen?" Master Zachiros looked at the floor around the desk.

"It's tucked behind your ear," Jeriah informed him.

Nevin came back up the steps and announced, "Goodman Adder of Grimble Mill petitions the Sunlord for the return of three fields, seized for nonpayment of taxes two seasons past. The goodman offers the taxes he failed to pay and taxes for the next season, in hopes that the land may be returned to him."

Nevin faced the Hierarch, but his gaze slid sideways to Master Zachiros. "Well?" he asked softly.

"Whose estate is he from?" murmured Master Zachiros, writing busily.

"Lord Solverscourt."

"Hmm. Honest enough, but rigid as a splint. We take the taxes Goodman Adder failed to pay and half his taxes for the next season, leaving the other half for the goodman so he can get a last crop in before he has to relocate. The Bright Gods are merciful and all that."

Nevin bowed to the Hierarch, turned to the crowd, and announced the decision. Throughout, he had stood so his body hid the fact that the Hierarch hadn't spoken, and had kept his face turned so it looked like he was talking to the Hierarch instead of Master Zachiros.

The chill in Jeriah's heart spread, and his hands began to tremble. He clenched them and knelt before the Sunlord, looking up at his face. The blue eyes were serene as the sky . . . and as empty.

Makenna

THEN THE STREAM DIED.

"I just woke up and found it like this." Tobin's voice was steady; a soldier making a report. Makenna wondered why he'd awakened half an hour before dawn, but no one asked questions like that these days—she had enough nightmares of her own, without adding other people's to the load. And he'd had the sense to fetch just her and Miggy, instead of rousing the whole camp to panicked wonder.

Gazing at the puddles lying between the rocks where a swift stream had run, Makenna was grateful for that. She felt a bit panicked herself, and she didn't need an audience.

"There are things can stop a stream," she told them. "Even sudden, like this. A big enough rock fall can create a dam and hold the water till it overflows and the stream runs again."

"So all we have to do is wait a bit?" Miggy sounded both dubious and relieved.

"That might be all we need to do," she said. "But I'm not

going to gamble on it. I need two scouting parties, Mig. One will go with Tobin and find us another stream, just in case. Tobin's wandered a fair ways from the camp, scouting and timbering, so he'll have the best idea which direction to go."

Miggy looked troubled, but the young knight simply nodded.

Makenna didn't give orders if she didn't have to, but when she did, he accepted her command. It was one of the things she liked about him. Along with that quiet steadiness when bizarre things happened, and the way one corner of his mouth quirked up when the goblins said or did something that was perfectly natural to them but looked ridiculous to human eyes.

"The second party will go up the streambed with me," Makenna went on. "I'll want a Stoner, a Greener, a Flichter to find routes through thick brush, and whichever Bookerie knows the most about geology and water engineering."

"And I'll go—" Miggy began, but Makenna cut him off.

"You need to stay here, in charge of the camp while I'm gone. Someone has to, and you're the one I trust most for it."

"But mistress," Miggy protested, "the others won't take orders from another goblin. You know they won't."

"They will if I order it," Makenna said. "As they used to take Cogswhallop's orders."

"But we were at war then!" Miggy wailed. "It's not the same."

Makenna's gaze went to the empty streambed. "Isn't it? I'm beginning to wonder."

It took them the better part of two days to hike to the place where the stream had been blocked—but once they reached it, there could be no doubt what the problem was: a whole hill, almost a small mountain, complete with trees and wildflowers, filled the gorge the stream had run down, cutting across the bed as if a giant had scooped it up and dropped it there.

"How is this possible?" Makenna stared at the green-clad slope, half expecting it to vanish when she blinked. But it hadn't yet.

A few raw, dirty rocks had spilled into the streambed from the hillside's edge, but the rest of its grassy soil looked undisturbed. And the trees . . .

"Not possible." The Stoner glared up at the hill as if its existence were a personal affront.

"Possible or not," said the Greener grimly, "I can tell you that most of those trees are decades old, some nearing a century. Even the smallest have been growing there for years."

"This hill hasn't been here for years." Makenna stamped a booted foot in one of the puddles. The splash was small. The puddles were already drying.

"Amazing," the Bookerie breathed. "It is clearly impossible for this hill to be here. But here it clearly is. A genuine, incontrovertible paradox. Which in reality can't exist! But here it is!"

He was clearly thrilled, and Makenna almost turned her glare on him. But Bookeries were what they were, and perhaps his scholarly obliviousness was just as well.

Makenna was terrified. And beginning to get angry. If they hadn't been the only ones in this world, if it wasn't completely impossible for *anyone* to move an entire, intact hill—complete with trees!—she'd have thought they had an enemy.

CHAPTER 8

Jeriah

NEVIN AND MASTER ZACHIROS SPENT the morning answering petitions—the deception was brilliant. No one even suspected that the Hierarch sat mute and mindless as a doll. When he became restless, Master Zachiros suddenly discovered that he was out of paper, creating a break while a clerk ran to fetch more and another brought refreshments.

Jeriah served the Hierarch with his own chilled hands.

Finally it ended. Nevin led the Hierarch, tired, querulous, and beginning to mumble, back to his rooms. Jeriah caught Master Zachiros' arm and drew him aside as the others went in.

"Master, I would *really* like to be told about my duties. Now."

The secretary sighed and led Jeriah over to the fountain, where the splashing water would cover their voices.

"You've just seen your duty—to keep anyone from guessing he's no longer a whole man."

"What happened?" It took all Jeriah's self-control to keep

his voice low. "Surely he wasn't like this when the priests chose him!"

"Oh, no. He became ill seven years ago, a terrible fever. We were certain it would kill him, but he clung to life so hard . . . We all prayed he would live. Sometimes the Gods answer prayers in ways you don't intend." Master Zachiros shrugged. "Or maybe it has nothing to do with prayer, maybe it's all random. I'd rather believe that."

Sunlight sparkled on the water. Flowers scented the air. Birds sang. Jeriah tried to still his shaking hands.

"The fever destroyed his mind?"

"Yes. His body recovered, for the most part, but his mind . . . didn't. And a hierarch's reign can only be ended by his death."

"Bright Gods. But how could you conceal that much damage? *Seven years?*"

"We added a few layers of formality. Instead of dealing with anyone personally, the Hierarch sends his squire. That part was Nevin's idea; he was only a page then. We've dispensed with pages, since few children can keep a secret. The guards admit no one to the Hierarch's presence without permission—we've told them we have reason to fear assassins. His menservants all know, of course. And myself, the Priests' Council, his healer priest, and perhaps a dozen of the highest lords and priests of the court since we had to let his personal friends in on the secret. A handful of others we trust. The brighter members of court were sent away, on one pretext or another. There's almost no one here who was at court seven years ago. He says the Sun Prayers well enough. It may be hard to get him through the Equinox Ceremony this year. We've divided most of the ritual between various priests, so all he has to do is the hourly obeisance, but . . . Well, we'll manage."

Jeriah didn't care about prayers. "Who runs the Realm?"

"The Landholders' Council. It's not such a big change. The Hierarch has always consulted them in secular matters."

And Master Lazur now controlled the Landholders' Council. The shaking in Jeriah's hands spread to his body.

"But the day-to-day decisions . . . the petitions . . . you do all that?" He gazed in astonishment at the bespectacled secretary in floppy slippers.

"Yes, with help from Nevin and others who are in on the secret. I'll need your help as well."

"But . . ."

"Lad, we need you to do this," said Master Zachiros. "Nevin's father wants him working in a more influential job, but whenever we've tried to replace him, the Hierarch . . . He doesn't adjust well to changes in his staff. The first time a new squire tried to serve him, he became hysterical—it took Nevin hours to calm him down. The next few times we tried to introduce the new person more gradually, but he still couldn't accept them. And he has to be kept stable and calm if we're to keep up our illusion."

"But why me?"

Jeriah wondered what had happened to the squires who'd failed to keep the Hierarch calm. Sent away, like the brighter members of the old court? How far away? Assigned to the army? To the farthest corners of the Realm? Jeriah had to stay in the palace, or Tobin would die.

"Why me?" He tried to keep the fear out of his voice.

"The Hierarch liked you," Master Zachiros said. "When the servants took him the tea you brought, he asked about 'that nice boy' he'd sent for it. So we hoped . . . And it seems to be working, Bright Gods be praised! Lord Brallorscourt understands the importance of keeping the Hierarch's situation stable, but he was becoming impatient."

"Surely I'm not—" Jeriah didn't finish. It sounded like he was the only one for this job. And if he failed . . .

Master Zachiros patted his hand. "Go for a walk and give it a chance to sink in. The Sunlord rests in the afternoon— only his menservants attend him then, though we keep a clerk there for appearances. He's supposed to be considering affairs of state. You won't be needed till it's time to dress him for dinner. He dines before the court when it's possible. So go for a walk and think about it."

Jeriah walked numbly down to the wooded parks of the palace grounds, but the tumbling chaos in his mind could hardly be described as thinking. This job was a *lot* more complicated than he'd expected. Would it interfere with his search for the spell notes? And what if he failed? Jeriah would bet that the others who'd tried to take Nevin's place were no longer serving in the palace. This secret was far too important to risk it slipping out.

Master Lazur's cadre was running the Landholders' Council, and with the Hierarch incapacitated, the council ruled the Realm. Was that such a bad thing? They'd accomplish the relocation—get everyone to safety. No, this . . . shadow government wasn't bad for the Realm, only for Jeriah. Master Lazur would never have allowed Jeriah to learn about this unless he believed Jeriah could be controlled. Could Master Lazur have evidence of his involvement with the conspirators?

Yes, he could. Jeriah's hands began to tremble again, and he tucked them under his arms.

"Did you find them? Are you ready to cast the gate now?"

Jeriah jumped. "Don't sneak up on me like that!"

"Well?" Daroo was perched on a limb above Jeriah's head. "Tell me! I saw that other one throw you out of the priest's rooms. He must have gone in before I started watching. He stayed till the priest came and they talked for almost half an hour, but the charm kept me so far away I couldn't hear them!" Indignation filled the goblin's voice. "I don't know where your room is, and during the day you were dashing all over the place or with that poor old man. And I'm *dying* of curiosity. You owe me a button for watching."

"Why should I pay for something I told you not to do? I'd pay you to go home! Although . . . You say you've been watching me for days? No one's seen you?"

"Of course not," the boy said smugly. "With all those flowers and bushes it's easy to get around. There's even trees in those planters, so I can go from one level to the next without using the stairs. But what's happened?"

Jeriah hesitated. True knights didn't confide in children. But if he called the Hierarch "poor old man," Daroo must have seen what the humans had missed. Besides, Jeriah had to tell someone.

He sat, leaning against a tree, and Daroo climbed down to sit beside him. The boy listened without interruption as Jeriah told him what had happened that first night, and briefly about his discoveries concerning the Hierarch. When Jeriah finished, Daroo put his small finger right on the heart of the problem.

"You believed this Nevin when he said the spell notes weren't in the priest's rooms?"

"Yes. He might have lied about that, but I'm sure he was about to let something slip when he told me that if I found them I couldn't . . . couldn't what? Can you think of anything? It has to be something that would give me a clue, because if it didn't, he would have finished the sentence."

"No. And if it's not in the priest's rooms, you'll have to search the whole palace. And maybe beyond. And to do that you have to be here, so you'd better make sure that old man likes you!"

"I need a clue," Jeriah fretted. "Searching the whole palace will take years, and Tobin doesn't have a month!"

Just over two weeks until Tobin became ill. Maybe less than that—no illness, not even a magical one, was completely predictable. After that, perhaps as little as a week before he was dead. Jeriah had to find those spell notes soon, but how?

In the stories, if the knight didn't know where to go, someone appeared to guide him. Usually a beautiful girl. But Koryn, who might have guided Jeriah, was working for his enemy.

"And maybe beyond the palace," Daroo repeated gloomily.

"I don't think Master Lazur would let those notes too far out of his reach," said Jeriah. "Suppose he needs them? But I can't . . ."

True knights also didn't ask for help. Especially not from vermin. Untrustworthy vermin, too.

Then Jeriah must not be a true knight, because he couldn't see any other way. Whatever the goblins were concealing, he'd come to believe that Daroo cared about Tobin. *Try.*

"Daroo, you seem to get around the palace pretty easily. Could other goblins do the same?"

The bright eyes glinted. "Does this mean you'll stop telling me to leave? During the day we'd have to take care, but by night we could run an army around. The guards are looking for big folk, see?"

"No," said Jeriah. "But I'll take your word for it. Could your people search the palace for the spell notes?"

"Aye. A few dozen Bookeries could go through that priest's office in an hour if it weren't for the charm. All the papers in the palace would take a while, but Bookeries could do it."

"Bookeries?"

"Their gift is writing and language, things like that. They're the ones you need for this."

"Then I'm going to have to ask you to leave." Jeriah grinned at the goblin's squeal of protest and continued: "Go home, and convince your father to come back with enough . . . Bookeries? . . . to search the whole palace. Will you do that?"

"I will," said Daroo. "For a button. But whether *they* will is something else again. What are you going to trade for it? They'll want even value, not just a token."

"I'll think of something." Jeriah rose and brushed himself off. "Your job is to bring them back. Can you do it? Fast? Tobin's running out of time."

"Sure." The boy held out his hand.

Jeriah looked around, and dropped a pinecone into it. "I need my buttons, if you don't mind."

"I'll do the trip for a pinecone, but I want a button for the watching, like we agreed."

"I never agreed to any such thing! I didn't ask you to stand watch. I didn't even want you to!"

"But I did it, so you're indebted. I'll do no errands for an indebted man. I want a button."

"But . . ." The foolishness of it overcame Jeriah's indignation and he laughed. It took only a moment to twist off a button. "There, demon, are you happy?"

Daroo sniffed. "It's an uphill fight to civilize some folk, but I suppose you'll get there. Eventually."

"Civilize? Why you . . ."

Daroo grinned, shot into the bushes, and vanished.

"Be careful," Jeriah called to the empty woods.

He went back to the Hierarch's rooms and was intercepted by Nevin, who immediately took him in charge. Jeriah's wardrobe was inspected and found wanting. "You haven't spent much time in civilized places, have you? Look at you— you're missing a button on the tunic you're wearing right now!"

Jeriah was taken to the seamstress for new tunics and tabards, to the baths for a haircut, and back to the Hierarch in time to help him dress for dinner.

As he handed the old man his shoes, the blue eyes dwelled on his face with troubled curiosity.

"Who . . . ?"

"Jeriah Rovan. I brought you some tea, remember?"

The Hierarch frowned, trying, and Jeriah's throat tightened with pity. "I'm Jeriah. Just remember Jeriah."

The frown vanished. "Ah, Jeriah. Good."

"It's time to go in, my lord." Nevin was scowling, but as long as the Hierarch accepted him, Jeriah didn't care. He was getting tired of Sir Nevin.

Still, he had to admire the young knight's competence. The Sunlord dined alone, at a table on a dais at the end of the huge hall. He was weary in spite of the afternoon's rest, his hands unsteady. But when he spilled his wine, Nevin was there in an instant, apologizing loudly for "his" clumsiness. The old man nodded, his confusion taken for graciousness by those who watched. Yes, this job was complicated. Jeriah hoped he could cope, along with everything else he had to do. What could he offer the goblins in exchange for their aid? And even if he found the notes, he couldn't . . . what?

The Hierarch was very tired after dinner. He sat on the bed, running a gold necklace around and around in his hands.

"You brew his medicine like a tea," Nevin was explaining. "One scoop of the leaves in a cup of boiling water, and steep it till the sand timer stops. Master Kerratis, his healer priest, says he has to drink it all. It helps him sleep and . . . well, it helps him."

Jeriah knelt before the old man. "It's time to take your medicine and go to bed," he said gently. "I have to put the necklace away."

The blue eyes gazed at him blankly. "Who?"

"Jeriah. Remember? Jeriah."

"Ah . . ."

Jeriah sighed and reached for the necklace, but the old man held on with surprising strength. "No."

"I have to put the necklace away. It's time for bed."

"No." The Hierarch's lip began to tremble and his eyes filled with tears. One of the menservants started forward, but it was Nevin's hand that grabbed Jeriah's collar. Jeriah was crouched on his heels, and the yank sent him sprawling to the floor.

Nevin stood over him and hissed, "He is not a backward child who must do what you say. He is the Holy One, Chosen of the Bright Gods themselves. If they've seen fit to afflict him, it is not ours to question. *Your* place is to treat him, always, with the respect he deserves. You may go."

He turned his back on Jeriah and knelt before the Hierarch. "My lord?"

Jeriah fled.

By the next morning the Hierarch hadn't simply forgiven Jeriah, he'd completely forgotten the incident. And Jeriah's name as well. But he did seem to like Jeriah, the Bright Ones be thanked.

As the days passed, Nevin forgave Jeriah for his disrespect—only one in three sentences was an insult, instead of all of them. And Jeriah overcame his own anger enough to study Nevin's methods for handling the old man. Nevin never actively thwarted the Hierarch, he simply distracted or confused him until the ruler was willing to do what was needed. When Nevin wanted to get something out of the Hierarch's hands, he gave him something else and waited until he became involved with it before taking the first object away.

Jeriah, whose pity was often laced with impatience, found Nevin's unfailing gentleness rather shaming—but it didn't make him like the arrogant knight any better.

When Nevin served the Hierarch, Jeriah could eat with his friends. From them, he learned that Nevin had been knighted not on the field of battle but for "service to the Sunlord."

The other squires held him in contempt for that.

"With his father being who he is, all Nevin had to do to get knighted was pick out the right clothes," Harell told him.

Jeriah, who knew why Nevin had been knighted, kept his mouth shut. But Nevin's father really was a power in the Realm. All landholders were technically equal in the sight of the Gods and the government. Lord Brallorscourt's influence came not only from his vast wealth, but also from his willingness to use that wealth in pursuit of political power. As Ranan put it, "Those who don't owe him either money or political favor are afraid of him."

Jeriah, whose father's influence sprang from his neighbors' respect for his integrity, was a little afraid of that kind of power too. He sometimes encountered Nevin's father, dealing with the council or other lords, but Lord Brallorscourt ignored lowly creatures like squires and Jeriah was grateful for it.

He'd almost forgotten about his mother's plans when Senna's letter arrived. The first page was full of family chatter. The tenants from the flooded village had been resettled, and his father was planning how to save more grain for seed, to take with them when they were forced to relocate. Jeriah was smiling over Tami's campaign to trade her pony for a full-size horse when he turned the page and his blood froze.

Mother got some disappointing news from her old friend, his sister wrote. *But she hasn't given up. She hopes you're doing well in your new post—says she'd love to hear some palace gossip again! So write if anything interesting happens there.*

The rest of the letter consisted of local news, with a brief note at the end that Senna might be doing a bit of traveling herself soon—and what in the Dark One's name did *that* mean? Jeriah thought he'd translated the rest of her hints correctly—Master Lazur had resisted whatever pressure his mother had brought to bear, and Jeriah was to stay at his post and report if the priest did anything unusual.

What was his mother up to? Confined to her own estate, surely she couldn't do too much harm. . . .

Jeriah shuddered. His mother could create world-shaking havoc confined to her bed!

He wrote back to Senna, filling his own letter with his recent promotion. *So don't worry about me—I'm delighted with how things are going here. I'm sorry Mother's old friend let her down, but maybe it's for the best. Try to keep her from worrying about it. And you might consider staying home too. It's too early in the year for good traveling weather.*

He hoped that would be enough to rein in his mother's scheme, whatever it was, but he doubted it.

As the Hierarch slowly became accustomed to Jeriah, Master Lazur began to pull Nevin into his own service. Although Nevin still turned up frequently to harass Jeriah—and, Jeriah admitted, to reassure the Hierarch with his familiar presence. Jeriah was heartily tired of introducing himself to the old man every morning.

Unless Master Zachiros drafted him to run errands, in the afternoon when the Hierarch slept Jeriah was granted free time. He came to like and respect the elderly secretary— though calling him a secretary was a joke. Master Zachiros exercised more power than any man in the Realm outside of the council. Except for Master Lazur, whose cadre held sway in the council.

Listening to the talk around him, Jeriah began to realize how tenuous the shadow government's control was. Everyone disliked the relocation, even those who had fought the barbarians themselves and *knew* it was necessary. Most of the daily petitions had to do with landownership. Master Zachiros said that the moment it had been announced that the amount of land a person owned in the Realm would determine how much land they were granted in the northern wood, every man who owned more than a few acres started scheming to get more.

Jeriah couldn't tell what Master Zachiros thought of

Master Lazur, though he was sure the secretary was aware of his power. But Jeriah wasn't even certain if Master Zachiros' absentmindedness was real or a clever act to fool those who watched the Hierarch. He only prayed that he would never have to deceive the foolish-looking "secretary."

Jeriah also met Master Kerratis, the Hierarch's personal healer priest, when he performed the Hierarch's weekly examination. The man's darting, birdlike gestures made the Hierarch uneasy, and Jeriah's distaste for the healer intensified when Master Kerratis made it clear he found the Hierarch's case hopeless and unworthy of his time. Even the fact that Nevin detested the finicky healer didn't make Jeriah like him. He resolved to continue Nevin's policy of never leaving the Hierarch alone with the man.

Between errands for Master Zachiros and his free afternoons, Jeriah was able to explore the parts of the palace where Master Goserian hadn't sent him. He found no papers in the unlocked storeroom under the chorus steps behind the altar, and he spent several minutes staring wistfully at the small, locked storage compartment under the lowest steps. He also bluffed his way into the wine cellar, one level above the furnace room, from which yet another staircase led down to the palace vault. Because of that, several guards were posted there. They escorted Jeriah as he selected the Hierarch's wine and prevented him from looking for the secret tunnel that was rumored to come out of the hill near the guards' barracks.

Jeriah kept hoping that one of the Lesser Ones would contact him. He knew enough about the goblins now to be certain Cogswhallop had passed on his letter—surely the tinker would have relayed his request. But no one tried to get in touch with him.

In fact, the only one who seemed interested in his movements was Master Kerratis—Jeriah encountered the Hierarch's healer in several odd places, and his eyes followed Jeriah during meals. But that might have been chance, for the palace was stuffed with people. The relocation, on top of the normal business of ruling the Realm, brought clerks, lawyers, and petitioners flooding in. It occurred to Jeriah that Master Lazur didn't need to set anyone to watch him; there wasn't a private corner anywhere! But Jeriah soon realized that although many people might see him, as long as he didn't act suspicious, hardly anyone noticed him. In some ways the crowded conditions made his search easier than it would have been if the palace had been empty.

In spite of what Daroo said, Jeriah thought Master Lazur would keep his spell notes in the palace. They were unlikely to be on the second level, which held only the Hierarch's rooms, Master Zachiros' offices, and the petitions court. (Unless Master Lazur had access to a strongbox in one of the offices?) They certainly wouldn't be in the temple. (Unless they were in the locked storage area under the chorus steps.) They wouldn't be in anyone's bedroom. (Unless the priest had asked someone to keep them for him.) They wouldn't be in any of the servants' rooms, or workrooms, or public hallways. (Unless they were hidden inside some object.) It seemed likely they'd be hidden among other papers, and Jeriah thought the palace library was a more promising place than the public offices. (Unless Master Lazur had asked one of the clerks who worked in those offices to hide them for him.)

He tried to search the library himself, avoiding the librarians, since he didn't dare tell them what he was looking for.

The amount of information in the vast tangle of shelves was staggering—and if it had been organized, Jeriah couldn't figure out how. He was in the middle of a shelf of books that discussed the nature of magic, and experiments on it, when he came across a brief history of the Sunlord's life before he was chosen. Jeriah suspected the long account of the old man's exceptional holiness was mostly lies, but he discovered one shocking fact—the "old man" was only forty-four. Younger than Jeriah's father. The fever must have changed him terribly.

But tragic as that was, it wasn't what he was looking for. Jeriah finished that section, turned around a corner into the next aisle, and ran into a gray-gowned woman perched on one of the step stools that allowed people to reach the taller shelves. She squeaked and started to topple, and Jeriah steadied her.

"I'm so sorry," he began, and then looked up to meet Mistress Koryn's wide gaze. "What are you doing up on a stool like that? Don't you know better than to . . . I mean, with your . . . ah . . ." The awkwardness of their last meeting flooded back, and his voice trailed into silence.

"I can still climb a step stool." Her voice was cool. "And what I'm doing is my job."

She clearly hadn't forgotten their last meeting either—and her job was working for Master Lazur. Jeriah released her and took a step back. She seemed secure enough.

"Then I'll leave you to it, mistress." He turned to go.

"They're not here," she said.

Embarrassing himself with this girl—again—was the last thing Jeriah wanted, but . . .

"What's not here? I'm just looking for something for the Hierarch to read."

"Master Lazur doesn't keep any of his notes here," she said as if he hadn't spoken. "Particularly not the ones you're looking for."

Heat flooded Jeriah's face. "I don't know what you mean."

"The notes about opening gates. I don't know where they are, but I do know Master Lazur put them somewhere safe. Safe from you. And the library isn't, so they won't be here."

Was there a hint of pity in those cool eyes? Jeriah, retreating in confusion, wasn't sure.

The fact that Mistress Koryn claimed the notes weren't there meant nothing. In fact, her denial might mean the notes were *more* likely to be in the library. Or not. Jeriah sighed.

Without the goblins' assistance, a thorough search of the book-, scroll-, and paper-filled room would be impossible—particularly under the observant eyes of Master Lazur's own clerk! He would simply have to wait for the goblins' arrival.

He tried to be patient, but it was hard. More days went by, and the goblins didn't come. Almost two months had passed since Tobin had gone into the Otherworld—he had roughly a week before the sickness began to affect his brother, and then . . . Master Lazur had said the illness could last for several weeks—but what if the sickness moved swiftly with Tobin? It might only take another week for him to die!

Jeriah had to get into the Otherworld with those spell notes now! But until the Lesser Ones and the goblins contacted him, there was nothing he could do but continue his search.

The other squires speculated about why he was so snappish, and also why he ignored the inviting glances his good looks won him from the young girls at court. Jeriah snapped at them.

One of his friends' idle conversations about the barbarians reminded Jeriah of something he could offer the goblins—but even if he gained their services, where should he have them look? Start with the library, despite what Mistress Koryn had said. Then the locked temple storage? The public offices? The wine cellar, the food storage, under Master Goserian's bed . . . Even if he found it, he couldn't *what*?

What in the Dark One's name was keeping Daroo? And where were the lesser magic users who were supposed to contact him?

More and more, Jeriah's thoughts turned to Koryn—she might not know where the notes were, but he'd bet she could make a pretty good guess!

He was looking across the dining hall at her table, again, when Marof said, "Don't bother. She's not interested in anything but dusty notes."

Marof was the most annoying of Jeriah's friends—of course he'd be the one to notice.

"I don't know what you're talking about." But he couldn't control the hot color rising in his face.

"I'm talking about the fact that you've been watching the nettle queen for the last week," Marof said. "And I grant you, those eyes of hers—"

Jeriah didn't want to listen to comments on Koryn's eyes. Particularly from Marof, whose descriptions of a woman seldom focused on her face. "The nettle queen?"

"Prickly as nettles." Marof grinned at him. "And cold as ice. Not even you could make that one bloom. And if you've tried . . . well, that certainly explains why your temper's been so short!"

"Why does everyone always assume that all I want from a girl is—"

"Don't let him get to you," Ranan interposed hastily. "He only says that because he got nowhere. And small blame to her, if she's not feeling . . . Well, I'd give a girl who's lost that much some time to recover before I made a move."

"Lost what?" Jeriah asked. "I thought . . . I assumed she was born crippled. Was there an accident?"

If she'd just lost the use of that leg, no wonder she wasn't interested in flirting!

Three sets of eyes turned to him.

"You don't know?" Harell asked. "But it was the talk of . . . Oh, that's right. You were in the north when she arrived."

"What don't I know?" Sometimes it was hard to keep his friends on track.

"Mistress Goserian is one of the Southlanders displaced by the barbarian surge," Ranan told him. Then he grimaced. "'Displaced' is a euphemism. She lost her whole family in the attack. That's why she came to live with her uncle. And that's why flirting with her now is a really stupid—"

"She might have been ready to forget about grieving for a while," Marof snarled. "Sometimes people who've been hurt need to laugh a bit, or—"

Jeriah wasn't interested in Marof's mistakes—he was too busy being appalled by his own.

"Is that what happened to her leg? Did the barbarians . . . ?"

The barbarians cut the tendons in their prisoner's legs to keep them from escaping. The thought of that happening to a girl he knew, even slightly, sickened Jeriah. He pushed his plate aside.

"No, her leg was just broken," Harell said. "Though I

shouldn't say 'just.' It took two healer priests working in shifts to get the bone to knit even half straight, and they say it will never heal completely. They carried her up from the Southlands on a stretcher. Reward for what she'd done."

With a badly broken leg that journey would be a nightmare. With all your family dead . . . Jeriah remembered what he'd felt like when Master Lazur told him Tobin was doomed, and his heart went out to the girl.

On the other hand . . . maybe that accounted for the hint of pity he'd seen in her eyes? She'd lost her family. Surely she'd be willing to help him save his. He just needed to figure out how to approach her.

"How did her leg get broken?" Jeriah asked. "And how did she escape, when the rest of her family didn't? Since I wasn't here when she arrived . . ."

Four more days dragged past. His friends hadn't known many details of Mistress Koryn's ordeal, but what they knew was bad enough. Jeriah was still looking for an excuse to approach her, but the need to do something was becoming intolerable. His temper grew so short that his friends began avoiding him. He felt as if everyone were watching him, or trying to delay him in everything he did. It was almost a relief to be in Nevin's company—he *knew* Nevin was his enemy.

Jeriah thought about the goblins' arrival all the time, so he should have been suspicious when he started to follow the Hierarch back to his room after Sunset Prayer and found the hem of his tabard tangled in the thorns of a flowering shrub. But as he bent to unfasten it, there was no thought in Jeriah's mind except care for the fragile trim . . . until he saw Daroo's eyes gazing at him from the depths of the bush.

Alarm jolted through him. Jeriah was horribly aware of the crowd around them; the chatting priests and lords. The alert guards. *Of all the stupid, reckless, dangerous . . .*

"The woods where we were before." The voice was so soft, Jeriah couldn't have made out the words if he hadn't seen the child's lips move.

He nodded, trying to control his expression, his breathing, the rapid beat of his heart. Jeriah slipped his tabard free of the thorns and followed the Hierarch without a backward glance. Every muscle tensed, expecting the outcry that would mark the demon brat's discovery. It didn't come.

The door swung shut behind Jeriah, cutting him off if the boy needed rescue. He'd have to trust Daroo to escape as unseen as he'd arrived—how did they *do* that?—and get to the woods himself as soon as he could.

Jeriah followed the Hierarch into his bedchamber, where the menservants were already helping him out of his ceremonial robe.

"There's something I need to do this evening." Jeriah pulled off his tunic, folded it rapidly into the chest, and put all his nervous energy into making his voice commanding. "You are to put the Sunlord to bed. I'll see you in the morning."

"Yes, sir, but—"

"Just do it!" He dared not let them question him, or worse, send for Nevin. By morning he'd have made up an excuse. By morning it wouldn't matter. Daroo had returned. He could finally *do* something!

Down and down the torchlit central stairs. No uproar. No goblin children being hauled off by the sunsguard. The woods' concealment embraced Jeriah, and some of his tension drained away. Where had he been when he'd talked to Daroo before? He hadn't bothered to mark the spot, and now, in the darkness—

"Too-too-wheer." It could have been a bird call, but Jeriah had never heard one like it. "Too-too-wheer." He followed the sound, struggling blindly though the underbrush.

"Hello, hero. I understand you need our help. Again."

It took Jeriah several moments to find Cogswhallop's sharp face amid the shadowy foliage above him. "Yes, I do."

Needing help embarrassed him less than it had before, perhaps because Daroo had already helped him so much. Was he becoming accustomed to goblin allies? Had Tobin felt like this?

"Well then, have you got that cursed Decree repealed? I haven't heard about it."

If Tobin had felt that way, then his brother had never been forced to bargain with them. "No, I haven't."

Cogswhallop rose as if to leave. Jeriah was almost certain the goblin was bluffing, but he added swiftly. "There's something else I think you'd be interested in. Something you'll need soon. At least in the next few years."

"And what might that be?"

"Do you know about the barbarians who are invading this land?" Jeriah asked. Cogswhallop snorted, and he hurried on, "Yes, of course you do. How do goblins get along with the barbarians?"

"No worse than your kind does, but that's not saying much. As far as we can tell there's no goblins in any land the barbarians control. They regard us as a delicacy, I'm told, and they're better at catching us than your folk are."

"So when they come, it'd be good if you had some defense against them."

"We don't intend to be around when they get here." But the goblin looked interested, anyway.

"There's an amulet their shamans make—it bestows the protection of their blood gods, or maybe it protects the wearer from the blood gods. We've never found a barbarian who didn't wear one. And if you're wearing one, they won't hurt you."

The goblin shrugged, setting the leaves rustling. "It'd take more than an amulet to disguise one of us as a barbarian— we're a bit shorter, you'll note."

"It isn't a matter of disguise. Some of our spies have been wearing these amulets when they've been discovered. As long as they've got the amulets, the barbarians won't harm them. Even if they know what they are. I heard a witness talk about it once—they followed a spy all the way back to our lines, hoping he'd lose the amulet, but they never attacked him."

"Then why doesn't your army wear them? Sounds like a sure way to win any battle."

"We considered that, but they're very unholy. The priests say that if we wore them, we'd forfeit the Bright Gods' favor. . . ." Jeriah suddenly remembered that the Decree of Bright Magic had been passed so the army could keep the Bright Gods' favor, and fell silent.

"Aye. They're powerful keen on that," Cogswhallop drawled.

"The amulet's magic comes from human sacrifice," said Jeriah. "I wouldn't want to wear . . . Ah, that won't bother you, will it?"

The goblin thought about it. "It might bother us some, but it wouldn't stop us. It's not like we did the killing. It wouldn't bother us at all to wear a copy—"

"You can't fake them," Jeriah admitted. "We did try that. Their shamans detected it instantly."

"Humph. They're not made of iron, are they?"

"Copper."

"How many of these amulets are you offering, for a search of all the papers in a large guarded palace?"

"Just one, but it will protect the person who wears it from any barbarians they meet, so—"

"One? I've got *thousands* of folk to protect." The goblin

started to climb back up the tree. "One is almost worthless, hero."

"You don't know that! One might save your life. Save lots of lives! Wait! I . . . I only know where one of them is."

The goblin paused. "If your army's been collecting them, there must be hundreds, maybe even thousands, about."

"I suppose, but I don't—"

"Two hundred of these amulets, and we'll search the palace for you."

"I couldn't possibly get that many! I don't—"

"You're the one who wants our help, human."

Cogswhallop was leaving.

"Twenty!"

The goblin turned back. "A hundred and twenty, perhaps."

They finally settled on "as many over fifty as you can get." Jeriah was left with a nagging feeling that it had been too easy—though it hadn't been easy at all!

This time the goblins' help would cost no one their home. All Jeriah had to do was find, and steal, fifty blood amulets. No, not easy, but the waiting was over. Jeriah only hoped this attempt at burglary would go better than the last one. He wasn't incompetent. He had to start getting it right, getting it done . . . before Tobin's time ran out.

Makenna

"A WHOLE HILL? WITH TREES? That's impossible!"

Makenna couldn't tell which of the goblins crowded around her had voiced that indignant cry—and she couldn't blame them.

"Possible or not," Tobin said calmly, "the stream is gone. And we've been ready to leave for the new site for days, so I don't see that the why of it makes much difference. We know what to do, and where we'll go next."

This practical approach reassured the goblins so much that the whole lot of them burst into complaint.

"You can moan all you want," Makenna told them. "I'm fairly peeved about it myself. But moaning won't get us to fresh water any sooner. So if I were you, I'd stop yapping and start taking down tents!"

She put enough tartness into her voice that they departed, showing far less panic than she'd expected. That was largely because as soon as Tobin had returned, with news of another site, he'd started them packing. Learning why the stream had stopped had shaken them, but they were already prepared to move on.

"You did a good job, making them ready to move," she told Tobin as the last of the grumbling goblins departed.

"I didn't have to do much," he said. "They'd already realized there was a good chance we'd have to leave. They started gathering up their possessions as soon as I told them I'd found a new stream. They're not children—though it took me longer than it should to realize that."

"No, they're not. But I have to wonder how they'll react if this new stream of yours disappears too."

"Why would . . . ?" Tobin's voice trailed into appalled silence. "I'm sorry. I hadn't thought it through that far. But if one mountain can move . . ."

". . . so could another. You've only had five minutes to think about it," Makenna said. "I had several days. And if our enemy— If something like this could happen to one stream, then *anything* could happen to the next."

"Enemy?" Trust him to pick up on the one word she hoped he'd miss. "We've seen no sign of anyone, anywhere in this world. And I've been looking."

Makenna sighed. "Maybe I've been fighting too long. Maybe I'm seeing enemies where there's nothing but accidents, and this new stream will run for a thousand years or more."

"If this was an accident, it's the strangest I ever heard of," Tobin said. "So maybe 'enemy' is the right conclusion.

But at least it proves one thing."

"What?"

"There's plenty of magic somewhere in this world. Because I can't think of anything else that could move a hill like that."

Makenna snorted. "I don't think the Hierarch, with all his priests assisting, could summon enough magic to move that hill. If that's magic, it's like none I've ever heard of."

Baffled silence fell between them. Makenna had been in command so long, she was surprised how much the worry and depression were lightened when she could share them.

"Are you sorry you came jumping through that gate after us?" she asked softly. The Bright Gods knew he should be.

"No." There was no hesitation in the firm reply. "Are you?"

"Since the immediate alternative was execution . . . no," she said. "At least, not yet."

CHAPTER 9

Jeriah

"I *TOLD* HIM ONLY THE Hierarch's squire could give him his medicine," Nevin snarled. "I told him several times!"

Master Lazur looked thoughtful. Master Kerratis looked angry.

Jeriah didn't remember Nevin saying anything of the kind. But he had to admit, at least to himself, that he ignored most of Nevin's lectures.

Nevin had been waiting outside the Hierarch's room that morning, and had dragged Jeriah down to Master Lazur's office all but breathing fire in his indignation. Trust Nevin to choose this morning to check on him. Jeriah didn't mind being scolded—the bad part was still to come.

"So the Hierarch didn't get his medicine last night," Master Lazur said neutrally. "What do you think, Kerratis? Will this cause problems?"

"Missing one dose will do no harm, but to entrust this careless young—"

"He should be whipped!" Nevin snapped. "Whipped and

dismissed in dishonor. How could he—"

"Calm down, Nevin. Master Kerratis says missing one dose won't harm him. Though you did right to report it, and I thank you." Master Lazur's tone held a dismissal. Nevin ignored it.

"Master, he isn't fit to serve the Sunlord! He neglects his duties, he's disrespectful, he—"

"Master Zachiros says he's doing well. In fact—"

The warning chime sounded though the open window; ten minutes to Dawn Prayer. The priest shook his head and visibly changed his mind about what he'd intended to say. "Nevin, you may attend the Hierarch today. Jeriah's going to be busy."

"But—"

"If you don't go now, he'll be late for the Dawn Prayer— and that's unacceptable," said Master Lazur.

Nevin gave Jeriah a final scowl and hurried out.

"I agree with the boy," said Master Kerratis. "Oh, not about the whipping. I don't care if you whip him or not. But you can't place the Hierarch's care in . . . unreliable hands. Dismiss him from the palace."

"With whom would you replace him?" the priest asked. "You know how hard it's been to get the Sunlord to accept a new squire."

"A squire who fails in essential duties does no one any good," the healer replied. "There's bound to be someone else he'll accept. If we introduced them very gradually, I think that would turn the trick. We just tried to move too swiftly before."

"Hmm. If you're right about that . . ."

If they sent Jeriah away now, Tobin would die.

"Masters, I swear it won't happen again. I thought the servants would take care of his medicine."

Master Kerratis ignored him. "I know young Rovanscourt's reputation, Lazur. How could you entrust him with—"

"You make too much of it." Master Lazur's voice was firm. "I'll handle the matter."

The healer priest glared at Jeriah. "I think you should question him under a truth spell."

Jeriah's heart lurched. If they put a truth spell on him, they'd learn everything!

"But . . . but that's for criminals! I'm not a liar. Though if you feel you must persist in this insult, over nothing more than a misunderstanding, I will submit." Jeriah tried to look haughty and offended, praying from the bottom of his soul that they wouldn't insist.

Master Lazur finally stirred. "No, this is a trivial matter when all's said. We shouldn't overreact."

Master Kerratis shut his mouth with a snap. "Then I'll stop wasting both our time. Good day." He glared at Jeriah again and departed.

Jeriah relaxed slightly.

"It's not that trivial," Master Lazur told him. "But Master Zachiros says you're doing well, for the most part. Have there been any other problems?"

"No, master. Though it's more complicated than . . . well, it's complicated."

"So except for last night I have no complaint of you." The priest's expression remained bland, but his eyes were intent. Jeriah's nerves tightened. He'd relaxed too soon.

"Where were you last night?"

"I was meeting someone, master. I hope you'll forgive me but I can't, in honor, give her name. It wasn't . . . We only talked, but . . ." Jeriah wished he could blush but feared his face was white instead. If Master Lazur changed his mind about that truth spell . . .

"But you've only been here . . ."

The priest's eyes swept over Jeriah and his expression changed from surprise to resignation. Jeriah let his breath trickle out, careful not to sigh with relief. There were advantages to inheriting his mother's looks.

"As long as it doesn't interfere with your duties, your personal life is none of my business," Master Lazur said. "But I'd advise you . . . Oh, why bother? Jeriah, you were given this job in spite of your past because it was convenient for me. If you fail in your duties again, we'll dismiss you. Understand?"

Jeriah nodded—he didn't dare speak.

"After Dawn Prayer you'll apologize to the Hierarch. And then"—the priest's lips twitched—"Master Goserian will give you a little work."

"I'm sorry, Sunlord, that I failed to attend you. I hope you'll forgive me." Jeriah studied the old man's face with some concern—he really hadn't intended to neglect him—but the Hierarch looked the same as always.

"All right." The old man patted his arm. "All right, Jeriah."

Jeriah! The Hierarch had learned his name. Maybe now he wouldn't have to introduce himself every morning.

"Thank you, my lord."

After his apology Jeriah reported to Master Goserian, who gave him a bucket of soapy water and a scrub brush and showed him the temple floor.

"Generally I assign eight servants to clean this. It takes them less than an hour. It will take you longer."

Was there laughter in that pompous voice?

"But there are advantages to that," Master Goserian continued. "By the time you get down the steps to the second level, the petitions should be over."

Jeriah eyed the stairs falling gracefully down the hill. Four flights. They grew wider as they descended. "The stairs too?"

"The steps that lead to the temple are part of the temple," Master Goserian confirmed. "I'll assign someone to bring you fresh buckets. If you had to fetch water yourself, you'd still be scrubbing when the Sunset Prayer was called."

He strolled away. Jeriah gazed at the vast expanse of marble and winced.

The stone came clean fairly easily, but there was a lot of it. Jeriah's rolled-up sleeves kept falling down and soon became wet. The knees of his britches were soaked. The maidservant who brought him fresh buckets smiled sympathetically . . . and brought more buckets. Jeriah smiled back—and waited till she was out of earshot to swear.

By midday he'd started on the stairs, and his good manners paid off; the girl brought him a meal and sat on the step beside him while he ate. Jeriah listened politely to her chatter, and ignored the flirtatious smiles for several minutes before he recognized an opportunity. Had she seen many of the palace treasures? When she dusted, for instance?

It turned out she'd cleaned most large objects in the palace, but if she'd seen a pile . . . chest? . . . sack? . . . of blood god amulets, she didn't mention it.

Jeriah returned to his scrubbing in a better mood. He'd known worse punishment for past pranks, it was just . . . there was something humiliating in being punished like a child. The legendary knights who had to neglect their duties to perform great deeds were praised, not set to scrubbing the floor. But talking to the girl had given him some ideas. Mistress Koryn might know where the amulets were kept. Jeriah's sudden shiver had nothing to do with his wet clothes. Mistress Koryn would also remember Jeriah's interest if anyone noticed the amulets were gone. Was there anyone else . . . ? He had to find them as soon as he could. The goblins would need time to search for the spell notes, and in less than a week Tobin would began to sicken.

The hours passed more quickly while he planned, but Jeriah was tired by the time he neared the bottom of the stairs.

"I see you've found a task that suits your capabilities."

Nevin stood three steps above Jeriah, and his malicious grin spoke volumes.

He's only trying to provoke you. Don't . . . Jeriah couldn't resist. "You, on the other hand, don't seem to have anything to do. Pity they've got enough stable muckers."

Nevin smirked. "You should know—I understand you've performed that task more than once."

Jeriah's lips tightened, but this time he managed to keep his mouth shut. If his reputation as a prankster made Nevin and Master Lazur underestimate him, then thank the Bright Gods for it. "Don't you have anything to do, Sir Nevin?"

"As a matter of fact I need to pack. I'll be doing some traveling soon."

He wants you to ask where and why, and be envious. "How nice for . . ." Jeriah's brain finally awoke, and Nevin's pricking became irrelevant. "Where are you going?" *And for how long, and is Master Lazur going with you?*

"The western coast. I understand it's beautiful this time of year."

"It is. My mother comes from that area."

Could this be some part of her scheme? Jeriah didn't see how, but if he was suspicious, what would Master Lazur be thinking?

A frown was forming on Nevin's brow—Jeriah had been silent too long. "It's a pity I have more important things to do than take pleasure jaunts. I could show you around."

"It's not entirely for pleasure. There's some rather odd unrest there. People are asking why we have to relocate instead of fighting the barbarians. It's probably nothing, but Master Lazur thinks we should kill it before it grows. He's taking me to be his eyes and ears when he's not present."

Jeriah's heart leapt. Whatever his mother was up to, she'd accomplished one thing—Master Lazur was leaving!

"I'm sure you'll make an excellent spy," Jeriah told him. "Eavesdropping, lying, sneaking around. You'll have a wonderful time."

Nevin's face darkened. "And when I get back, I'll check to be sure you've managed to perform your simple duties properly."

He turned to go. No time for subtlety.

"I'll be counting the days. When do you leave?"

For a moment Jeriah thought he wouldn't get an answer, but Nevin had to have the last word. "Day after tomorrow. Enjoy your afternoon." He gestured at the remaining steps and strolled off, leaving Jeriah torn between fear for his mother and quivering excitement. There was no way to know how long they'd be gone, but in their absence . . .

✧ ✧ ✧

Three hours past midday Jeriah finished scrubbing. He felt as sore as if he had been beaten as he clambered wetly to his feet and stumbled off to the baths. He might not know where the barbarian amulets were, but he knew who to ask—and he'd finally figured out an excuse that wouldn't rouse her suspicions.

Mistress Koryn was easy to find. Today she sat at a library table, with a small, old-looking book in front of her and a sheaf of notes to one side. Ink smudged both her right hand and her nose, and her gown was a drab blue that was even less flattering than the last two.

Jeriah knew better than to wait for her to notice him. And she seemed the kind of girl who wouldn't mind if he went straight to the point.

"Mistress Koryn, I need information about the barbarians. As much as I can get. They say you're the person to ask."

She jumped when he spoke, and her extraordinary eyes studied him for a long moment before she replied.

"And you're suddenly taken with a burning desire to learn about the barbarians because . . . ?"

"Because I want to get my brother back." Jeriah met her gaze steadily. "If I could figure out some better way to fight the barbarians, maybe I could make the relocation unnecessary. And if I did that, I think I could persuade Master Lazur to open a gate for me. He'd owe me that much."

"And you plan to accomplish all this in what . . . less than a month?" Koryn asked.

"He could become ill in less than a week." Fear tightened Jeriah's voice as he spoke. "He might even be ill now. He'll live for several more weeks, but that's all. Please. My brother is going to die!"

She'd lost her whole family—she should have melted with sympathy. Any other girl would have. Koryn eyed him suspiciously for a long moment. "I guess it depends on what you want to know."

It was much too soon for Jeriah to blurt out that he wanted to know about the barbarian amulets.

"I understand why getting everyone behind the great wall would help so much, as a matter of tactics." Jeriah pointed to a map of the Realm of the Seven Bright Gods that had been painted on a high wall, above the level where shelves were practical.

The great southern desert, which the barbarians had to cross in order to attack the Realm, was a yellow blur at the bottom, flowing into a wide crescent of golden green marked with roads and towns. The Southlands. Moving up the map, the Realm broadened even more through the green Midlands, rimmed by rocky hills to the west and the scattered lakes and marshes of the wetlands to the east. In between lay the finest farmland known to man. The dark green forest of the north began just after the Realm started to narrow abruptly, like the neck of an off-center hourglass.

Looking at a map like this made it perfectly clear why that narrow neck of land that joined the Realm to the woodlands beyond the wall was the perfect point of defense—even without the great stone wall that spanned it. Still . . .

"This map doesn't show all of the woodlands," Jeriah said. "But they're smaller than the rest of the Realm, and uprooting all those trees would be a farmer's nightmare. No one wants to go. Half the Realm's population will probably just sit on their own land, no matter what the Hierarch says, until it's too late. There's got to be a way to stop them in the Southlands. That's what you're trying to find, isn't it?"

"If I find a way, I'll certainly let you know," Koryn said dryly. "But there's no place short of the wall where the border is less than hundreds of miles across. And now that they've got bases in the Southlands, bases they can occupy year-round . . . I'm sorry about your brother. I really am. But, Jeriah, there is no way to stop the barbarians short of the wall. The border there narrows to less than thirty miles, and the wall is—"

"I've seen it," Jeriah told her. "And that wall will need a lot of repairs to make it into a solid barrier. We've held the barbarians on the southern border for years now. I know their army has been growing, but why not just bring in more of our own men to match them?"

"Every landholder in the council is already screaming that they're not going to be able to get the planting done with the men they have," Koryn told him. "And the number of men the Hierarch can demand for army service was set when the Realm was first formed."

"So what?" said Jeriah. "If the choice is between sending more men or relocating, the landholders will find men to send. And the Hierarch . . . the Hierarch speaks for the Seven Bright Gods. If the first Hierarch set the limits for army service, why can't this Hierarch speak for the Gods again and change it?"

This Hierarch was a mindless husk, and the Gods' will was currently being interpreted by Timeon Lazur, but Koryn might not know that. How deep in Master Lazur's confidence was she?

"If we had the men," he went on, "surely we could wipe out enough of their army to drive them away. Yes, it might be hard to get the crops in if we sent more men to the border. Yes, it would mean changing the ancient laws about army service. But that has to be better than trying to move the entire Realm!"

He was panting when he stopped, but he'd had the sense to keep his voice low. To question the Hierarch's decrees was to question the Bright Gods themselves—both heresy and treason.

"It's not just numbers," Koryn said. "Our army outnumbers theirs right now, by about five percent as nearly as we can estimate."

Jeriah brightened. "If we already outnumber them, then we wouldn't need many more troops! We can—"

"It's not a matter of numbers! You served with the army for almost a year. You have to know what I'm talking about."

This wasn't something Jeriah ordinarily admitted to girls, but . . . "I was only on the border for one summer. I went out with several patrols, but I never actually fought the barbarians. And I don't know what you're talking about."

"But you must know about . . ." Koryn eyed him warily. "Never mind. We'd need more men than you think, because the barbarians aren't going to get discouraged and go home. They can't. There's a terrible drought in their own lands. Not a natural drought, either—it's lasted more than ten years now, and it's getting worse every year. Their rain has vanished. Their lakes are gone. Their rivers are gone. They have no crops. Even the grass is dying. Their only chance for survival is to conquer a new land. And the only land available is ours."

"But that's impossible. No drought lasts that long."

"As I said, it's not natural. The priests say the Bright Gods are punishing them for giving themselves over to the Dark One."

"Right," Jeriah said dryly. "Isn't there some way we could negotiate—"

"It's not nonsense! I don't claim to know what the Gods are thinking, but the barbarians are evil."

"If they're all going to starve, if they just want to survive, then surely we could work something out."

"That's what the Hierarch thought when they first attacked us, years ago," Koryn told him. "He was going to offer them the northern wood. Safe passage through the Realm—escorted by the army, to make sure it was safe for everyone. The land would be hard to till and settle, but better for everyone than war to the death."

"That sounds like a good solution," said Jeriah. "Why didn't it work?"

"Because the barbarians turned it down," Koryn told him. "And ate all but one of the diplomatic party who carried the Hierarch's message. Which made it a bit hard to repeat the offer. The one they left alive—he was only a boy, somebody's page. He came back to our lines, draped in one of their filthy amulets, and told the generals that the barbarians said they didn't want useless woods. That they could take the land they needed, for they had nothing to fear from us. Later that night"—her voice was very quiet—"the boy killed himself."

Jeriah's stomach was churning. "All right, but that was before this war had really started, before so many of their own warriors died. Maybe now—"

"Aren't you listening?" Her calm voice was rising. "The barbarians are *evil*. We have no choice but to fight them to the death—theirs or ours! Because this can't end any other way."

The words echoed in the quiet room, and Jeriah looked around. There was no one nearby.

"I'm sorry," he said softly. "I heard about what happened

to your family. But you have to admit that might be influencing your judgment. It would influence anyone! So I have to—"

"You know nothing about what happened to my family." Her voice was quieter, but contempt flashed over her face. "*You* never even fought them."

"Neither have you," Jeriah pointed out, nettled. "Your father put you up on a horse before the attack, and it bolted. Which is good," he added hastily. "You'd have died, otherwise."

"So that's what they think happened?" She considered this a moment, then shrugged. "Close enough."

"That's not what happened?" The story his friends had told about Mistress Koryn's escape had some holes in it. But they were all clear that her horse had bolted, and that was how she got away. How she'd broken her leg in the process wasn't entirely clear.

"It's true as far as it goes. We had almost no warning. We were far enough from the border that we never expected them to reach our estate, but my father set watchers on the edge of our land, just in case."

"So you did get some warning?" Jeriah asked. Her golden skin was pale—but Jeriah wanted to learn about her, and this was his chance. Besides, he had a feeling that she ought to talk about it. That she might be ready.

"You could say that," Koryn said. "They screamed. Warning enough. A barbarian war band was swarming across our fields by the time we all ran outside.

"My father was organizing the men to fight." Her voice quivered for the first time. "But he told our steward to get the rest of the family on horseback, to put me up on Snake. Snake was his own horse, the fastest in the stable. I was still arguing that my father would need him when old Rinnie threw me into the saddle."

She had been staring off into space. Now she turned to Jeriah, and he flinched at the agony in her eyes.

"I was a good rider, better than my mother, but when the barbarians attacked . . . No one could have kept Snake from bolting. I tried to turn him back. I did."

"You shouldn't have," Jeriah said gently. "And no rider can stop a bolting horse until it's ready to stop. You couldn't go back."

"Oh, but I could." The smile that touched her lips chilled Jeriah to the bone.

"I fell off when Snake jumped the north ditch," she continued. "But my left foot got caught in the stirrup. I remember being dragged for a while. Then nothing till I woke up, just before sunrise, with my leg twisted three ways and my head hurting almost as bad. I was tangled in a big clump of brush," she added. "That's probably what pulled my foot out of the stirrup. And it must have kept the barbarians from finding me, because I was only a few fields from the house."

Jeriah's whole body tightened when he realized what would come next. "You went back?" He couldn't raise his voice above a whisper. "You went back there?"

She eyed him curiously, as if she were seeing him for the first time. "Most people assume I crawled away."

Jeriah shook his head.

"Well, you're right," she went on. "I crawled back to the house and found them. Everyone. Even the servants . . . I'd grown up with them, too. So you see, I know *exactly* what happened to my family. Although you're right," she added. "It certainly influenced my judgment."

"Why aren't you crying? You should be hysterical by now."

In fact, Jeriah was wondering if he should send for a healer.

"You think I didn't cry? I screamed my head off. I cried my eyes out. I spent the whole trip to the palace, and most of my first month here, bathed in tears. I finally got tired of it."

She didn't claim she'd healed, Jeriah noted. She might never heal. On the other hand, she was clearly able to talk about it, and that might help.

"So how did you escape? With a badly broken leg, behind the battle lines, and no horse?"

"A horse wouldn't have done any good," she said. "I couldn't have mounted something that tall. We had an old donkey, in a pen under the stable that the barbarians missed when they were stealing the rest of our livestock. I managed to get myself onto his back. As for getting through the lines, I'd been riding through that countryside my whole life.

I knew every ditch, back road, and trail. It wasn't hard to avoid the war bands. They were noisy."

Her voice flattened on the last words. Jeriah could all but hear the screaming, the sound of carnage drifting over the grape fields.

"I'd probably have lain down and died," he admitted.

"I thought about it." Was there a note of humor in her voice? "But I wanted revenge more. So I made my way to the regional headquarters and told the commander that his pickets had been massacred, and the whole barbarian army was ravaging the Southlands. They were quite surprised," she added. "And even when I told them, they didn't—"

She rubbed her face and sighed.

"No, that's not fair. Once I got word to them, they did all they could. No one can stop the barbarians."

"But why?" Jeriah demanded. "I don't care how many barbarians there are—every man in the Realm who can carry a weapon would turn out for that fight!"

"It wouldn't matter," she said. "Come on, Rovan, think! Even if you were recalled before the fall skirmishes began, you must have heard rumors!"

"I heard dozens of rumors," Jeriah said impatiently. "Maybe hundreds. What *are* you talking about?"

She hesitated a moment, then said softly. "About their magic."

"I know the barbarians have magic. And I heard plenty of wild rumors about it, too. So what? Our battle priests serve the Seven Bright Gods, and their power is more than a match . . . for . . ."

The hard stillness in her face stopped him. This scholarly girl, who'd faced so much, was now facing something that frightened even her.

"Nothing is more powerful than the Seven Bright Gods!" For all his shock, Jeriah's voice dropped. This was a conversation no one should overhear.

"So they say." Koryn might be frightened, but she didn't retreat. "I don't know what gods the barbarians serve. I've been trying find out, but the bits of information I'm reading don't make much sense. What we do know is that the barbarians have a magic our priests have never encountered before. It comes from human sacrifice, from death and blood and pain. And it makes the barbarians so strong in battle that our troops cannot defeat them. No matter how many men we send to the front, the Realm's defeat is inevitable. Unless we find a position of overwhelming tactical superiority. Like a very small border"—she gestured to the map—"defended by a big stone wall."

"No magic is stronger than that of the Seven Bright Gods," Jeriah repeated. "It can't be. If it was . . ."

"Then one of the founding tenets of the church, the bed-rock beneath the whole Realm, turns to quicksand," said Koryn softly. "And on the eve of invasion by an army we can't defeat, we'd be faced with anarchy and rebellion as well. Inconvenient, isn't it?"

If that was true . . . It couldn't be true.

"But suppose . . . suppose the barbarians' magic is just some new trick of the Dark One? Something our priests could easily counter if they could figure out how. Suppose figuring it out is the Bright Gods' test?"

"Suppose all you want," Koryn said. "Why do you think I'm studying every scrap of any document that even mentions the barbarians? Our battle priests have been trying for years now to find a way to negate their magic. If this is one of the Bright Gods' tests, we're failing."

Jeriah struggled to gather his scattered wits. The barbarian invasion had suddenly become much more real. But even if their magic was stronger than that of the Bright Gods— which he still couldn't believe—he had a brother to save. He'd wanted to learn about Koryn, in order to find a lever to use against her. And he had.

"The priests," Jeriah said softly, "aren't the only ones in the Bright Gods' Realm with magic."

Koryn snorted with unladylike force. "You think hedge-witches and herb-healers can defeat barbarian battle magic? You're dreaming."

"Maybe," said Jeriah. "Or maybe that's part of the test. Has anyone tried it?"

He already knew the answer. So did Koryn. "They got rid of all the lesser magic workers because they might have encouraged resistance to the relocation. So we'll never know, will we?"

"There might be a few left," Jeriah said carefully. "If some-one could find them."

The gray eyes fixed on him with the intense focus Koryn gave the books she studied. It wasn't a comfortable feeling.

"You know some of the lesser magic workers? You could contact them?"

"No," said Jeriah truthfully. "I don't know any of them, and I have no way to contact them. Even if I did, even if I wanted to give them a handful of barbarian amulets, say, to see if they could tell us anything about barbarian magic, I couldn't do it. Because I don't know where the amulets are, either."

He had no doubt she'd take the bait—there was nothing this girl wouldn't do to destroy the barbarians.

"I don't know what you're up to," Koryn said slowly, "but they don't have the power to disrupt the relocation now, so I can't see how it would do any harm. And if you could find a better way for us to fight—even something that would buy us a little more time—that's worth some risk. But, Rovan . . ."

"Yes?"

"If you do anything to hinder the relocation, anything at all, I will stop you and all your friends. Permanently. No matter what it takes."

The cold fervor in her voice left Jeriah speechless.

"The amulets are stored in chests under the chorus steps."

Koryn rose awkwardly to her feet and limped away.

Guilt washed over him, so intensely that he almost called her back. Jeriah would have felt guilty using a tragedy like that against anyone, and Koryn . . . she was a hero! She'd overcome agony, and a grief he couldn't even imagine, to warn the army. Every life they'd saved from that attack was to her credit. No knight in the Realm's history had done more. In an earlier, more romantic age, Jeriah would have knelt and offered his sword to her service. A part of him wanted to do it anyway—she deserved that kind of tribute. But Jeriah had a brother to save. That intelligent, driven young woman was his enemy.

Tobin

"BIRD TRACKS, MICE, SOME SQUIRRELS. But that's all."

The reporting Tracker was as muddy as Tobin, and he looked almost as tired. He couldn't be more tired, for these days weariness seemed to drag at Tobin's bones.

Today he had a headache, too. But this long marsh was the best water source in miles, and anything that approached it would leave its mark in the mud. Tobin had hiked along one section of the slippery shore himself—though even with their magic drained, the goblin Trackers were better at it than he was.

When Tobin had scouted around their previous camp, it had mostly been as part of another task; wandering away when the log cutters didn't need him, or accompanying the Greeners who hunted foodstuffs farther and farther afield.

When they reached the new village site, Makenna had sent him out to search the area before he'd even had a chance to unpack. And she'd sent a handpicked band of Trackers and

Flichters with him. It was a perfect scouting team . . . had there been anything to find.

No predators larger than a fox. No sign of building, of any intelligent life. No trouble even from the weather, except that it was hot in the afternoons.

Tobin rubbed his aching temples gently.

"We're going to head back," he told the Tracker. "All the way back to the main camp. I'll send the Flichters to round up the others and bring them in."

"That's assumin' none of them found anything either, right?"

"If anyone's seen anything, then of course we'll investigate," Tobin assured him.

But in his heart he knew they hadn't. And it wasn't because he wanted to get back to Makenna, although he did. Despite being surrounded by goblins, as she'd been most of her life, her connection with her own humanity was growing every day. Every time he looked at her, Tobin sometimes thought.

That was why he'd followed her through the gate; to keep her human. He needed her human.

But the real reason he wanted to return was his nagging conviction that the goblin camp was the *reason* all these strange things were happening. Erebus had pointed out that peculiar events could be taking place all over the Otherworld, all the time, and they'd only know about the things that affected them. Tobin was certain that even that mountain had been moved just to drive them out.

If they had an enemy, the new camp was where it would strike.

Tobin rubbed his aching head again. "Round up the others," he repeated. "We're going home."

CHAPTER 10

Jeriah

THE DAY BEFORE MASTER LAZUR and Nevin departed seemed eternal. The night, most of which Jeriah spent reviewing his plans, was even longer.

He caught a glimpse of their departure from the dais as he carried petitions from the crowd to Master Zachiros, but dealing with the Hierarch under the secretary's sharp eye took all his attention. To his disappointment the old man had forgotten his name again, but Jeriah hoped he'd start remembering it soon.

After the petitions he helped the menservants put the Hierarch to bed, and then pulled Mohri, the most senior of them, aside.

"Before he left, Master Lazur asked me to conduct some business for him. It was scheduled before his departure and can't be delayed."

"Yes, sir." The man didn't even look curious. *Don't say too much.*

"The problem is, I may not be back by sunset—can you

attend the Hierarch at prayers?"

"Yes, sir. But what about his medicine?"

"I'll be back in time to give it to him," Jeriah said. He'd better be finished by then! "But if I'm not, I'll brew it for him when I get in. I'd have done that before, if I'd realized . . ."

"All right, sir." Mohri turned away, and Jeriah hurried to the stable to put his plan in action.

He saddled Glory and rode into the city in case someone checked his story. Was he making this too complicated? He had to make people believe he'd left the palace, or he'd be forced to attend the Hierarch this evening. Jeriah wished he knew how to pick locks. He hoped St. Cerwyn, the patron of wild and desperate ventures, would favor him once more.

He was going to need the help of all the saints to get into the Otherworld in time to save his brother. Tobin could become ill any day now, and the Lesser Ones still hadn't contacted him!

At least after tonight he could set the goblins searching for the spell notes. While they were doing that, Jeriah would track down that cursed tinker and choke the information out of him! He'd have to make some excuse . . . What excuse could he make to abandon the Hierarch? Especially if Nevin wasn't there to take his place. Could the menservants alone keep the Hierarch's condition secret? And if they couldn't, would that be so terrible?

Yes, Jeriah realized grimly. Only a divinely guided Sun-lord could have convinced the Realm that relocating was truly necessary. That the barbarians couldn't be defeated in battle. If the Hierarch and Master Lazur's shadow government fell, the relocation would fall with them. And then, if the barbarians won . . .

Catastrophe. A catastrophe beyond imagining.

Jeriah thrust the thought away. He had to save Tobin. The servants could make some excuse for the Hierarch's non-appearance, claim he had some minor illness until Nevin returned.

Half the government was looking out for the relocation—Jeriah was the only one who was trying to save his brother.

A different guard shift was stationed at the gates when Jeriah added himself to the crowd that came to the palace to attend the Sunset Prayer. The few grooms still in the stable paid him no attention when he returned Glory to her stall. Jeriah joined the people climbing the temple stairs, concealing his identity simply by pulling up his hood and keeping his eyes lowered.

The warning chime sounded as Jeriah got off the steps at the fourth-level terrace—he could have been rushing to change his clothes before the prayer. He dashed into his room and shut the door behind him, then he changed his mind and cracked it open. When the ceremony began, he could hear the distant murmur of prayer and response clearly.

Jeriah slipped around the terrace to the dining chamber, hugging the wall. Everyone was supposed to be in the temple, but what if someone was late? Or was using this emptying of the palace for their own purpose, like he was? Jeriah grinned. *I won't tell if you won't*. It was a bargain he'd made several times, working pranks in the past. He hoped he wouldn't need it tonight.

If anyone else was shirking their pious duties, Jeriah didn't meet them. He took the laundry stairs to the third level, and the narrow servants' staircase to the corridor that ran between the Hierarch's rooms, Master Zachiros' offices, and the petitions court. At the end of that corridor, a ladder with a hatch at the top gave access to the crowded storeroom under the chorus steps.

Jeriah quietly opened the hatch—the Hierarch's strong voice and the chorus' rumbling response came clearly through the steeply angled ceiling. The first third of the prayer was already over. When Jeriah had been in this room before, he'd been looking for spell notes, not chests of amulets. The high wall held narrow cabinets, where the priests of the chorus kept their robes. They were labeled with their owners' names, and Jeriah took a few seconds to read down the line. If one belonged to a friend of Master Lazur's, he'd take a moment to check it for the notes—but the only name he recognized was Herb Mistress Chardane's. If Jeriah could find those cursed notes, he wouldn't need the amulets—but that wasn't going to happen now.

On to the storage compartment. Jeriah had to shift several crates to reach the small door. Quietly—if he could hear the prayer this clearly, they might be able to hear loud sounds he made.

The last crate he pulled aside revealed a keyhole, but Jeriah reached out and tugged the handle anyway. Locked! Jeriah swore under his breath. But at least he knew where these keys were probably kept.

He climbed down the ladder and ran down the hall to Master Zachiros' office. No locked doors here. Jeriah had been in the secretary's desk several times, fetching things he'd "forgotten." He knew exactly where the keys were.

Snatching them up, he ran back to the chorus storeroom and began fitting keys into the lock. The prayer was almost two thirds done now. *Come on, one of you, fit!*

Key after key—he was halfway through the ring when he heard the sweet click.

The locked compartment was a narrow wedge, the ceiling too low for anyone to stand inside. It was full of chests, crates, boxes. Jeriah tore them open, desperately balancing silence against speed. At least each needed just a glance to tell him it held only prayer books, crockery, pennants—an infinite number of things he didn't care about. This was taking too long! Chests of medallions, copper medallions. Jeriah grabbed the next chest and shook it. No sound. The next chest thudded dully. Jeriah kicked a crate but nothing jangled. No sound. No sound. Wood on wood, like a child's blocks. No sound. The next chest was only medium sized, but so heavy Jeriah could barely shift it. Metal, lots of small pieces of metal, jangled within. Please, please, *please*.

It was locked.

"Dung!" He slammed his fists on the lid. There were several small keys on Master Zachiros' ring, but the prayer was almost over. He was so close! *Try!*

Jeriah snatched the key ring back out of his pocket. His fingers shook as he searched the smaller keys.

"Praise the Bright Gods."

It was ending. Next key.

"Praise them."

"Praise their rule, whose justice gives order to our land."

"Praise their rule."

"Praise their sun, whose light gives life to our land."

Key, key, key. They clattered in his trembling hands.

"Praise their sun."

Come on, you demons, one of you fit!

"Praise their love, which lights our souls."

"Praise their love."

One more try.

"Praise and farewell."

Just one more try!

"Praise and farewell."

The lock clicked open.

Footsteps rang on the steps above him as the chorus began to descend, but Jeriah couldn't quit now. Most people spent a few moments chatting after the ceremony. He flung open the lid, sobbing with relief at the dull green and brown of tarnished copper. He yanked open the sack at his belt and thrust in handfuls of amulets, as fast as he could, careless of the noise. No less than fifty, curse them. His sack was full. Slam down the lid, snap the lock shut. Jeriah grabbed the keys and scuttled to the low door—no one there! He shot into the storeroom, the sack dragging at his belt. It took several precious seconds to relock the door. If he could make it to the Hierarch's rooms, he could hide the sack of amulets, pretend he'd just arrived . . .

Jeriah dashed across the storeroom and opened the hatch in the floor, but just as he started down the ladder, three priests came down the east stairs, talking easily among themselves. Jeriah had no excuse to be seen coming out of this room! He closed the hatch and gazed around frantically—the chorus would come through the main door in seconds, the only other door besides the hatch led to the locked storage area, and there was no time to reopen it. As the door from the temple swung open, Jeriah rushed to Chardane's robe cabinet, crammed himself in, and pulled the door shut—it closed on the hem of his tunic. He could hear people coming into the storeroom, talking, banging cabinet doors. He didn't dare to free his tunic—someone might notice the movement.

Would the grandmotherly herb mistress, who'd been so sensible about the Hierarch's tea, turn him in? Why wouldn't she? If she was anything like Jeriah's grandmother, she'd thoroughly enjoy the drama of his exposure. How could he have been so stupid? He might have made some excuse for being in the storeroom, but there was no possible excuse for hiding in a cabinet! He had panicked. Maybe Chardane was ill today. Maybe she'd be delayed outside until the others left. And maybe Master Lazur would personally present Jeriah with the spell notes, and offer to create the gate himself! He was still panicking and it wouldn't help. *Calm, calm.* What could he say when the door opened? Jeriah's heart pounded. He was breathing in gasps. Calmness was a joke. What could he—

The door opened.

Herb Mistress Chardane gazed at him for a moment, draped her robe neatly over his head, tucked his tunic into the cabinet, and closed the door. Jeriah heard the latch click shut.

Why hadn't she exposed him? Why hadn't she screamed, pointed, cried out? And why in the Dark One's name had she locked him in?

He didn't dare to move—not that he could have moved far. The robe cabinets' latches were simple, but they were on the outside of the doors.

Jeriah waited until the last voices had faded away before he stirred. Crushing the robe into a corner, he wiggled around till he could run the tip of his dagger up the door seam—it didn't penetrate far enough to reach the catch. He tried until his muscles began to cramp before he resigned himself. St. Cerwyn was *not* going to help him this time.

Until she came back and released him, Jeriah was stuck here. Pray gods she'd be back before the Hierarch's servants missed him in the morning!

The knights of legend never got stuck in closets. But those knights were more competent than Jeriah—as his father would attest!

Jeriah stretched as much as he could and tried to sit down. The cabinet was too narrow. He tried to stand, but even with his head bent the cabinet was too short. He ended with his knees braced against one wall and his back against the other. If Chardane took too long to return, he was going to pay for his sins.

Why had she trapped him here, instead of raising the alarm?

Jeriah had plenty of time to think about it as the hours passed. There was a grilled vent at the top of the door, so breathing was no problem, but even though he shifted position as much as he could, his muscles spasmed and ached. He tried carving away the door beside the latch, but the wood was too hard—Dawn Prayer would arrive before he succeeded. Jeriah tried to distract himself by speculating about the woman's motives, but his guesses led nowhere and the pain was beginning to disrupt his concentration. He'd have tried to break the door, but the guards who stood night watch outside the Hierarch's rooms would investigate the noise. As more time passed, Jeriah began to think that his screams would draw them just as surely. He had to get out of here! His back muscles burned; his thighs cramped and shook.

He heard a door open, and light steps crossed the floor—if this wasn't the herb mistress, he would pound on the door, demand release, think up some excuse.

The door opened. Jeriah burst out and would have fallen if Chardane's plump hands hadn't caught him. She was awfully strong for a grandmother.

"Sorry it took so long," she said softly. "Some of Zachiros' clerks were working late. Try to walk a bit."

She didn't look sorry, demons take her; she looked amused, and a bit rueful. But she supported Jeriah as he staggered back and forth until his trembling legs would support him and he could straighten his neck. If she noticed the clinking sack at his belt, she didn't mention it.

As the pain eased, Jeriah's curiosity returned. "Why didn't you expose me? Why trap me there?"

"In a minute," she said. "Can you walk without falling?"

"I think so."

She opened the main door and peered out before leading Jeriah out to the temple. Moonlight coated the flagstones, and the fresh night air felt wonderful after the cramped cupboard. Chardane took him down the west stairs, where the Hierarch's guards wouldn't see them, then entered the third level and crept down several servants' stairs to a room Jeriah thought was somewhere behind the kitchen. The herb mistress opened the door confidently and whisked him in.

The scent struck Jeriah first, green and spicy. The darkness rustled in the draft from the door. Chardane lit the lamp without fumbling—she knew the room well. The flaring light winked on rows of jars, sitting on the shelves that lined every wall with small sacks nestled between them. The ceiling, hung with bunches of drying herbs, resembled an upside-down meadow. A worn worktable with a pump and a sink at one end completed the small herbery.

"I thought priests worked magic to cure themselves," said Jeriah softly.

"It's easier to drink a tea than cast a spell," the woman replied. "At least for small things. And sometimes herbs work better. The priests come here with their stomachaches, just like the other palace folk." Her voice sounded loud in the stillness. "No need to be quiet now. If anyone comes by, we can say you came for a headache tea. And speaking of tea . . ." She gestured him to one of the stools by the table, filled a kettle, and lit the fire pot beneath it. Jeriah wondered what the tea would have in it and resolved to watch her closely when she chose the herbs.

"You're an unusual sort of priest," he began cautiously.

"I came to it late." She moved easily in the cluttered room, gathering cups and a wicker tea sieve. "The chooser missed me when I was first tested—said my 'holiness' was insufficient. When I grew up, I became an herb-healer—a good one. So good that the village priest began to wonder. He had them out to test me again and behold! My holiness turned out to be sufficient after all, and they whisked me into the priesthood. By that time I was over thirty and set in my ways. They were a bit miffed that when I got my robe, I just set up as an herb-healer again. But they've found me useful over the years. No one likes going to kill-or-cure Kerratis."

The jar she took the leaves from was labeled "ambermint," and the familiar scent spread through the room as she poured boiling water over the sieve. Jeriah began to relax.

"Why didn't you raise the alarm when you found me in your cabinet?"

"Oh, I knew you were there. I'd noticed you weren't at the prayer and wondered a bit. When I saw your tunic sticking out of the door, I decided it was time we had a talk."

She handed him the steaming tea. This woman had noticed his absence at prayer and been alert enough to spot his hiding place. She'd taken some trouble to save him . . . and she wouldn't tell him why.

Jeriah set the tea down, untasted.

There was a moment of silence while she studied him; then she sighed. "All right. Todder Yon asked me to look after you. And give you a hearing, if I would. This seemed a good chance."

"Todder Yon?" Astonishment rang through Jeriah's body. "Then you're . . . You can't be one of the Lesser Ones! You're a priest!"

"I was an herb-healer before I became a priest. Old loyalties don't vanish just because you gain new ones. The Decree of Bright Magic only came about seven years ago."

"But . . ." Lesser One. Right in the heart of the palace for seven years. As a priest her magic would be legal. She didn't have to help the Lesser Ones. And if the priests caught her, she'd be tried as a traitor.

"If you've talked to Todder Yon . . . Did he tell you what I need?"

"Aye. We're old friends, Todder and I. He tells me most things. But I'll not be able to help you."

Jeriah's heart plummeted. "Why not? Makenna was only a hedgewitch, and she cast a gate. If I got the spell for you . . ."

She was shaking her head. "Lad, in order to create that gate, Makenna drained a power sink that held the magic of more than a hundred priests. Casting even a small gate would take several powerful priests—who knew what they were doing! Using lesser wielders it'd take a dozen or more. We'd be bound to get caught gathering that many, and Master Lazur's always watching for some clue as to who we are."

"Master Lazur doesn't really care about the Lesser Ones. As long as you don't challenge . . ." Jeriah's breath caught. He stared at the plump graying woman with the soft peasant accent. Everybody's grandmother.

"You were one of the conspirators," he whispered. "They didn't catch them all."

"No." Her voice was lower too, and held grief as well as caution. "They didn't catch all of *us*."

"Why didn't you tell me?" Jeriah demanded. "If you'd come to me when I first arrived—"

"When you first came to this palace, you'd been working as Timeon Lazur's assistant," said Chardane. "All of the conspirators they caught were hanged . . . except you, Jeriah Rovan."

"Only because Tobin took my place. And the only reason he didn't hang was because Father paid off the tribunal."

"Others tried to bribe the tribunal," Chardane told him. "They failed. What made your family so special?"

Jeriah frowned. "Nothing. I wasn't in very deep, and the others confirmed that. And Tobin was my father's heir . . ."

Other landholders' heirs had been executed. He stared at Chardane in baffled silence.

She shrugged. "Todder Yon gave his word for you, and he's a fair judge of men. I've been watching you myself these last weeks, close enough to know you're not working for Master Lazur anymore, so I decided to take a chance. I only hope I've not made a mistake that'll get me hanged!"

"You haven't," Jeriah assured her. "I'm sorry the conspiracy failed, and I still believe reforms are needed. But Master Lazur's right when he says we have to complete the relocation before we reform the laws."

Chardane snorted. "He's likely right about the relocation—I believe he's wrong about the laws. But there's no use arguing about it. There's not enough of our folk left to do anything but hide for our lives, and hope to try again someday. So I'm afraid I can't help you."

"But Tobin has to get out of the Otherworld! He could be getting sick right now—in a few weeks he'll die! Surely you could gather enough people to cast the gate spell?"

"Not without getting caught. Timeon Lazur has spies from one end of the Realm to the other; that's the source of most of his power. I'm sorry, for you and for your brother, but the answer is no."

"Isn't there some way I can change that?" Jeriah asked desperately. "There has to be something."

"You could overthrow Timeon Lazur's cadre, so we wouldn't be at risk anymore."

"But that's *impossible*."

"I know. That cadre's power goes so deep, it'd take a team of horses to uproot it. That's why the answer's no."

"Wait—is Master Zachiros part of the conspiracy?"

"There is no conspiracy anymore. But no. Zachiros serves the Sunlord and the Realm, and he doesn't get involved in who controls the council. Which is likely why he's lasted so long."

"But . . ."

"Give it up, lad. The council's under Lazur's thumb now—his enemies daren't stir. Even if I was willing to risk my own life, others would be endangered if they got their hands on me. I know too many names."

She rose abruptly, went to her shelves, and began shaking herbs into a folded paper.

There had to be a way to make her help him. Jeriah was certain she could find the people he needed to cast the gate. But what she'd said about getting caught was true. Tobin would be appalled if saving him cost dozens—hundreds?—of conspirators' and hedgewitches' lives.

He remembered his conversation with Koryn. "Is there any chance that you, the Lesser Ones, could find some way to help defeat the barbarians' magic? If we could somehow make the relocation unnecessary, then maybe we could convince Master Lazur . . ."

Chardane was already shaking her head. "Lad, letting that girl convince you of anything is the biggest mistake you could make. If she suspects you're working against the relocation in any way, she'll have your hide for belt and boots! She's obsessed, and she's no fool—and that's a dangerous combination."

"How come you know her so well?" Jeriah asked. "I didn't think she had any friends, except maybe Master Lazur."

"I helped treat her when she first got here," Chardane said. "They'd already set her leg, but I brewed something for the pain and a mild soother for when she had nightmares. She stopped taking both of them before I thought she should, but she's a strong girl. She'd be dead if she wasn't."

"Will she always be lame?" Jeriah asked. "Or will her leg eventually heal?"

He knew she'd always have nightmares.

"I don't know," Chardane told him. "Her bones are as

straight as healing magic can make them, but soft tissue can go on mending for a long time after an injury that severe. She'll always limp, but the pain may lessen. Most pain lessens. Eventually. But the reason she's attached herself to Master Lazur is because she believes the relocation is the best way to prevent what happened to her family from happening to the whole Realm. I don't think there's anything she wouldn't do to help the relocation along. Or anything she wouldn't do to prevent someone she thought was trying to stop it. So you stay away from Mistress Koryn. Right?"

"I will," Jeriah promised. No matter how much he admired what she'd done, Koryn was his enemy.

"Here's a packet of headache tea." Chardane handed him the folded paper. "It's a good excuse for being about so late, if anyone stops you on the way to your room."

"What time is it?"

"About an hour before midnight."

Jeriah could smuggle the keys back to Master Zachiros' desk, but it was too late to give the Hierarch his medicine— going there now, so long after the palace gates had closed, would surely make the guards suspicious. If the shutters hadn't been latched, there was a tree outside the Hierarch's bedroom window Jeriah could have climbed—probably the same tree from which Daroo had observed "that poor old man." But the nights were still too cool for open windows, and there was no other way into the Hierarch's room that wouldn't take him past the guards. Skipping a dose hadn't seemed to hurt the Hierarch last time.

"Is there nothing I can do to change your mind?"

"I'm sorry, but no. If there was some way to help that wouldn't put me in danger, I might try. But Timeon Lazur's too sharp. I don't dare make a move as long as he has power."

She hustled Jeriah gently out of the herbery and closed the door.

Makenna

"SHOULDN'T WE START BUILDING AGAIN?" Miggy fretted. "We've been here four days."

"Harcu hasn't found any good rock," Makenna told him. The Stoner also hadn't been able to tell her what was wrong with it. Makenna didn't think he really knew himself—but he was certain it wasn't right, and that was enough for her. "I want to wait for the scouting party's report before we settle in for good," she added.

It surprised her how much she missed Tobin's presence. It wasn't as if she couldn't manage without him—as she always had! It was just . . . things were easier, calmer, when he was there.

"They won't find anything," said Miggy. "We lost two months of labor at the old village. If we're to get even one crop out of the summer, the Greeners need to get their seed in."

"I know. But if we have to leave this site too, I don't want them wasting any more seed, and the rest of us more effort."

Besides, the wait was giving her time to study the priest's stolen spell books. Makenna thought she might actually have figured out how to cast a gate—if anyone had enough magic left to cast it.

Miggy sighed. "That's what the Greeners and the others are thinking as well. I'm just afraid that in trying to save seed and effort, we may be wasting too much time."

Makenna feared it too. Even in this strange new world, the signs of summer settling in were all too plain. And without their growing magic, the Greeners' crops couldn't be hastened. Still . . .

"We'll wait for Tobin to come back."

CHAPTER 11

Jeriah

JERIAH RUSHED UP THE CENTRAL stairs, shivering in the predawn chill. If they discovered he'd failed to give the Hierarch his medicine a second time, he'd probably be dismissed! Though even if the goblins found the spell notes, he still had no one to open a gate! Tobin could be ill by now—but Jeriah trusted his brother to hang on to life until he got there. There had to be a way. He'd found one of the Lesser Ones—that was a step forward, right? One step at a time. But to help the goblins search for the spell notes, and to persuade Chardane, he had to be here, and if they learned he hadn't given the Hierarch his medicine . . .

He was running when he reached the Hierarch's door and he wasn't even late. *Slow down. They'll be suspicious if you race in panicking.*

When his breathing had slowed he went in, smiling at the Hierarch as if nothing could possibly be wrong.

The Hierarch smiled back. "Jeriah!"

"Yes, my lord. Good morning." In spite of his worries, he

was pleased. Perhaps this time the old man would remember for more than a day. The menservants smiled at him too.

Helping the Sunlord into his robes, Jeriah expected one of them to ask about the medicine any minute. Perhaps he should lie, say that he'd come in later and . . . No, the guards would know he hadn't. Better to confess as soon as he was accused. Perhaps they'd only set him to scrubbing the steps for a year. He'd scrub them forever if they'd let him stay. Though if Chardane refused to help . . .

Jeriah barely heard the morning prayer. Was being in charge always like this? An endless succession of defeats and insoluble problems? The knights of legend never banged their heads against the wall and howled, but that was what Jeriah felt like doing.

After the Hierarch had disrobed and dressed, they ate breakfast. Mohri asked Jeriah how his business had gone. Jeriah said fine and added that Master Lazur would be pleased. He suppressed a desire to babble, waiting tensely for the next question—it never came. Gradually Jeriah realized that they all assumed he'd done what he'd promised and given the Hierarch his medicine later. They weren't going to question the guards, or mention it to anyone. They trusted him.

A stab of guilt poisoned his relief, but the Hierarch seemed no worse this morning.

During the petitioning Jeriah tried to thrust his problems out of his mind. It took all his self-control to keep from looking guilty when Master Zachiros remarked that the Hierarch seemed to be having one of his good days.

When the Hierarch lay down for his afternoon rest, Jeriah tackled the next problem: How could he tell the goblins that he had the amulets? He hadn't thought to set up a method to contact them, so all he could think of was to make himself available and hope they approached him. Daroo had first done so in the woods near the barracks, so Jeriah set off for the stables to visit Glory and take Fiddle out for a ride. Being around horses might soothe his fraying nerves. But what if the goblins didn't contact him? Then what?

Jeriah thumped his head gently against a nearby tree, moaning with frustration. No wonder knights in the stories did everything themselves—trying to organize helpers drove you mad!

Fiddle seemed pleased to see him, and he felt guilty again for neglecting Tobin's horse. Jeriah rode around the lake, problems spinning through his mind: the spell notes, the gate—the days were racing by. Once Tobin began to sicken, there was no way to know how long he might survive.

No goblins popped out of the trees. No contact. And every day counted now!

Jeriah unsaddled Fiddle and began to curry him, trying to come up with some way to let the goblins know that he'd gotten their cursed amulets and was—

"Congratulations, hero. Why'd the lady priest lock you up in that cupboard?"

Jeriah jumped and swore, and Fiddle gazed curiously at him. Cogswhallop was perched on a corner of the manger.

"That's none of your business. Were you watching me last night? Wait a minute. If you were watching, why didn't you let me out? I was in agony in there! I could have been caught!"

The goblin grinned. "The trade is amulets for the search—we charge more for a rescue. Though if you're interested, we might—"

"No," said Jeriah hastily. "I'll rescue myself. You know I've got the amulets—are you ready to start tonight? I don't want you running around in . . . What are you doing here in broad daylight? If you get caught—"

"Keep your voice down and I won't be. Don't worry so much. There's enough cover on this tier to conceal a goblin village. That palace is another matter—we did some exploring last night. We'll be safe enough once folk have gone to bed, but during the day it'd be risky."

"Don't even think about going there during the day," Jeriah told him. "It'd be suicide. You can't—"

"Then we're in agreement, and if you'd stop yammering and arrange a time to hand over the amulets, we could begin the search tonight. Any particular place we should start?"

"The library." Jeriah explained his reasoning, and Cogswhallop nodded.

"Makes as much sense as anywhere else. Bring the amulets to the terrace in front of the library door. When will you be there?"

Jeriah had lost control of this conversation, but the goblin's plan was sound. "I'll meet you around midnight. Everyone should be asleep by then, and—"

The stable door opened and a groom backed in, pulling a wheelbarrow over the sill.

Jeriah whispered, "You'd better get . . ." But when he turned back to the manger, the goblin was gone.

Jeriah crept around the third-level terrace, carrying the sack of amulets and thanking St. Cerwyn that the sunsguard was posted by the steps, on the other side of the palace from the library. He wondered how the goblins were getting in and out, but he had no doubt they'd manage. If they were vermin, at least they were *competent* vermin. And this time the Hierarch had been given his medicine and put to bed, just as he should be. So why was Jeriah so nervous?

The waxing moon shed enough light to see where he was going. The amulets jingled if he moved too fast, forcing him to creep along instead of rushing like a fool. Like he wanted to.

He reached the library doors. The fountains were shut off at night. The metallic rattle as he set down the sack sounded clearly in the stillness.

For once Jeriah didn't jump when dark forms crept from the bushes. Most of them hovered in the shadows—a dozen, perhaps—but Cogswhallop and Daroo approached him.

Daroo was grinning. "I brought them, just like you asked.

We'll have those notes right soon. If they're in the palace, that is."

If they're in the palace. But Jeriah couldn't help smiling back. "I brought my half of the trade, too."

Cogswhallop gestured, and a couple of goblins darted out to seize the sack and bear it off.

"You're not going to count, to be sure there's at least fifty?"

"I'll trust you that far. Besides, fifty'd make a smaller bag."

Daroo snorted, and a murmur of amusement rippled out of the shadows.

"We'll get our own back if you cheat us." The words were threatening, but Cogswhallop's voice was neutral, almost approving. Perhaps he thought Jeriah was becoming "civilized."

With some surprise, Jeriah realized that he had no doubts about the goblins keeping their part of the bargain. It wasn't particularly honorable to demand payment for everything, but once you paid them, they'd do the job.

"So let's get on with it." He gestured to the library door.

"If someone's fallen asleep over a book in there, it'd be better if you opened it. You can make excuses—we can't."

Jeriah glanced at the dark windows; that possibility hadn't occurred to him. He tried to turn the handle, but it didn't budge.

"It's locked!" He shook the handle furiously. "I hope you

can pick it, because I sneaked Master Zachiros' keys back into his desk last night."

"Keep your voice down. I'll handle the locks. And if it's locked, it's likely empty." Cogswhallop drew a slim probe from some inner pocket and inserted it into the keyhole—he had to stand on tiptoe to reach it. Jeriah heard him murmuring—magic? curses? senility? He couldn't make out the words.

A familiar tug at his britches drew his eyes down.

"While you and Fa and the Bookeries do this, the rest of us are going to give some other rooms a proper search. I know the palace best, so I'm in charge of that."

Jeriah winced, but Daroo looked so proud, he couldn't bring himself to spoil it. "Good luck." He fought down the impulse to add, *You'll need it.*

"Ha!" Cogswhallop's grin flashed and he eased the door open. Jeriah suddenly understood why the goblin had wanted him there—if he hadn't been present, from inside the library it would look like the door was opening by itself. Which might make someone look down.

Daroo darted away. The rest of the goblins streamed into the library, and Jeriah followed. They'd obviously planned this, for they split into two groups and began tacking sheepskins over the windows. The scent of ink and paper was sharper in the dark.

"Won't someone notice that the windows are covered?"

"They'd be more likely to notice a light. Not even Bookeries can read in the dark, young hero."

"We shouldn't be working at night at all," said a prim voice. The room grew darker as the windows were covered, but the light from the open door enabled Jeriah to see the plump shadow approaching Cogswhallop. "I've always objected to this whole mad venture. And it's not as if he's trading us information. Shiny stones and buttons! That's—"

"That's a sight more useful than a bunch of scribbling," Cogswhallop snapped. "Hero, this fool is Master Hispontic. He's the Bookeries' leader—"

"High scholar," the shadow corrected.

"—who led them right into catastrophe, trying to save their books when they should have been saving themselves!" Cogswhallop finished.

"Information," hissed the shadow, "is what will save us all in the long run, not your mad schemes. It's your kind's short-term thinking that—"

Jeriah wondered what scheme the Bookerie was talking about. He wished he could let them go on quarreling, but their voices were beginning to rise.

"There's lots of information in here," Jeriah interrupted softly. "You can't take the books away, of course, but you're welcome to read—"

"No!" Cogswhallop howled in a whisper.

"Read them," Jeriah finished, baffled.

"Ready," a voice whispered from the darkness.

Cogswhallop moaned and shut the door, and light sprang

from half a dozen lamps. Jeriah blinked down at a bespectacled goblin with a neat beard and ink-stained fingers. The gratification in his round face outshone the lamps.

"Thank you, sir. We're in your debt. Gentlemen"—his voice lifted in triumph—"we have *full permission*!"

Gasps of astonished joy came from a dozen throats, and the goblins darted for the bookshelves.

"Now you've done it," said Cogswhallop through gritted teeth. He stalked to the nearest goblin, grabbed his collar, and spun him face-to-face.

"You're looking for Lazur's spell notes *first*, understand? We've got a bargain, and you're not to read another thing till it's fulfilled!"

His captive's eyes were straying over Cogswhallop's shoulder to the shelves. Cogswhallop shook him. "Understand?"

"Oh, aye, aye. Lazur's notes on the Other . . . Is that . . . It is! Marcabus' treatise on the forming of rock!" He pulled free of Cogswhallop's grip and shot back to the books like iron to a magnet.

Cogswhallop sighed. "It's the best I can do. You shouldn't have given them permission, hero—they'd have been bad enough without it."

Watching the Bookeries scramble nimbly up the shelves as if they were goblin ladders, Jeriah remembered Koryn perched so carefully on her stool denying the notes were there. Of course, she'd have denied it whether they were there or not. If they were there, would she have reported that conversation to Master Lazur? And would he have moved them? Or would she think Jeriah believed her, and decide that the spell notes were even safer in the library? Not that Jeriah could have found them—that would take a small army of scholars, which was precisely what he now had.

"As long as they find the spell notes first, I don't care if they read every book in the place," said Jeriah. "They will find the notes first, won't they?"

"Maybe, but . . . Oh, don't look so panicked. I'll keep 'em in line. Is there another way out of here?"

Jeriah led him across the shadowed room. "What did you trade the Bookeries for this?" Master Hispontic's comments about mad schemes had made him curious.

"None of your business." A haunted look flickered across the goblin's sharp face. "Where does that door go?"

"An inner corridor to some offices. There won't be anyone in them now." Jeriah opened the door and peered through. "Empty, just as I said."

The few corridor lamps that burned all night were turned low, creating pools of soft light every twenty steps. You could walk without running into anything, but there was plenty of shadow.

"This corridor ends in the record room," Jeriah murmured. "No one's likely to be there this late."

"We'll still post a watcher. Pity the Flichters won't do it, but they didn't . . . The gen'ral's the only one who could ever get sense out of them. This isn't bad—if someone comes to

260

one door, we can scoot out the other."

The goblin wasn't telling him everything, but that was nothing new. They'd do their best to find the spell notes. That was what mattered.

"Suppose someone comes down the corridor?" Jeriah asked. "And someone comes to the library door at the same time."

"Then we hide."

"What if they see you?"

"Then we run," said Cogswhallop impatiently. "You're jumping about like your fleas had declared war. Don't be so nervous, *hero*. This is easy."

"You think that now," said Jeriah. "I've been breaking into places ever since I got here, and I've been caught every time."

"We won't be. Go back to bed. I'll come by before sunrise and tell you what we found."

"Go back to . . . I'm going to help you! I can search, or stand guard, or . . . or . . ."

Cogswhallop was shaking his head. "I was afraid you'd be wanting that. Then I noticed your clothes, and I thought you might be sensible."

"What's wrong with my clothes?" Jeriah asked, gazing down at his plain dark tunic.

"Nothing, if you're sneaking up on an enemy camp. But no one who sees you is going to believe you just got up to go to the privy."

Jeriah's mouth opened, but he couldn't think of anything to say. "If I put on a night robe, can I watch the corridor? If anyone comes I can greet them, which will warn you."

"Is the privy in this corridor?"

"Well, not the nearest one. But I'll go mad shut up in my room all night! I have to be here."

"I can't stop you," Cogswhallop admitted. "But if someone gets suspicious when you yawn all day, don't say you weren't warned."

"I'll be back," Jeriah promised.

He hurried down the corridor praying he wouldn't meet anyone. Cogswhallop was right—these clothes were suspicious in the palace this time of night. He reached his rooms unseen, pulled on his night robe, and had just emerged onto the terrace when a shriek shattered the night—but the shouts that followed came from the other side of the palace by the main staircase. Had someone caught one of Daroo's searchers? Daroo himself? Jeriah ran.

Several people clustered at the top of the third-level steps. The guards' torches covered the scene with flickering light.

"I swear I saw it," a bony woman in nightclothes protested as Jeriah joined them. "It ran into those flowers. Right there!"

Two guards were searching the flower bed. Jeriah tried to swallow the lump in his throat. He should have realized that others might visit the privy!

"What's going on?" he asked.

"This lady—"

"I saw a goblin!" she insisted. "It darted into those bushes when I screamed, but I saw it!"

"But that's im . . ." *Careful, don't protest too much.* ". . . incredible. Would they dare come into the palace?"

"Didn't your brother get rid of all the goblins, Jeriah?"

Master Zachiros was standing behind him. *Careful.*

"He got rid of the ones in the Goblin Wood, but there might be others. I just find it hard to believe they'd be here."

"I know what I saw." Even in the torchlight, Jeriah could see the stubborn anger in her expression.

"I'm sure you did, mistress," Jeriah said politely. "Though sometimes the moonlight plays tricks. Could it have been a rat?"

"Impossible," Master Goserian's frigid voice declared. "Rats aren't allowed in the palace." He was dressed in his night robe, like the rest of the growing crowd. Thank St. Cerwyn Cogswhallop had sent Jeriah to change—he'd have been horribly conspicuous in his tunic.

"Come now, Goserian," Master Zachiros murmured. "You know we've had rats before. I admit you dispose of them quickly, but . . ."

The Master of Household stiffened. "There are no rats in *my* palace. She must have imagined it."

"I saw something scuttle into those flowers," the woman

insisted. "If it was a rat, it was a cursed big one."

"A *big* rat, mistress?" Goserian huffed. "Was it pink, perhaps?"

The crowd snickered. The guards had stopped searching the flower bed to listen to the quarrel. Jeriah's racing pulse began to slow.

Koryn hobbled up to the crowd, panting, her uncle clearly having outpaced her.

But while everyone else's eyes were on the altercation, her gaze went straight to Jeriah and stayed there.

She suspected him. She couldn't know what he was doing, but she suspected him all the same. Jeriah hoped his face showed only the excited curiosity that everyone else was expressing, and turned his attention back to the argument.

"They'll put out traps in the morning," Master Zachiros murmured. "But Goserian will never admit it, even when they catch the thing."

Jeriah needed to get back to the library. He murmured good night to the secretary and departed—still feeling Mistress Koryn's gaze on his back.

Creeping down the corridor, he jumped at Cogswhallop's whispered greeting.

"Do you know what happened? Someone saw—"

"I know. Some woman caught a glimpse of Konno, but thanks to you they think it was a rat. Not bad, hero."

Ordinarily the praise would have pleased Jeriah—he knew

the goblin didn't offer it lightly—but now he was too anxious.

"If your people get caught, Master Lazur might figure out that I'm involved. And then—"

"Ah, hero. Go to bed."

"But—"

"If anyone else sees you wandering about, they'll know you're up to something, and what will your priest think of that? You're about to twist out of your skin. Do us all a favor. Please."

"But . . ." The goblin was right. The guards would be suspicious if they found him up a second time. He was doing no good here, his stomach was in knots, and his nerves were tight as lute strings. He wasn't cut out for this. Jeriah went to bed.

He surprised himself by falling asleep after only a few hours of tossing. The small hand shaking his foot barely roused him, but the jolt that shot though him at the sight of the rolled-up paper in Cogswhallop's hands brought him wide awake. Jeriah blinked as his eyes adjusted to the light; the goblin had kindled the lamp without waking him.

"Is that it? Did you . . . ?"

The goblin was shaking his head. "Sorry, lad, they're not in the library."

Disappointment clawed at Jeriah. But even through it . . .

"Lad?"

Cogswhallop scowled. "Do you want to see what they found, human, or chat till sunrise?"

"What did they find?" Jeriah pulled himself up to sit with his back against the headboard. If it wasn't the spell notes, he didn't care.

"Something that'll make our job easier." The goblin unrolled the paper across Jeriah's lap. It was upside down, but . . .

"A map of the palace?"

"Not a map, want-wit! A builder's plan, complete with heat and water tunnels. The place crawls with 'em, too. For folk our size those are like private corridors; they'll make the search a lot safer."

"Tunnels. . . . Is there a secret tunnel from the wine cellar to the outside?"

Cogswhallop looked down. "Aye, it's marked right here. Humph. Some secret."

"If you didn't live in the palace, you wouldn't have access to the plan. Are there any secret rooms or compartments near the priests' quarters?"

Cogswhallop peered at the paper for several moments. "None that I can see."

"I suppose it was too much to ask." Staring at the drawing, he found the thought of searching that complex maze overwhelming. Jeriah hadn't realized how much he'd hoped the notes were in the library until those hopes were crushed.

"Well, hero? Where next?"

"They could be *anywhere*." How could he find the notes in time? Despair closed like a fist around his heart.

The goblin let the papers roll closed. "Are you giving up?" His voice was surprisingly mild.

"No," said Jeriah. "I can't give up. Not while there's any chance Tobin's alive. Though the Bright Gods know what I'm going to do next, because even if you find those accursed notes, I can't get anyone to cast the gate! But I'm not giving up—and neither are you, goblin. You owe me a search of the whole palace. And you owe me for saving your friend tonight, too!"

"Maybe Konno owes you, but . . . Oh, keep your skin on, we'll do it. But you shouldn't have given those pen pushers permission; they want to spend part of each night copying in the library. They say that after the record room and offices have been searched, anyone can do the rest of the place and only call the Bookeries if they've got papers to look through."

"I still say you're indebted for what happened tonight, but as long as the search is completed as quickly as possible I don't care who does it. And I don't care what the Bookeries . . . copy?"

"Aye. That's how they take what they want, they copy the books. I'll admit they're quick about it. It's part of their gift. They've even got some sort of fast-drying ink. "

"Then this"—Jeriah gestured to the builder's plan—"is a copy?"

"Of course. How else could we keep it without a search being raised? And speaking of searching, where do we look next?"

"The record room and public offices, just as your Bookeries said. After that . . . what do you think?"

"That they could be anywhere," said Cogswhallop. "Including outside the palace. That priest's crafty. Once the offices have been searched, we'll start at the top and work our way down. If it's in this building, we'll find it."

"How long will that take?" Jeriah demanded.

"Four days to a week, depending on how it goes."

"Tobin is probably ill right now—he might be dead in a week! And we still have to open the gate, and then find him in the Otherworld. That's not good enough."

"It takes the time it takes. Unless you've got some idea where the notes are hidden?"

Even if you find them, you couldn't . . .

"No." Jeriah rubbed his face wearily. "And even after we find Tobin, and your sorceress casts the spells to keep him alive, we still have to get back, which means she'll have to make another gate, which she probably doesn't have the power to do. Gods, what a mess."

"Don't worry too far ahead. If you can get that first gate cast, you can have others cast as well. Once we've found them, we can bring them back to the gate site and wait . . ." He noticed Jeriah's expression and his voice trailed off.

"I guess I forgot to tell you. The gates come out in different places in the Otherworld. You can open two gates here, in the same spot, and they'll come out miles, maybe hundreds of miles apart in the Otherworld. At least, that's what Master Lazur said. That's another reason we need his notes."

"So if we get in, we may not be able to get out?"

"Not for a while, at least. That's why we need the notes about keeping people who don't have magic alive, in case it takes a while to figure out . . ." His voice faded under the weight of the goblin's glare.

"Oh, that's fine. Any other little thing you forgot to mention?"

"I told you, didn't I?" Jeriah glared back. "You owe me, goblin. You're not quitting and neither am I. We *will* get them out."

"You're a hero, all right."

"I don't need your sarcasm. I know perfectly well that all I am so far is a failure. Failed conspirator, failed burglar. But Dark One take me if I'm going to be a failed brother!"

"Aye, that's what I meant. It's not entirely blather. You're reckless, you think fast on your feet—if nowhere else—and you're stubborn as a pig. What more does a hero need?"

"How about succeeding?" Jeriah asked bitterly. "Instead of having everything go wrong, every time I try."

Lightweight. And this time, Tobin's life was in his hands.

"You know"—the goblin's voice was oddly gentle—"even the gen'ral didn't always get it right the first time. It's a matter of trying again and again till you find a way to make it work.

I'll be back on and off, to tell you how the search is going." Cogswhallop rolled up the plan and went to the door.

"Can I help?"

"You can be thinking of a way to get that gate cast once we have the notes." Cogswhallop's grin held all its old malice. "Not to mention the rest of it. Sleep well, hero." And he was gone.

Jeriah arrived early to attend the Hierarch, for he couldn't go back to sleep after the goblin had left.

The spell notes could be anywhere in the palace. They could be *outside* the palace, and Tobin's time was running out. *Even if you found them, you couldn't* . . . What? It wouldn't matter, if he couldn't find the cursed notes in the first place. Jeriah sighed and tried to force his mind off the circling dilemma as he approached the Hierarch.

"Good morning, my lord."

The old man gazed blankly at him. "Good morning, ah . . . ah . . ."

"Jeriah, my lord." Curse it, he'd *had* his medicine last night! Yesterday he'd been . . .

Jeriah's breath caught. The idea swelled slowly, like an enormous bubble. When it burst, the implications left him shaking.

Twice Jeriah had forgotten to give the Hierarch his medicine, and each morning after that the Hierarch had *remembered*. He'd been better, more alert, more conscious of the world around him.

"Sir?" The menservants were staring at him.

"Ah, sorry. Let's get him dressed."

Jeriah barely managed the robing, handing the Hierarch the wrong garments twice. He couldn't imagine what the servants thought of his performance. He didn't care.

Could it be true? The Sunlord wore enchanted jewelry to protect him from evil magic and was surrounded by guards to protect him from violence—had no one thought to protect him from plain, nonmagical drugs? His menu was approved by Master Kerratis and prepared in the palace kitchen. Surely there were a thousand precautions and safeguards . . . if the drug came from outside. What if it came from inside the palace? The guards' attention was directed outward, so if the drug came from within . . . But who would do such a thing? And why? Careful. He had to be absolutely certain before he spoke of this.

Jeriah fumbled through the morning. Master Zachiros looked sharply at him when he forgot part of a petition and had to go back and have it repeated. It didn't matter.

One of the jars that held the Hierarch's medicinal tea was almost empty. When he was finally free to leave for the afternoon, Jeriah took it with him.

Tobin

THE FOOTPRINT WAS LIKE NOTHING Tobin had ever seen, resembling the imprint left by a twig broom more than anything else. All the scouting they'd done and now, in the sand of the new stream's bed not a hundred yards from camp, he'd found what he'd been searching for. He'd have to find other tracks. If he hadn't been looking for this, almost from the moment he set foot in the Otherworld, Tobin wouldn't have recognized this scraggly imprint for what it was. But whether he found more tracks or not, Tobin knew, with the certainty of a hunter and a soldier, that their enemy had finally made a mistake.

He'd decided to keep watch himself, confiding in no one, not even Makenna. The headache that had plagued him on and off for several days was back, and he was so tired he could have lain down under the bushes where he was concealed and gone to sleep. But the moon was nearly full tonight—there would never be a better chance.

The goblins had looked at him like he was crazy when he'd insisted they use the last of the straight lumber to build a storage shed for their food supplies. What food supplies? They wouldn't need a storage shed till the harvest was in.

It was Makenna who had settled the matter, casting a long look at Tobin and then curtly ordering them to "Do it."

All the Bright Gods bless her—she hadn't even asked him why.

She was sleeping now, in the tent her goblins had pieced together, sacrificing precious bits of leather and canvas from the old world, materials that wouldn't rot within days. Looking across the meadow at the sturdy shed the Makers had built so swiftly, Tobin wondered if everything in this world wasn't rotten at the core. He couldn't blame the goblins for not wanting to build it. Either the wood would warp or someone would plunk another mountain down on—

He heard it before he saw it, though the rustling in the grove on the far side of the clearing was softer than the great, shambling shape that stepped out of the shadowy trees should have produced. It looked rather like a tree itself, with twiggy protuberances sprouting in all directions, but it waddled over to the carry carts on two legs . . . or maybe three legs . . . and began running twiglike fingers over the wood.

His brother Jeriah would have drawn his sword and tried to capture the thing. Or at least have sneaked off to bring back some witnesses. But the fact that it had moved slowly didn't prove it couldn't move quickly, and the creature was a lot bigger than Tobin was.

Jeriah was crazy.

Tobin stayed still in the bushes and watched until the creature had run its hands over all the straight timber. He had no doubt that it would be warping by morning. He was even more interested, and worried, when the thing walked backward into the grove, using its twig-broom hands to sweep away its own tracks.

At least that settled the question of intelligence. And Tobin thought Makenna would accept his wild story, even without proof. Which was good, because he didn't feel up to arguing.

She came awake all at once, the minute he shook her foot, and her voice held the professional calm of a battlefield commander when she spoke.

"What is it? The stream?"

Tobin understood her concern—having another stream die would terrify the goblins. Though he knew they half expected it, just as he did.

"No, it's the wood," he said hazily. "I'm sorry, I mean—"

"Sprung your trap, did they?"

She didn't seem surprised, but Tobin's headache was too fierce for him to care.

"It's big. It looks like a tree, but it walks like a man. And it brushed out its own tracks."

"Intelligent, then. Though a brute beast would hardly have come up with the idea of cutting off our stream, and I don't know how even a walking tree can be moving the hills about. But we'd best set a watch, at least. Come with me." She laid a hand on his arm. "We'll wake Miggy. And I think . . ."

The hand left his arm and pressed against his forehead, then his throat.

"You're burning up! How long have you been feverish?"

"I don't know," Tobin admitted. "The headache comes and goes." He felt pleasantly distant from the question.

Makenna scrambled out of her bedroll, a pale shadow in the dim light. "Dark One curse this place—sickness is the only thing it hadn't thrown at us! You lie down—yes, on my bed, want-wit. Where else? Charba is the one who nurses me when I fall ill. I'm going to fetch her. And then we'll set a watch against the tree boggles."

She was gone before Tobin could reply—though he had no idea what he'd have said. He lay down on her bedroll. He wasn't sure he should, because he wasn't sure he could get up again. He'd feel better when this headache passed.

But even through the pounding in his temples, and the sluggishness of his thoughts, he realized one thing: she hadn't been surprised by the existence of their enemy.

CHAPTER 12

Jeriah

"YOU SAID IF YOU COULD help me without endangering yourself, you'd do it. Did you mean that?"

"Probably," said Chardane cautiously. "Within reason."

As he'd knocked on the herbery door, the horrible thought that Chardane herself might be supplying the drug had flashed through Jeriah's mind. But the conspiracy had started only a few years ago; the Hierarch's illness was seven years past. She had no motive . . . he hoped. He pulled the jar, dark-glazed pottery with a wide cork stopper, out of his tunic and set it on the table. Chardane's face showed nothing but mild curiosity.

"What's this?"

"It's the Hierarch's medicine."

She looked up, startled. "I don't make any medicines for the Hierarch."

"We brew it into a tea he drinks nightly. One scoop of leaves in a cup of boiling water, steeped for a minute and a half. I thought you were the only herb-healer in the palace."

"I am. Kerratis thinks herbs are beneath a real healer. Where did he get this?" Her eyes narrowed, suspicion dawning. She was either innocent or a brilliant liar. Lesser One. Conspirator. Jeriah knew she was a brilliant liar.

"I don't know. There are several jars of it. I haven't been here long enough to need replacements."

"Let's see if I can tell what's in it. It might just be a mild soother." She poured some of the leaves onto her palm and peered at them. Then she sniffed, and her expression stiffened.

"What is it?" Jeriah asked.

"It smells like . . . No, that's not possible! I'll wet it—that will make the scent stronger."

"Smells like *what*?"

"Well, it smells like green vervallen. But yellow vervallen smells much the same, and it's harmless."

"What does the one that isn't harmless do?"

"Just what you're guessing—it clouds the mind, the memory, the ability to think."

"All the symptoms the Hierarch's been displaying for the last seven years." Anger seethed in Jeriah's voice. "Seven *years*. And no one suspected? No one even bothered to check—"

"His personal healer is the only one who examines him." Chardane focused her full attention on Jeriah for the first time since she'd smelled the herbs. "If this is what I think it is, do you realize how deadly your discovery could become?"

"Of course I do. I'm not stupid."

"Then go now, and let me test it." She was already hustling him toward the door. "The scent isn't enough—we have to be absolutely certain."

Jeriah grabbed the door frame on his way through. "I'll go if you promise not to do or say anything until we've talked about it. You promised to help me, remember? Anything within reason."

She stopped shoving at him. "Aye, though I'm not sure this falls within reason. I promise not to tell anyone till after we've talked. Come back tonight."

She pushed him out and shut the door before he could reply— but she'd promised.

Two of Jeriah's friends had been here seven years ago, when the Hierarch became ill, but they'd been children at the time. That was probably why they'd been allowed to stay.

Jeriah found the first in the tilt yard, helping the arms master teach some pages to use a lance.

"Seven years ago? Who remembers anything that long ago, much less council stuff?"

But with a little prompting the second one, who was polishing his master's armor, did remember what was going on in the council when the Hierarch had fallen ill. And what side of that debate the Hierarch had been on.

While they dressed the Hierarch for dinner, Jeriah told the menservants that one of the medicine jars was empty. How to get it refilled? Just mention it to Master Goserian.

That surprised Jeriah, but he had to pursue it.

He mentioned the empty jar to Master Goserian, who said he'd order more. It was natural to ask where it came from.

After dinner Jeriah gave the Hierarch his medicine, feeling like a murderer as he handed him the cup. Then he claimed a headache and went straight down the servants' stairs to knock on Chardane's door.

She cracked it to identify him before letting him in. The tidy workshop was awash in dirty crockery and open jars, the air thick with the cloying scent of the Hierarch's medicine.

"Well?"

Chardane brushed a straggling wisp of hair away from her tired eyes. "It's green vervallen. I could prove it to any competent herb-healer—except that all the ones who don't serve the church are under a death sentence. Even so . . . Did you find out where this 'medicine' comes from?"

"Master Goserian buys it from 'a very reputable' herb seller in the city, recommended by Master Kerratis. I didn't have time to go to his shop."

"Doesn't matter; I know that one. He's not what I'd call reputable, but he doesn't have the nerve to raise the stuff himself. He probably gets it from someone else, who pays him well and whose name he doesn't even know. At least, not the real name."

There was a moment of silence.

"Dead end?"

"Bet on it."

"I can't believe Master Kerratis would—"

Chardane snorted. "I believe it. Kerratis . . . I'd be lying if I said he was a bad healer, but it's the healing itself he cares for, the art, the magic of it. The people he works on are just 'subjects.'"

"The Sunlord is a dangerous subject to play with unless he has a very strong motive. And I don't think Master Kerratis does." Jeriah paced the crowded chamber. Had she already guessed the truth? "I talked to some people this afternoon. People who were here seven years ago and remembered what was going on in the Landholders' Council."

"I've been thinking about that myself."

"They said that a handful of priests had gotten some spy's report on the barbarians, and they wanted to move the whole Realm into the north. Everyone thought they were crazy, and the Hierarch opposed it."

Another heartbeat of silence passed.

"I wouldn't say he opposed it," said Chardane. "It had just been proposed and he . . . resisted the idea. He was never a decisive man. But it was becoming clear that he was going to oppose it."

Even to imply that the Hierarch was an indecisive man instead of a divinely inspired leader was a minor heresy, but Jeriah brushed that aside. She knew. Would she help?

"Was his illness natural?"

"Aye. I helped treat him and I'd stake my life on that. I was a little surprised when his mind didn't recover, but it was a terrible fever. I didn't know he was taking *medicine*." Anger hissed in her soft peasant voice.

"So Master Lazur didn't set out to kill him. He just saw an opportunity . . ."

". . . and he took it."

Jeriah almost expected something to explode when the words were finally said aloud, but nothing happened. At least, nothing visible.

"Can we prove it?"

"How?" Chardane asked. "By this time Lazur will have buried his tracks so deep, it'd take an earthquake to uncover them. If he needs to, he can throw Kerratis to the wolves. There's nothing to connect Lazur to the drugs except our suspicions. The question is, can we use our knowledge without proving it? And Dark One take me if I know the answer."

Jeriah's plan began to take shape. "I think I can. But first, you said green vervallen clouds the mind. Is the effect permanent? He got better, a little, the few times I missed giving him his medicine."

"It isn't usually permanent, but I'm talking about one or two accidental doses. I've never heard of it being given to someone for seven years! The effect of that . . . I don't know. I've also no idea how long it would take to wear off, but I'd guess it would take weeks for his mind to clear completely. If it ever does."

"And the moment we stop drugging him, Master Kerratis

will notice. He keeps a close eye on the Hierarch's condition. He'd notice any change within days. No wonder he was so upset when I missed the dose. And Master Lazur . . ." Jeriah gazed blindly at the disordered room, remembering.

"Was he upset too?"

"No, dead calm. He must have thought it would make me suspicious if he overreacted. In fact, he said something like that to Kerratis. Why didn't I notice? But he seemed so confident . . ."

"A formidable enemy. Who else was there?"

"Just Nevin, and he doesn't . . . Surely he couldn't . . ."

"Did he overreact?"

"Yes, but he would because he loves the Hierarch. I'm sure Nevin doesn't know about the drug. Almost sure."

"Hmm. They'd tell as few as possible. Nevin was a child seven years ago, so you're probably right. Who else might know?"

They thought for a moment.

"Some of Master Lazur's cadre, perhaps," said Jeriah. "Though he wouldn't tell anyone he didn't have to."

"Some of the landholders as well . . . perhaps. So we can't simply go to the council and announce our suspicions. The straight path is barred—we need a twisty one. I think I can use this."

"So can I, and I want to use it first. You said you'd help me."

"Not by giving up the best weapon that's ever come to

my hand! This could uproot that cursed cadre!" Her hands twisted against each other. It was the first time Jeriah had seen her serenity broken, but he couldn't yield.

"I'm not asking you to give it up, just let me use it first. Once I've got the notes and gone into the Otherworld to find Tobin, you can do anything you want. I'll approach Master Lazur as soon as he gets back. You wouldn't lose any time at all."

"Approach him? I can give you some time; three of the folk I need won't be able to get here till the Equinox Ceremony, which gives us a week. But I can't let you warn Lazur!"

"Tobin doesn't have weeks!" Jeriah snapped. "He's probably ill already! You can't stop me. Besides, what can Master Lazur do? Quit drugging the Hierarch? That's the last thing he wants."

"He might kill him." Grim determination sat oddly on her plump face. "If the Hierarch dies, our weapon no longer matters."

"Is Master Lazur ready to have a new hierarch chosen?"

"If not, I'll bet he could get ready. Don't do this, lad. I don't want that poor man's blood on my hands."

"Me neither. But I don't think I'll frighten Master Lazur that much. All I want is a chance to save Tobin, and he knows it."

"You're thinking to blackmail him?"

"Why not? If what I wanted was really dangerous to him or the relocation, it might not work—but he shouldn't see much risk in letting me go after Tobin. Lots less risk than revealing that the Sunlord is being drugged, and a shadow government has been running the Realm for the last seven years."

She picked up a dirty cup, turning it in her hands. "I might be able to stop you, but I don't think either of us can afford to start fighting the other. If I let you go ahead, you mustn't give him the slightest hint that I know *anything*."

She was going to agree! Fear and excitement shook him.

"That should be easy."

"I doubt it. Lazur's a great one for laying traps."

"Then you might find it useful to watch me spring them."

"Aye, I might. Very well, you have till Equinox to do what you will—just keep my name out of it! In fact, we shouldn't meet again." Once more she was hustling him out. "And be careful. The Hierarch isn't the only one Lazur might think to kill, and I want don't want your blood on my hands either."

"I'll be careful," he promised. "The last time . . ." The last time Jeriah had been careless, his brother had been convicted of treason in his place. "I'll be *very* careful."

Two days dragged past as Jeriah waited for Master Lazur's return. It was absurd to be eager for an event that just a few days ago he'd been praying to put off. But Chardane's people would arrive for the Equinox Ceremony in less than a week. How long would it take Master Lazur to retrieve the notes and arrange to cast a gate? Hours? Days?

Tobin was almost certainly ill by now—his days were running out.

Each night Jeriah gave the Hierarch the drug. He told himself that after seven years a few more doses would do no additional harm. Then he tried telling himself that he had to do this to get Tobin back. At least that was true—but it didn't make Jeriah feel any better as he watched the old man drink.

Cogswhallop woke him before dawn each morning—no success. Jeriah thought about calling off the search, but he wasn't certain his plan would succeed. And the goblins had already been paid for it.

He was beginning to understand why the sorceress had taken up the goblins' cause—but she still had no excuse for dragging his brother into it!

Nevin arrived on the evening of the second day, when Jeriah was helping the Hierarch dress for dinner. He told Jeriah that he'd serve the high table tonight; Master Lazur wanted to see his ex-assistant. Malice glittered in his eyes. Jeriah was too preoccupied to spend much thought on Nevin, although anything that pleased Nevin probably meant trouble for him.

He detoured by his room to pick up the empty medicine jar, its glazed surface cold in his chilly fingers. Jeriah felt cold all over.

The flowers were blooming riotously. Marble gleamed in

the mellow light. How could this palace be so beautiful, run so smoothly, when its heart was rotten? Maybe the rot was only in Lazur's heart. Or his own? Blackmail and lies. Tobin would be ill by now—this was Jeriah's only chance to reach his brother before he died. He drew a steadying breath and knocked on Master Lazur's door.

"Come." The priest's face was lined with weariness from his journey. "Come in, Jeriah, and sit down. It seems"—his smile was wry—"that I underestimated your mother."

"My *mother*?" It was so far from any of Jeriah's expectations that it took him a moment to understand. He dropped into the offered chair.

"Yes. In her last letter she threatened to . . . What was it? Make my life a lot more difficult. Well, she's done so."

Good for her. "How did she do that?"

The priest's lips thinned. "Nevin told you about the unrest on the coast? Where people were suddenly questioning the need to relocate?"

Jeriah nodded.

"Your mother's behind it. I only hope the damage hasn't spread beyond the coast. But if it has, we'll deal with it. I'm going to need your help with her after all."

"I told you I can't control my mother."

"I can control her. What I need you to do is to find out if she planted her dangerous little seeds anywhere else. I've taken care of the western coast, but it will be easier to stop the same trouble in other places if I can get to it before it sprouts. I'm going to write to her, demanding she tell me who she's contacted and giving her reasons to answer. Your job—you'll carry my letter—will be to talk to her confidentially and make sure she gives me a complete list. She's not above forgetting one or two, or a dozen, of her fellow conspirators."

Outrage warred with disbelief. "You want me to spy on my mother?"

"You know how important the relocation is, but resistance to the idea still exists. We need to start moving Southland towns this summer, and the rest of the Realm will have to follow in the next few years. Your mother made a lot of friends when she served the Hierarch's mother, and many of those people hold influential positions. If she continues throwing out her little arguments . . . For all I've accomplished, the relocation is still balanced on a knife edge. If your mother stops the relocation, she could be responsible for the death of the entire Realm—and I'm sure you don't want that any more than I do. You can go . . . Hmm. It'll take both you and Nevin to get the Hierarch through the Equinox Ceremony. That's four days from now. You can leave for your home the day after."

Master Lazur was already turning to the pile of papers that had accumulated during his absence. Anger burned through Jeriah—how easily this man dismissed his scruples.

"I'm afraid you have more to deal with than my mother, sir."

Jeriah pulled the medicine jar from his tunic and rapped it down on the desk. The priest's eyes widened. His face stilled. Jeriah cherished a heady sense of power.

"What's this?" Master Lazur asked.

"You know what it is."

The priest sat for a moment, eyeing the plain dark crockery. Then he rubbed his face wearily and rose to his feet. "I'd hoped I wouldn't have to do this."

Jeriah turned to face Master Lazur as he came around the desk, but the priest went over to the door. A single gesture summoned a passing page, and Master Lazur bent to murmur in his ear. The boy cast Jeriah a startled look and dashed off.

Was he going for the guard? For someone else to help Master Lazur? Any kind of disturbance would draw attention to Jeriah's accusation, and that had to be the last thing the priest wanted!

Master Lazur returned to his seat behind the desk, leaving the jar in plain sight between them.

"I deny knowing what that is. If I go on denying it, can you prove I do?"

"Do I need to? The accusation alone would make your life a *lot* more difficult. I don't think you want the Hierarch to recover, no matter who gets blamed."

"I'll admit my life is difficult enough right now." Mockery danced in the priest's eyes. *Why wasn't he frightened?* "I take it you haven't found my spell notes."

"What makes you think that?" Jeriah asked.

"Because you're attempting to do it this way. Though that doesn't necessarily follow. You could be trying this because you've discovered that no one can steal the notes."

No one can steal them? Even if he knew where they were? Where . . . ? Of course! Even if you found them, *you couldn't get them out*! But he couldn't be certain. Test it!

"Oh, I gave up trying to steal them when I learned you'd put them in the vault."

"I thought you would; that's why I put them there. But how did you learn . . . ? Ah! From me, just now. Very good!"

He leaned back in his chair, laughing. Jeriah's elusive sense of power had evaporated, leaving dread in its wake.

"Don't count on doing that again, lad. You know, Tobin's probably ill already—he'll be dead in a few weeks. Did it ever occur to you that if I'm arrested for treason, all my papers will be confiscated? There's no way you could save your brother if that happened."

"True, but I doubt you'll let it go that far."

"You're right about that. In fact, I'm going to stop this right here. I suppose you've written out your suspicions and given them to someone in the traditional sealed envelope, to be opened if anything happens to you?"

"I wrote to a friend and enclosed the sealed note. It's not anyone in my family. You'd never find him." A safe statement, since Jeriah hadn't sent any such note. He hoped the fabrication would draw Lazur's attention away from the palace and Chardane.

"That's a pity, because you're going to want that sealed note back. Because if anything happens to me, and there's the slightest evidence you had a hand in it, Lord Brallorscourt will open *my* sealed envelope and find papers that will condemn your father to disgrace and probably death. Unlike you, I have proof—not just suspicion."

Master Lazur's gaze was steady, the sardonic humor gone. Jeriah remembered how he'd felt when the dike started to tremble beneath his feet.

"Proof of what? My father never did anything wrong in his life!" Jeriah tried to sound contemptuous, but the quaking in his belly found its way into his voice.

"Didn't you ever wonder what price your father paid for your brother's life?"

"He bribed the judges. He had to sell a lot of land."

"Others sold land and offered bribes. It didn't save them. But in your brother's case there was a favor we needed. A favor from a man of impeccable integrity. A man no one would ever believe would give false testimony."

"What are you saying?"

"Lord Glovinscourt, Jeriah. He opposed the relocation, and he was rich enough to stir up trouble. Unfortunately, he wasn't involved in the conspiracy—a sign of good taste on the part of the conspirators, I might add. He was a despicable man. When it was his word against your father's, no one believed him for a minute. He went to his death on your father's oath, but your father lied. And to lie a man's life away is a crime for which your father would be stripped of rank and lands. If they let him live at all."

"I don't believe a word of this! My father would never lie under oath." But it accounted for so much: why he'd taken Tobin's disgrace so hard; why he'd become a recluse—he'd been trying to protect the rest of his neighbors. Even his anger at Tobin . . . Jeriah wiped his hands on his thighs. "I don't believe you."

It was a lie, and the priest knew it.

"It doesn't matter whether you believe me or not; I have—" Someone rapped politely on the door, and the priest rose to answer. "I have proof. Though I don't blame your father—no one practices honor when it matters. I'm not being unreasonable about this, either; Brallorscourt will only act if he believes that you're behind my . . . difficulties. Give up trying to blackmail me, lad. You're an amateur." He opened the door.

Senna stood there, with two guards gripping her arms. Her face was streaked with dirt and tears.

"I'm so sorry," she whispered. "So sorry."

"What's going on here?" Jeriah's voice sounded hollow in his own ears. Did this have something to do with his mother's scheme? Had she used Senna—

"Your mother was using your sister as her agent," Master Lazur said calmly. "And there are dozens of witnesses who'll testify to that—truthfully, as it happens. She's only doing it to put pressure on me, but conspiracy to thwart the Hierarch's orders can merit the death penalty if it threatens the safety of the Realm. And trying to stop the relocation definitely qualifies."

Senna's face went white. Jeriah drew a shuddering breath. "Let her go."

"Unfortunately, I need her to make your mother behave. I was going to confine her to a room in the lady's maids' quarters, but with all of you Rovans being so . . . active, I think she'd better go to a cell. At least for the next . . . three weeks? No, make it a month, so everyone can be certain. See to it," he told the guards.

In a month there would be no chance that Tobin was still alive.

"Wait! You don't have to lock her up. I'll . . ."

He'd what? Give up trying to save his brother?

Senna was crying as the guards dragged her away. Every muscle in Jeriah's body shook with the need to follow, to wrest her out of their hands and keep her safe—but that wouldn't keep her safe; it would only end with him in a cell beside her. He had to keep his wits, to stay free. To find some way to prevent this priest from destroying everyone he loved.

"Did you blackmail Tobin into helping you in the first place? Did you . . ." He stopped, but not in time.

"Did I use your involvement in the conspiracy against

him? There was no need—his own problems were lever enough. And I've never found proof of your guilt. I haven't tried very hard. You don't believe it now, but we can still work together."

"I'd rather die than serve a man like you!"

Master Lazur shook his head. "A man like me . . . because I'm willing to make sacrifices for the good of the Realm? What are you doing right now, except sacrificing the Hierarch to save your brother?"

Jeriah was silent.

The priest went on. "You're not evil, and neither am I. You have courage and intelligence—and when the relocation commences, we'll need all the brains and courage we can get. Once you've gotten those names from your mother, I'll send your sister home. By then enough time will have passed that you'll have no further reason to defy me, but—"

"Because Tobin will be dead!" Jeriah put in bitterly.

"Precisely. And you might bear in mind that I didn't send him into the Otherworld—in fact, I was trying to stop him! Hmm. This will be hard for someone your age to accept, at least for a while. I believe I'll let Nevin return to the Hierarch and send you to the border for a time. Brallorscourt may object, but I can use someone to keep an eye on things there, and it will remind you why the relocation is important. You can go there straight from your home—I'll send a courier to bring back your mother's list. It's almost summer on the border, but since the barbarians took the Southlands there's still some action. I'll probably bring you back before the winter campaign—though you might be needed more in the south. Anyone who can lift a sword will be needed for that, I fear. You can leave for your home right after Equinox."

"That's only four days!"

Tobin would have been ill almost a week by then—Jeriah's time was running out.

"Which will leave you no time to hatch futile, dangerous schemes. Because if those spell notes vanish from the vault, I'll use my evidence against your father. And if anyone in your family stirs up inconvenient rumors, I'll charge your mother and sister with conspiring against the Bright Gods' will. Give it up, lad. Tobin will be dead in week, two at the outside. Accept his death." He came around the desk and opened the door, ending the interview. "There's no way to reach your brother in time. Unless . . ."

"Unless what?" Jeriah was on his feet, shaking with rage.

"You've tried blackmail. Had you thought to try bribery? Some of the conspirators survived, and we know at least one of their leaders escaped. If someone you know—your friend who holds the envelope perhaps?—could name a few of those survivors, I might be persuaded to give up my spell notes. If we capture the leader, I'll forget about the charges against your mother and sister and cast your gate spell myself!"

"Why should I believe anything you say, demon spawn?"

"Because the conspirators, even the small number that remain, are more dangerous to the Realm than a handful of goblins and a hedgewitch. And with your brother home, your mother would have no reason to cause more trouble. I'm always willing to trade up. Think it over. Just don't think too long."

Jeriah found himself walking in the wood that covered part of the palace grounds without remembering how he got there, but he desperately needed to be alone.

Trapped. He even knew where the cursed notes were! Master Lazur must have enjoyed watching him blunder around the palace, knowing the notes were safe in the heavily guarded vault. No wonder he hadn't been worried when Jeriah broke into his office. Even if the goblins *could* steal them, Master Lazur would destroy his father.

His father, who had lied a man to his death! Admittedly, Glovinscourt wasn't much loss. . . . But with that on his own conscience, how dared the old man be so angry with Jeriah over an accident! Although flooding that village might have cost lives. That was why his father had been so angry.

Was Master Lazur right, that no one practiced honor when it mattered?

The trees began to thin, moonlight shining on the surface of the ornamental lake. Jeriah turned and plunged back into the woods at a different angle. Even if he could get the notes—out of a stone vault with iron doors surrounded by the sunsguard—Chardane wouldn't cast the gate spell unless he destroyed Master Lazur. Which he couldn't do, because the priest would then destroy Jeriah's family.

Senna had never been in serious trouble in her life—much less locked up in a cell! She must be sick with terror.

Tobin was probably sick already. How long would it take the goblins to find him in the Otherworld? Jeriah might be too late, even if he got that gate cast tomorrow!

In four days Chardane would move against Master Lazur herself. As soon as it came out that the Sunlord was being drugged, Master Lazur would know Jeriah had been part of it, and then . . . He had to stop Chardane. But how?

There was one way. A cold hand wrapped around Jeriah's heart and he pushed the thought aside. He came to another edge of the wood; the Hall of Justice loomed through the trees. He turned back, walking faster, but the idea intruded again.

If he turned Chardane over to Master Lazur, he could save both Tobin and his family. But Chardane would die, taking dozens, perhaps hundreds with her. That would be as bad as anything Master Lazur had done. To destroy property was one thing; for destroying lives there was no reparation. Tobin wouldn't want to be saved at such a price!

But if Jeriah didn't stop Chardane, most of his family would die. What would happen to Tamilee, if everyone she loved was executed?

That was what Koryn had experienced. No wonder she was obsessed with avenging her family—it was a miracle she was walking around sane!

But how many people would Jeriah have to kill to prevent it? And wasn't condemning the Hierarch to his drugged half life as bad as killing him?

The branches snatched at Jeriah's face and hands as his pace quickened again. Could he destroy Chardane and the Hierarch? Surely he owed Tobin and his family more. The lesser of two evils. How many times had Master Lazur been seduced by the lesser evil, committing one crime after another, sliding step after step into darkness? How many lesser evils had Jeriah already accepted? Maybe the priest was right. Maybe they weren't so different after all.

No. It had to stop. He refused to take even one more step down that terrible path. Not one more death.

Even if his family died for it?

Jeriah was almost running when something wrapped around his ankle and brought him crashing to the ground. He sat up, rubbed his throbbing elbow, and looked at the long root that stretched like a trip rope across his path.

"It was the only way to stop you." Daroo's voice came from a bush several feet away.

"You could have called my name."

"I tried that three times." The goblin scrambled out to crouch beside him. "What's wrong?"

"Everything. But there's nothing you can do."

"I suppose a hero like you has to solve it all alone?" Daroo snorted. "You're a fool, but Fa says a body has a right to make a fool of himself. He sent me to say we've finished the

297

third level, and is there anyplace on the fourth level you'd have us search first?"

"Nowhere. It doesn't matter anymore. I know where they are, but even if you could get them I can't let you, and you can't get them anyway, and in four days it'll be too late!" Jeriah buried his face in his hands.

"What?" The boy's eyes were wide with confusion. If Jeriah was going to call off the search, he owed the goblins an explanation. And sometimes Daroo had ideas.

He told the young goblin what he'd learned about the Hierarch, what his mother and Senna had done, and what Chardane and Master Lazur had said. "And Tobin's running out of time," he finished. "Any suggestions?"

"No. It's a fair poser," Daroo admitted. "Even if you do nothing, bad things happen. Though you've got a fine chance to be a hero when that poor old man gets saved."

"At the cost of my family's destruction? Dark One *take* being a hero! I don't want to be a hero! I just want my family to live."

"But to get that, you'd have to do worse than not-being-a-hero. You'd . . ."

He went on talking but Jeriah didn't hear. The idea filled his mind, blinding, deafening. "Not a hero."

"What? Jeriah, are you all right?"

"*I* don't have to be a hero. I don't! It might work!"

Daroo rose on tiptoe to feel Jeriah's forehead. "No fever. Maybe I shouldn't have knocked you down."

"No!" Jeriah grabbed the child and shot to his feet. "I'm all right, really. If *I'm* not a hero it might work! I have an idea!" He spun Daroo in a jubilant circle.

"Put me down! I suppose you'll try to work it all by yourself? Again?"

"No," said Jeriah, sobering. "To bring this off I'll need all the help I can get."

Makenna

ONLY A WEEK. ONLY A week they'd been camped beside the new stream before it too had died.

At least this time they were prepared. This time the watch called the alarm the moment the roiling stream began to flatten, and they had rushed into the water and filled every container they possessed before the stream's flow had stopped.

Makenna hadn't bothered to go upstream to search out the cause, but this time she'd told the scouts to find a lake, which wouldn't disappear the instant something cut off its source.

Something. Now that they knew what to look for, several goblins had seen the creatures—though they didn't all look like trees. One, they said, seemed to be made of grass, and another resembled a tumble of stone come to life.

All the creatures had departed before the goblins could speak to them, and however different their appearance, Makenna was certain they were one tribe, one clan . . . one enemy.

She could do nothing about that now.

Looking over the meadow they were about to abandon, Makenna saw that all the small tents were down and packed. In fact, most of the goblins seemed to be waiting for her, so Makenna swung the heavy pack onto her shoulders. She didn't dare leave Master Lazur's books behind, because the bridge out of this world had to be built with magic. Somehow. She had tried. She'd gathered the goblins into a spell group, and they had pooled all the magic they possessed and poured that power into the gate spell's runes—and watched it sink into the surface the runes were cast on as if this whole world were a magic-sucking sponge.

In truth, Makenna was beginning to believe that was exactly what was going on—or at least a pretty good analogy. Every goblin reported that their innate magic had been reduced to the merest trace. Makenna felt as if her own magic was evaporating the moment it was generated, like a trickle of water poured into a hot pan.

Of course, evaporating water was on her mind now. Once they reached the lake, she'd have time to experiment further—though if their enemies could move whole hills at whim, maybe she shouldn't be so certain of that.

But they needed time so badly. Time for the Greeners to build up their food supply, since they didn't dare plant. Time for Tobin to heal.

He'd wanted to walk to the lake, but Charba forbade it. Dozens of goblins had volunteered to carry him, not even demanding a token payment for the service. Charba was frankly baffled as to why he was so sick, but she said that given rest and nursing, most folks recovered from most illnesses, most of the time.

The lake would give him time to rest, to heal, Makenna resolved grimly. Time for her to scour Master Lazur's books and find some way to get them out of this world. For the Otherworld wasn't a refuge—it was a death trap. A trap into which *she* had led them. And she'd get them out, too. Every one of them. Somehow.

CHAPTER 13

Jeriah

JERIAH HAD THOUGHT HE WAS nervous the first time he broke into Master Lazur's office; his past anxiety was nothing compared to his bone-deep knowledge of the stakes he played for now.

The beginning of Sunset Prayer rolled over him, and he turned to the flowers where Daroo hid. "You're sure he's gone?"

"Five minutes ago, with the rest of them. Here are the jars. Hurry!"

Jeriah hesitated at the door, and then knocked softly before pushing it open. "Master Lazur? Anyone here?" This time he had an excuse ready, but the office and bedroom were both empty. They must have accepted his claim that his headache was too severe for him to attend the Hierarch at prayer—he'd been pale and tense enough to make it plausible.

First the jars. He opened the cabinet Nevin had caught him searching and felt around the top shelf. There was enough room to plant the medicine jars behind the stacked papers, but he had to slide the stacks forward several inches. Would Master Lazur notice the papers had been moved? No help for it.

The dark crockery blended with the shadows, making the jars almost invisible. Chardane had supplied them, along with the herbal mixture in them—guaranteed identical to the Hierarch's "medicine."

A plan that would destroy Master Lazur without putting her people at risk had delighted Chardane, and she'd willingly promised that once her cadre gained power, the Decree of Bright Magic would be revoked. With that promise Jeriah had bought the goblins' cooperation. His whole scheme was built on a tottering stack of promises, like the piles of paper on Master Lazur's desk.

It took a long time to find the documents that had been assembled for tomorrow's council meeting. Jeriah knew they were discussing the relocation, but there were so many sessions. . . . His lips tightened. They'd be having some meetings they didn't expect, if this plan worked.

By the time Jeriah was sure he'd found the right documents, the evening prayer was drawing to a close. He pulled one of the new maps of the Goblin Wood out of the stack— they'd certainly need that—and tucked it quickly into the papers on the cabinet's top shelf.

Jeriah was closing the cupboard door when a thought struck him. The muted rumble of praise and response signaled the end of prayer as he dug rapidly through the documents till he found another map of about the same size. Outside the office Daroo hissed a warning. Jeriah shuffled the map into the same place as the one he'd removed and fled, reaching his own room just before the crowd flowed down the steps from the temple. His heart was thundering and his stomach rolled. All his other plans had failed, and they'd been *simple* compared to this one. But he refused to follow in Master Lazur's footsteps, and it was too late to back out now.

Jeriah had to overthrow not only the priest, but the whole shadow government that would fall with him. Because if he didn't, sometime in the next two weeks, Tobin was going to die.

He tried to visit Senna in her cell, but the guards stopped him. No visitors allowed, by Master Lazur's order. Jeriah almost went back to argue with the priest, but he knew he wouldn't win. He did succeed in bribing the guard to deliver a pillow and a warm blanket to her cell . . . but only after the man had searched them and removed the brief note Jeriah had tucked under the pillowcase.

Finally Jeriah sent Daroo, who swore he could sneak the note into Senna's cell without being caught. He was sitting up in his bed, with the lamp burning low, when the small goblin returned.

"Is she all right? She's not too scared, is she? Did she recognize my writing? I didn't dare sign it."

"I should let you keep stacking up questions," Daroo said. "Just to see how high the pile gets. But it won't do you any good. She was asleep."

"You didn't wake her?"

"Don't be silly. What if she'd screamed? She's not accustomed to being visited by our folk."

"Then how can you tell if she's all right?" Jeriah demanded. "How can you tell if she recognized my—"

"Who else would send her notes saying, 'Don't worry, I'm working on a scheme, and if we don't all get killed everything will be fine.' You've written her letters before, haven't you? She'll recognize the writing."

"I just said I had an idea, and that everything would be all right. To keep her from worrying."

"If she knows you, that'll worry her more than anything else."

He might be right about that. Jeriah sighed. "But she was all right?"

"How would I know? She was sleeping. And me going back to talk to her in the daytime would put the rest of your plan at risk. You know that."

Jeriah did know it. And Tobin was in even more trouble than Senna, so he had to let it go. But the thought of his sister, alone and terrified, still haunted him.

The day before Equinox Jeriah hovered outside the door of the council chamber. He could hear muffled voices through the door but he couldn't make out the words—he could only wait, and pray to be standing there when Nevin emerged.

St. Cerwyn be praised there were no petitions today; the Sunlord was "meditating" before the holy ceremony. In fact, he was alternately resting and being drilled in the procedures. Jeriah had nothing to do but run errands for the attending priests, and he'd managed to make those errands last a long time. As far as he could tell, the busy priests barely noticed his absence.

Master Kerratis had come by yesterday, and contemptuously declared the Hierarch "as fit for it as he's likely to get." Nevin had gone around in tight-lipped fury for the rest of the afternoon. He couldn't know about the drugs. No one could fake the devotion Nevin showed the Hierarch . . . unless he had some motive Jeriah knew nothing about. Jeriah winced and pulled his mind back to the present. There was plenty that could go wrong right now.

This next step of his plan might even work without Jeriah's presence. But it was such a small thing, and so critical, the thought of leaving it to chance made his stomach cramp.

If I bring my family out of this alive, he offered up as a silent vow, *I will never involve myself in plots again.*

A few moments of general chatter came from the council chamber, then a single voice resumed speaking. Jeriah thought it was Master Lazur, who'd been addressing the council for most of the morning. There was still resistance to the relocation in many hearts. Chardane was wrong;

Lazur's grip on the council wasn't unshakable. Not yet. And knowing his own weakness only made the priest more dangerous.

There was another break in the flow of the speech, followed by a flurry of conversation. A new speaker? The doors opened and Nevin strode out. He clutched a roll of paper in his hand, and his mouth was tight with irritation. *Thank you, Bright Ones!*

Jeriah gave him a few moments' start, then dashed down the hall after him.

"Hey, Brallorscourt! Wait up. I've got some questions about tomorrow."

Nevin slowed but didn't stop. "I can't help you now—they're waiting for me. Ask me this evening."

"I'll walk with you. What's that?" Jeriah gestured to the map.

"The stupidest thing! I put the new woods map with his papers, I swear I did. But . . . I must have mixed them up."

"A new map? Of the Goblin Wood?" *Innocent, casual, easy.* "I think I saw something like that the night when you, ah, interrupted me."

"Oh, really? You remember every paper you glanced at?"

Calm down, he's not suspicious. If he was nice, you'd know something was wrong. Jeriah wished, passionately, that Nevin was a fool.

"I noticed it because I just returned from that area," Jeriah said coldly. "But if you want to go through every stack in

Master Lazur's office, that's fine with me. It should only take you half a day." He turned and began to walk away. *Don't let me go. Don't let—*

"Wait. It's your duty to assist the council as well as the Hierarch. Besides, ah, I thought you had some questions."

Jeriah's questions about the Hierarch's role in the Equinox Ceremony carried them to the door of Lazur's office, where he went straight to the tall cabinet.

"I'm sure it was here, on the top shelf. Let me get . . ." Jeriah pulled a small chest over, and stood on it so he could go through the papers—and his body blocked Nevin's view of the shelf.

"If you cared to think," said Nevin, "it might occur to you to bring the stack down and sort through it on the desk."

"No, I'm doing fine, but . . . Hold these for me."

He handed the crockery jars to Nevin, who put them on the desk without a second glance. "Demon's teeth! Bring those cursed papers down so we can go through them!"

"It's all right, I've got it." Jeriah passed the map down to Nevin. "Hand me those jars, will you?"

"Get them yourself." Nevin was already on his way out the door. "I'm not your servant."

Jeriah replaced the jars carefully at the back of the shelf. He'd called as much attention to them as he dared. And at least Nevin hadn't recognized them too soon, which could have been disastrous. Nevin had handled them himself—surely he'd remember. If he didn't, Jeriah could remind him, but to bring himself into the matter, even in a small way, would be horribly dangerous. Thank the Bright Gods Nevin wasn't a fool.

On the morning of Equinox Jeriah stared out of the Hierarch's bedroom window at the gardens, though calling it morning was a hideous exaggeration. The gardeners, who'd been ordered to make all perfect before the sun rose on this holy day, were working by torchlight.

"Come away from the window. You're supposed to be serving him, not sleeping."

Jeriah was too apprehensive for even Nevin to irritate him.

"Mohri's serving his breakfast. And I'm trying to straighten this." Jeriah held out a web of fine gold chain that would be draped over the Hierarch's robe. He'd spent the last five minutes twisting it into knots.

"Well, leave it for now and . . . Demons curse it! We've run out of caroliss tea!"

They wouldn't have, if Jeriah hadn't emptied the jar down the privy last night. "Those priests must have used it up. Can you give him something else?"

"The Sunlord is to be served nothing but the best. Besides, I don't want to change his routine any more than we must." Nevin looked nervous too. "Go down to the kitchen and get some."

Jeriah held up his hands, covered with tangled gold. So

many small things had to go right. The whole plan hinged on his next words. "This is a real mess—if I put it down, I'll have to start over. Besides, it's as much as your life's worth to go into the kitchen this morning. One of the cooks threatened me with a carving knife yesterday, I swear he did. Master Goserian wants the feast to be perfect and he's riding them hard. Why don't you go to the herb-healer? I bet she'd have some, and it's nearer."

"Would she be awake this early?"

Jeriah shrugged, trying to make it look casual. His shoulders were tighter than a drawn bow.

"Who knows? Lots of people are up; anything that gets done today has to be finished by dawn."

"I'll try her."

Nevin hurried out, and Jeriah tried to relax. It was all going according to plan. But this plan was so complex. Too complex to succeed. There were a thousand things that—

"Sir?"

Jeriah jumped, almost dropping the chains.

"Will you eat breakfast? It's ready."

"No! Don't sneak . . ." He summoned up a smile. "Sorry, we're all a little tense." The servant was staring at him. "I want to finish this. I'm not hungry, anyway."

"Yes, sir."

Jeriah tried to sort out the tangled chains of the Hierarch's ceremonial necklace—he shouldn't have done such a thorough job of twisting them up.

If even one of his allies got caught, the plan was finished. Jeriah also worried about the number of times Chardane came into it, but she didn't seem concerned. When she'd approached the council and offered to investigate the possibility of using drugs against the barbarians, no one had seemed suspicious. In fact, she'd told Jeriah, the council was so enthusiastic she'd probably have to come up with something no matter what else happened. If Chardane was so confident, why did Jeriah feel as if he was floundering on the brink of disaster?

Nevin hadn't returned—he would have, if it hadn't gone according to plan. It was still going according to plan, it was . . . it was going to drive Jeriah mad if he didn't get up and do something.

"Here, someone take care of this mess. I'm going to dress; then we'll start robing the Hierarch whether Nevin's here or not."

They'd almost finished by the time Nevin returned, carrying a tea tray . . . and wearing different clothes than when he'd left. Jeriah suppressed a gasp of relief.

"Where have you been? It's almost time."

"That woman spilled some concoction all over me! She said it was mildly toxic and insisted on hauling off my clothes and washing me—as if I were a two-year-old! But the stuff stank, so I had to change anyway. Have you got the gold on him yet? Where's my tabard? Where's . . ."

Jeriah let the stream of questions run over him. *Remember*

that scent, you arrogant toad. The pieces were now in place. Jeriah was shaking as he joined the procession that led the Sunlord to welcome the turn of the season.

The sun rose, spreading its glowing benediction over the land, and the Sunlord greeted it. As the day wore on, the sun beat down on Jeriah's head and shoulders. He fretted and sweated, paying as little attention to the ceremony as he could manage. Nevin had to nudge him into his assigned place several times.

The Hierarch had "honored" other priests by asking them to recite the twelve long prayers that lasted from sunrise to sunset, but no one else could recite the hourly invocations. As the day passed, his fatigue grew, but he never complained or tried to avoid the altar—not even when the words deserted him and he was forced to rely on the whispers of his prompters.

Courage. Even drugged, the courage showed through. Jeriah felt a piercing shame that he'd actually considered letting the Hierarch continue this loathsome half life.

Master Lazur watched along with the rest of the crowd. If he felt anything, it didn't show. How easy it was to sacrifice others to a personal obsession. At least Master Lazur's goal was noble—Jeriah couldn't even claim that. If his plan didn't succeed, he still might have to make that impossible choice. He glanced at Nevin, on whom his whole plan depended, and shivered despite the heat.

Tobin would have been ill for some time now.

Wait for me, brother. On this of all days, surely the Bright Gods would hear his prayer. *Just hang on till I can get there. I'm coming.*

Finally the sun set. Nevin and Jeriah helped the Hierarch inside—he shook with exhaustion, but he had less than an hour to rest.

"He has to appear at the feast," Nevin fretted, "and watch the dancing till midnight—it's traditional. But if he gets too tired, demons can take tradition! I'm putting him to bed when he needs to go."

A chill ran along Jeriah's nerves—he needed those hours before midnight. "He did well today, and did it bravely. All he has to do is eat, then sit and watch. Surely he can manage. Besides, you said Master Zachiros is responsible for him in the evening. We have leave to join the festivities as soon as the high table's been served."

"You can spend the night drinking and dancing if you want—and I'm sure you will. I'll stay where I'm needed."

"Suit yourself." Jeriah shrugged away the sting. As long as he was free between the end of the feast and midnight, nothing else mattered.

Nevin served the Hierarch himself, but helping to keep the exhausted ruler's true state from becoming obvious took all of Jeriah's attention. The senior council lord and the second-circle priest, who sat on the Hierarch's right and left, did their best as well. Hungry now in spite of his taut nerves,

Jeriah snatched a meal in bites as he passed to and from the kitchen. Finally, the last dishes were removed and the tables cleared away. Master Zachiros took Nevin's position at the Hierarch's shoulder, and Jeriah was free.

But Master Lazur's eyes kept straying to him. *Not yet. Not quite. Dance awhile, let him see you in the crowd, let him lose himself in his own conversations.*

Jeriah took his place on the dance floor. He smiled, laughed, and must not have mangled the sets too badly, though afterward he couldn't remember his partners.

The eighth set, also by tradition, was the threshing dance. The dancers took up their wands and formed a circle, no partners needed. No one to miss Jeriah if he slipped away.

The drumbeat throbbed in heart and bone as they danced their way through the plowing, sowing, reaping, and finally threshed the grain, their wands pounding the floor. If the Seven Bright Gods were the source of all life, why did dancers throughout the Realm take up wands every spring and do their best to dance the seed from the soil? Was this dance older than the Bright Gods themselves?

It was the kind of question that used to horrify Tobin. Suddenly, sharply, Jeriah missed his brother. If this didn't succeed . . .

Master Lazur was deep in conversation with what looked like half the council.

Even Master Kerratis, a cup of wine cradled in his thin fingers, was talking with friends, not watching Jeriah. In that whole, vast, crowded room no one was paying—

He saw her eyes first, luminous gray surrounded by small, sharp features and a cloud of dark hair—her pale gray gown as drab as ever. Maybe it did set off her eyes, but it made that warm skin look muddy. A deep red, or a really brilliant blue, would make her glow . . . though they might not have suited *her*. Koryn was a creature of shadows and corners. Dragging her into the light would be as unkind as driving a bat out of its cave.

And perhaps she preferred the shadowy corners because it made spying on Jeriah easier. She watched him openly now, making no effort to hide it, though she must have seen that he'd noticed.

He couldn't absent himself while she was looking. If he simply walked out and ran from her, she might report his odd actions to Master Lazur, and Jeriah's scheme would come to an end right there.

He had to make her leave him. But how . . . ?

It turned out someone else was watching him, after all. A strong hand clapped his shoulder so heartily Jeriah staggered a step.

"So." Marof's voice was thick with wine. "The nettle's looking at you. Got her blooming yet, Rovan?" He tried to wink, but both his eyes closed.

"No, I . . . haven't," said Jeriah. "Though I think . . ."

It would make him look like a total cad. Jeriah had sisters. He despised men who made that kind of bet. But it would get Koryn out of the way. And if he could get her to slap his face, in some spot she'd have difficulty escaping from, it might take her some time to report the matter. If she wanted to report it. And when Jeriah lost and paid—because he was going to say he'd lost, no matter what happened—her reputation would be spared. It was Jeriah who'd look like a callous, brutish idiot. But not a traitor.

". . . I think I could get her blooming tonight," he finished firmly.

It took only moments to set up a bet that tonight he would "make the nettle bloom." Even the drunken louts who were wagering weren't crass enough to get specific about what that meant. And since Jeriah intended to lose, even if it only referred to a passionate kiss, it hardly mattered.

Now, as he wove through the crowd to the corner where Koryn sat, he faced the hard part—he had to get her to go with him. And Koryn was neither drunk nor a fool.

"Good Equinox, Mistress Goserian."

"Good Equinox, Master Rovan." Her voice was dry. "You seem to be enjoying yourself."

"And you aren't? I know you can't dance, but half the women and three quarters of the men aren't dancing either, and they all seem to be having a fine time. If you'd just let yourself . . ."

Jeriah hadn't figured out how he was going to lure her to a secluded spot, but scolding her for sulking in the corner wasn't going to help.

"I'm sorry. Maybe sulking in corners is how you enjoy yourself. I have no right to judge."

That hadn't come out quite the way he'd intended.

"No, you don't." The gleam that leapt into her eyes at the prospect of a debate looked remarkably like enjoyment. Gods, she was prickly.

"As it happens," she went on, "I liked watching the threshing dance. Though it occurs to me that if the Seven Bright Gods are the only ones with the power to create life . . ."

"Why are we dancing for it? I thought the same thing!"

Here was someone who wasn't a bit shocked by his blasphemous musings. And there were things she enjoyed. Things she wanted. That was what he had to use against her. Suddenly, the solution fell into place.

"I need to talk to you," Jeriah told her. "Alone. Without anyone to see. I think tonight would be a good time for that."

"Why alone?" she asked reasonably. "There's no one listening now."

"Well, it's not me you need to talk to." Jeriah lowered his voice carefully. "I've . . . made contact with someone who might have some of the answers we talked about."

Koryn's eyes widened. "That night on the terrace . . ."

Jeriah leaned closer, the picture of someone whispering words of romance. "It wasn't a rat. But they're not about to come into the palace again, so you'll—"

Koryn held up her hand for silence. "We're going outside?

Let me get a shawl. This silly gown's too thin to go out at night."

"You should have warned me to get my boots too," Koryn grumbled as Jeriah led her through another tangle of brush. "If I'd known we'd be thrashing around in the wilderness, I'd have changed."

This pang of guilt was worse than the last three, but Jeriah suppressed it, too. Maybe he was a cad, or even worse, but he needed her out here in those ridiculous, slick-soled slippers.

"You knew they were goblins," he said. "Did you expect them to join us in the Hierarch's sitting room? Especially after what almost happened to their first messenger. Meeting us in the ravine guarantees their safety, because they can get in and out of it so much more easily than humans."

The small, steep-sided ravine that drained the ornamental stream would also be hard for a crippled girl in a formal gown to climb out of.

He hated using her injury as a weapon against her. Particularly when he remembered how she'd been crippled. She was the hero . . . so what did that make the person who betrayed her?

"What would goblins know about barbarian magic?" Koryn asked. "I never found any connection between them in my research."

"There's no connection." Jeriah had already decided to

tell as much of the truth as he could. "But I was looking for magic that didn't come from any of the Gods, and that's what the goblins have. It may not use the same source as the barbarians' magic. The goblins I spoke to said the barbarians are as quick to kill them as they are to kill us. Maybe quicker. 'They regard us as a delicacy' is the exact quote. That's one of the reasons they might be willing to help us."

"What's the other reason?"

"We're here." Jeriah paused on the brink of the ravine. The trees had thinned, revealing the steep banks. It wasn't some canyon she'd be trapped in forever, Jeriah assured his complaining conscience. Only a twenty-foot scramble. And having used this ravine to meet conspirators, before they'd all been hanged, Jeriah knew there were easier ways in and out of it. He just didn't want Koryn to find them quickly. "Let me help you. This bit's tricky."

She got herself down with less assistance than he'd thought she'd need, wrapping her skirt tight and sliding down the rougher sections on her butt. When they reached the bottom, the first thing she said was, "What's the other reason the goblins are willing to help us?"

The brush had reduced her hair to a wild tangle, and the moonlight softened the angles of her face. Jeriah wished it had softened her brain.

"I don't know how much you know about goblins," he said, "but they always demand a price for their services."

Koryn snorted. "Everyone knows that."

Was she standing more awkwardly than usual? Jeriah didn't want her hurt. Just delayed for an hour or two.

"Come sit down on this rock." He led her over to it. "We may have to wait awhile."

They'd have to wait forever, since his goblin allies were currently deep under the palace—and probably wondering what was keeping Jeriah so long!

He had to do this. He had no choice.

Had Master Lazur thought that, when he committed his first betrayal? Jeriah had sworn to take a different path, and here he was, doing something his whole being screamed was wrong . . . for the greater good.

But Koryn wouldn't die. And if he didn't get her out of the way tonight, Tobin would.

Koryn had followed him, but a frown creased her smooth forehead. "Are you stalling me?"

"No," said Jeriah. But he was stalling. He didn't want to lose . . . what? They were hardly friends. He would certainly lose her respect when he tried to kiss her, when he told her he'd lied and brought her to this isolated spot with seduction in mind. But he had no reason to suppose she respected him now. It was just . . . He didn't want to see her hurt, or frightened, or even made uncomfortable. And he'd have to do at least some, maybe all of that, to make her slap his face.

"The thing is"—he helped her settle onto the flat rock— "I'm not sure you're going to agree to what the goblins want. In exchange for their aid."

As much of the truth as he could tell. And being involved with one plot should make him look more innocent of being involved in another. At least, he hoped it would.

"So what do they want?" Koryn asked. "You'll have to tell me, sooner or later."

She was right.

"The goblins want their leader back," Jeriah said bluntly. "The girl who took my brother into the Otherworld. Think about it for a minute before you say no. Her army is shattered and scattered, and she told Master Lazur under a truth spell that she's only a hedgewitch—she hardly has any magical power at all! She couldn't even dent your precious relocation! And—"

"And your brother could come back with her."

Was it only the moonlight softening her face?

"Jeriah, I don't have their leader in my back pocket—or you brother either. I told you before, I don't even know where Master Lazur's spell notes are!"

But Jeriah did, and if Master Lazur ever heard about this part of the conversation . . . he'd believe Jeriah had lured her out here to win his bet. Particularly if Jeriah got his face slapped trying. And if he was going to get those notes in time to save his brother, he'd better start now.

Jeriah stepped forward, only a small step needed, and bent to press his lips on hers. He'd intended to be a little rough, a little intrusive. But he hadn't known her lips would tremble when he touched them. Or be so soft. Or cling so gently when he finally pulled away.

He stood staring down at her, at the wide, colorless eyes . . . that suddenly narrowed in suspicion.

"What are you up to?" she demanded.

Now was the time to tell her about the wager. Now he'd have to tell her, because that hadn't been a face-slapping sort of kiss.

"Nothing," Jeriah heard his own voice saying. "I just wanted to . . . um . . ."

"Rubbish!" she snapped. "You wouldn't drag me all the way out here for a kiss, and I already told you I don't know where those accursed notes are. Even if I did, I wouldn't tell you, and you know that too. So what are you—"

All Jeriah's seething emotions boiled over.

"You really wouldn't tell me, would you? You'd let my brother *die* rather than take the slightest risk that your precious Master Lazur might be wrong about something. They're right, what they say about you, nothing but nettles and ice, because you're so wrapped up in your own obsession, in your hate, that you can't even feel anything else!"

Her thin hand flew up and slapped his face, the sound echoing in the empty ravine.

Jeriah took a step back. Then another. Then he turned and scrambled up the slope as if the barbarian army were after him.

"Hey," she called. "Wait! I can't get out of here. Jeriah, wait!"

Jeriah kept walking.

She'd slapped his face. He looked like a total cad. He'd accomplished exactly what he'd come for, and he hadn't even had to maul her, physically.

Only to betray a friend. Only to hurt her heart.

A wind was rising and the new leaves whispered. The room Cogswhallop had showed him on the map was behind the kitchens, which were now full of servants enjoying their own feast. Jeriah had to circle around the terrace and work his way through several corridors. As well as he knew this level, it took him several minutes to locate the door, which looked more like a cupboard than the entrance to a room. The rattle of the chain washed over Jeriah as soon as he opened the door.

"They're running it fast tonight." Cogswhallop stepped out of the shadows. "Must have a lot of dishes to wash."

Jeriah eyed the dripping buckets the great chain carried to the cistern under the temple floor, from which water flowed into taps and fountains throughout the palace.

"Are you sure you can get into the vault from here?"

The goblin snorted. "I showed you the builder's plan three times. This shaft is where water's hauled up from the spring room—see that big bucket chain? All you have to do is climb down the ladder beside it and use those big muscles of yours to remove the grate that keeps folks like us from going past the dungeons."

Jeriah looked dubiously into the black pit—he couldn't see the bottom. "Isn't there an easier way down?"

"Of course. There's a great human-size door into the spring room from the wine cellar. It's right next to the vault's guard station. You could—"

"All right!" Jeriah gripped the ladder and descended into darkness.

The rungs were evenly spaced, and soon the rhythm claimed him. Down and down. The sound of splashing water grew louder. He stumbled when his feet hit the floor, then stood aside, clinging to the ladder. Cogswhallop came down and felt his way across the room, grumbling softly.

A starter scraped, and light bloomed from the lamp in the goblin's hand. It shimmered on the surface of a deep pool, as bucket after bucket sloshed in and out. The great wheel that guided the chain creaked. From the pool's rim, two shallow troughs led into the wall through culverts about three feet high. Water ran in one, but the gate that controlled the other was closed.

"I suppose it's too much to hope we go down the dry one?"

Cogswhallop grinned. "Best take off your fancy tunic. They're sewage culverts, hero. They open the gate when they've got prisoners on one side or other. So your sister's on the side—"

"Where the water's running. Naturally." Jeriah pulled off his tunic. "And someone might notice if we shut it off." There were worse things. He drew a resolute breath and pulled a crowbar from the pile of tools the goblins had placed near the culvert's mouth.

"Do I owe someone a button for these?"

Cogswhallop bit back a grin. "Part of the service—no payment required."

"You're joking. A goblin doing something for free?"

"Not for free; for getting the Decree of Bright Magic revoked. Don't forget that, hero. Not ever." The softness of his voice did nothing to diminish the threat.

"I won't. We'd better go."

"Wait." said Cogswhallop. "You can't hold that bar while you crawl—you'll clank all the way. Sound carries in stone, and there's an opening up to every cell."

They strapped the crowbar to Jeriah's back and he crawled into the culvert, trying to ignore the cold water flowing over his hands, soaking his knees and feet. It was no colder than the dread in the pit of his stomach. Jeriah tried not to think about the layer of slime that covered the stone—at least it made their progress quieter.

The culvert was dark, for Cogswhallop had left the lamp back in the spring room, but every ten feet a faint patch of light shone from above; sewer holes from the cells. They were only small square shafts with bars across the top, but that light meant there were prisoners in some of the cells above—and that meant guards, who might hear someone pulling out a grate or chipping through the culvert's wall.

Senna was in one of these cells. Terrified? Despairing? The goblins had delivered his second note hours ago, but Jeriah longed to stop and whisper up some words of hope. He didn't dare. He had no way to know if the guards were watching her. If Senna got into more trouble, would his father blame him for that, too? It hardly mattered—if Senna came to harm because of his schemes, Jeriah would never forgive himself.

Below the sixth shaft Jeriah's dark-adapted eyes caught a glimpse of something lumpy, crouched precariously above the waterline. He stopped so abruptly that Cogswhallop bumped into him and breathed a curse. The shape stirred and resolved itself into a grinning Daroo, who motioned them past. They must be beneath Senna's cell. Jeriah had hoped she'd be imprisoned near the grating he'd come to remove, but there'd been no way to arrange it. Yet another of the things that could go wrong. They'd been lucky—Jeriah passed only three more openings before he reached the grate, which blended with the darkness so well, he ran into it. "Ow!" He managed to keep it to a whisper.

"Shhh."

Hanging the crowbar quietly over one of the bars to keep from losing it in the water, Jeriah studied the barrier with his fingers—he could see almost nothing.

The bars stretched from one side of the culvert to the other. If they'd been drilled into the stone, Jeriah's plan would probably have ended there, but they were fastened to an iron rim that had been spiked to the wall. The spikes didn't feel too large.

"I can do it," Jeriah murmured, "but it's going to make a demonish noise."

"Isn't that why we passed that second note to your sister telling her to create a diversion? Give me a minute to signal Daroo. Then give her a minute or two to get it started."

The goblin moved away and appeared in the faint patch of light beneath the nearest shaft. He waved to Daroo, and moments later a muffled shout echoed down the culvert. Jeriah couldn't make out the words, but it was a girl's voice.

Cogswhallop crept back to Jeriah. "Wait for it. . . ."

Vigorous clanging joined the shouts. "What's that?"

"We gave her a rock to pound on the bars. How else could she make enough noise? Hurry it up. The guards will reach her soon."

Jeriah wedged the crowbar under the iron rim, braced himself, and heaved. Iron shrieked and stone cracked. Jeriah prayed that in the corridor above them Senna's clanging would be louder, but he had no time for finesse. He pried the grate free of the stone and pushed it to one side. Then he stopped, listening. He heard nothing but Senna banging on the bars and shrieking, and his own gasping breath. It had only taken a few moments.

Cogswhallop's eyes gleamed. "Good enough. Back out with you, hero."

"That was easy!"

"Humph. For a great lout like you, maybe. Not one of us could have done it, even if the others could touch iron. Come along, back to the dance. Your alibi, remember?"

Jeriah turned awkwardly and crawled out, grinning at Daroo as he passed. "Tell her she did great! Tell her—" But the child was already scurrying up the shaft to Senna's cell. As Jeriah and Cogswhallop passed the next opening, the clamor quieted—the guards, come to see to Senna's "illness." It really was going according to plan, St. Cerwyn be praised! With a little more luck, Senna could be out of that place by morning.

Jeriah emerged into the spring room, which now seemed brilliantly lit. Half a dozen goblins darted into the culvert, their tools wrapped in rags so they wouldn't clank.

Cogswhallop, who looked like he'd rolled in a pig wallow, watched them critically. "They'll do. Once you get past the dungeons, there's only three or four inches of stone between the culvert and the vault. It's a pity no Stoners were left behind; they'd have done it better. But we'll manage."

Jeriah looked down at himself. He not only looked like he'd rolled in a pig wallow, he smelled like it. "I can't go back to the dance like this. I have to change, but I haven't got time! I didn't think—"

"Then it's a good thing you've got us to think for you." Cogswhallop dug into the equipment pile and pulled out a clean shirt and britches. "You can get wash water from the pool. With your tunic over them no one will . . . Bend over."

He grabbed Jeriah's collar and pulled him down to brush at his hair. "Aye. Clean clothes and you'll do. I'd best get back to the action." He strolled into the culvert and disappeared.

Jeriah washed off the stinking muck, put on clean clothes, and climbed the ladder, leaving his muddy garments for the goblins to dispose of. If they wanted another button or two for their pains, that would be fine with him!

Nothing had changed at the dance when Jeriah slipped back in, and he was startled to realized that less than an hour had passed. Koryn wasn't there. He hoped she'd made it out of the ravine by now, but he didn't dare go in search of her.

He returned to the dance floor and spent the last hour till midnight avoiding the squires he'd bet with, and trying to look as if he hadn't a care in the world.

The next step might not go so smoothly; it depended on Nevin. Jeriah looked at the high table where Nevin hovered over the weary Hierarch. He was no fool and, arrogant idiot that he was, he loved the old man. It would work. It had to.

Nevin fussed about, putting the Hierarch to bed. The menservants had been dismissed, and Jeriah boiled water for the drugged tea. One level scoop of leaves . . . It would smell stronger if he added more. As Jeriah poured steaming water over the sieve, the leaves compressed. He grabbed a generous pinch of the tea and added it to the sieve, pouring again till the cup was full. He turned the sand timer and waited for it to steep. A minute and a half.

A minute and a half for Jeriah to realize that a stronger dose might harm the Hierarch. That someone might notice there was more tea in the sieve than usual. *Fool! Why did you have to improvise?*

Jeriah could smell the sickly sweetness of it. Would Nevin? He hadn't been wrong to try to strengthen the scent—if Nevin failed to notice it, the whole plan would collapse. And Jeriah's father would be destroyed.

So don't let him fail.

The last of the sand ran through the glass. Jeriah removed the tea sieve and carried the cup to the bed where the Hierarch waited, helpless. He couldn't let the old man drink such a strong dose. If worse came to worst, Jeriah could spill it. That would surely trigger Nevin's memory, but it would be cursed suspicious—twice in one day.

The Hierarch smiled at Jeriah and guilt pierced his panic. Nevin was reaching for the cup.

Jeriah wrinkled his nose like someone catching an odd scent. He lifted the cup, sniffed it and grimaced, then passed the cup to Nevin. His heart pounded in his throat.

Nevin sniffed the cup curiously, then offered it to the Hierarch. Jeriah tensed to knock the cup away. What excuse could he make? Then Nevin froze, his face a mask of astonishment.

The Hierarch reached for the cup, but Nevin pulled it back and sniffed again. The surprise in his face gave way to furious thought . . . and dawning suspicion.

That's it! Put it together.

Nevin moved to the medicine jars, opened one, and smelled the tea.

"Is something wrong?" Jeriah asked innocently.

"I'm not sure." He turned the jar in his hands, looking at it instead of its contents. "Do you recognize this?"

Yes!

"Of course I do. I've been making it for him for weeks. What's the matter with you?" Jeriah prayed he could keep his expression sober; his heart was singing.

"You fool! It was in Lazur's office! Don't you remember . . . Wait. Let me think." Nevin paced. "I have to talk to the council. My father too. Zachiros . . . You stay here. Don't touch anything. He'll be asleep in a few minutes—*don't* give him that medicine. Just stay here, don't touch anything, and don't let anyone do anything till I get back with the council."

"But why? What's going on?"

"Do it!" He hurried out, slamming the door behind him.

Jeriah drew in a sigh of heartfelt relief.

"At last! I thought the fool would never leave."

Jeriah spun to the window and met Cogswhallop's worried eyes.

"What are you doing here?"

"We've got a problem, hero. A bad one. You need to come with me."

Tobin

MOONLIGHT SHONE FAINTLY THROUGH THE canvas patches of Makenna's tent. It shouldn't have been enough light for Tobin to see, but he could. Charba was glowing, wispy streams of glittering dust trickling from her hair, her fingers, her nose.

Her hands were gentle, the damp cloth in them cool on his hot skin. It eased the aches when it passed, and Tobin was grateful. He decided to tell her so.

"It's nice that this tent is here," he said.

"Aye, aye, be easy, lad," she murmured.

Tobin had noticed that sometimes his nurses didn't understand what he said, but it hardly mattered.

He closed his eyes, but he could still see Charba, or at least, see the nimbus of light that surrounded her. Tiny comet tails shot off it, and when they came in contact with the trampled grass on which the tent had been pitched, the blades glowed brighter. Or was he imagining that?

Tobin opened his eyes and looked again, but he still saw

it. Whenever those trailing sparks touched the grass, or even the smooth stone they'd set the bucket on, they brightened for a moment.

"You're glowing," Tobin said.

"Easy, lad. It's all right." The cool cloth slid down the inside of his arm, and Tobin saw that even the water devoured those glowing wisps. But the tent didn't. Charba's clothes didn't. The blankets didn't.

Of course! All those things had come from the real world with them. It was only the stuff of the Otherworld that was absorbing Charba's magic into its own. Because it was made of the same glowing . . .

Wait a minute. Was this what was happening to Makenna's spells? He had to tell her! If the very fabric of the Otherworld, everything in it, was *made* of magic, that was how they could move a whole hill! That was why . . . why . . . It was important. He knew it was important.

"I have to tell Makenna she's important," Tobin said urgently. His head was aching again. It did when he tried to rouse himself, which was why he'd stopped trying. "I have to tell her about the magic."

"Shh, it's all right," Charba soothed.

"No!" Tobin made a great effort and tried to sit up. "Makenna. I need to talk to Makenna."

A lightning shaft of pain took him down to his pillow, assisted by Charba's firm hands.

"Is it Mistress Makenna you want? She's getting some

sleep. She'll be by in the morning, but she needs her rest now. And so do you, so no more thrashing about! Just settle down—there you are."

Tobin gathered his failing strength and spoke each word distinctly. "I have to tell Makenna about . . . about . . ."

It was something to do with magic, wasn't it? His head was pounding so fiercely he couldn't remember, but the cool cloth in Charba's hand eased the pain. Her hands were tiny, and little wisps of light drifted from her, making the water on his skin glow. It was pretty. Soothing.

Tobin let his eyes fall closed.

CHAPTER 14

Jeriah

THE BRANCHES OF THE TREE outside the Hierarch's window quaked under Jeriah's weight, and the bark scraped his palms. Cogswhallop slithered through the tangled leaves in near silence—unlike Jeriah! But there were no broken branches to mark his passage when he finally dropped to the terrace, and the guards who stood at the Hierarch's door would swear under a truth spell that Jeriah hadn't left . . . as long as he was back before Nevin returned with the council.

Cogswhallop was still grumbling as Jeriah snatched up the blanket he'd dropped from the window and wrapped it hastily around the goblin before lifting him into his arms. The goblin objected to being carried, but it was the fastest way to get both of them to the spring room, so Jeriah had ignored his protests.

Praying he wouldn't meet anyone who'd remember seeing him, Jeriah raced around the terrace, the awkward bundle clutched to his chest. Things were no longer going according to plan—time to improvise!

"How much of this charmed iron is there?" he asked softly.

"We can't get close enough to tell." The fabric muffled Cogswhallop's voice, but his words were clear enough. "It makes sense when you think about it, that they'd take extra precautions around the vault."'

A pair of tipsy revelers wandered through the dim inner corridor. Jeriah slowed his headlong pace—they'd surely notice a running man.

"You haven't even got *in* yet?" he muttered.

"I told you, it's spelled so no goblin can go near it." Cogswhallop's voice was now so soft Jeriah could barely hear him. "I could hardly drag you off the dance floor, and after that you were attending the old man. Keep your skin on. It'll take young Brallorscourt a while to gather up the council."

"Unless they're all still at the dance." Jeriah turned a corner and hurried toward the spring room—no one in sight now. "Unless he settles for a few of them. Unless—" He shifted the bundle into one arm to turn the knob, then ducked through the low door. "We're in!"

The moment the latch clicked shut, Jeriah dropped the blanket and started down the ladder, leaving the cursing goblin to fight clear of the fabric on his own. The bottom of the shaft was invisible in the darkness, but Jeriah knew how deep beneath the fourth level it ran. He was hurtling down, almost running, when his foot missed a rung and slid off into space.

Jeriah's hands clamped on the poles as his body slammed into the ladder. He dangled, sobbing under his breath, till his feet found the rung once more and then clung to the ladder, shaking, horribly aware of the drop below.

When Jeriah began to descend again he moved more slowly. He was still trembling when he reached the bottom, but his sense of urgency had returned. He grabbed the crowbar and headed for the culvert.

"Wait!" Cogswhallop called.

"What?"

"We've no more clothes for you—best put the muddy ones back on."

"But . . ." He was right. Jeriah dropped the crowbar, tore off his clean clothes, and pulled on the dirty britches, swearing as the wet cloth clung to his skin. Forget the rest of it. He had no time to spare.

Thrusting the crowbar through his belt, Jeriah scurried into the culvert like a rat. He counted off patches of light till he reached the sixth grating, where Daroo crouched.

"Tell her to start now," Jeriah hissed. "I'll be making a racket down here any minute."

"Aye!" The small goblin scampered across Jeriah's legs as he crawled onward, and his whisper echoed down the culvert. As Jeriah passed the next shaft, he heard Senna calling that she was sick, she really was. She needed help. A stone clanged on iron.

She might be a bad liar, but Senna always came through

when it mattered. Thank the Bright Gods for clever assistants. He couldn't imagine how the knights in tales got along without them.

Shortly after he passed the spot where he'd pried out the grate, the sewer shafts stopped, but Jeriah saw a faint glow in the culvert ahead of him. Since there were no openings to carry light to the surface, one of the goblins had lit a candle. There must have been a score of them perched above the shallow water. Jeriah didn't stop to speak as he splashed between them, but he heard Cogswhallop murmur something to Master Hispontic.

Jeriah's only concern was the charmed iron, and soon he saw it: half a dozen slim strips, arching against the culvert wall like a snake's ribs. Three spikes held each strip in place.

How long did he have before Nevin returned with his witnesses and found Jeriah gone? Not enough time for silence, that was certain. He'd have to rely on Senna to cover the noise. And pray this second disruption didn't arouse the guards' suspicion. If Jeriah's plan failed, it would certainly rouse Master Lazur's. *So don't fail!*

Jeriah flung himself down by the first strip, inserted the crowbar, and pried it off the wall. Iron squealed and spikes snapped, but he didn't care. It was taking too long. Even when the last strip was free he had to waste precious time hauling the charmed iron farther down the culvert so the goblins could approach.

They were already chiseling through the wall when Jeriah returned, tapping at the mortar with rag-wrapped wooden hammers that were . . . well, relatively quiet. Cogswhallop and another goblin were conferring over the builder's drawing.

"You'll have to hurry," Jeriah told them. "If Lord Brallorscourt gets suspicious—"

"Aye, we know. Best way to keep him lulled is for you to get back where you're supposed to be. And hero, wash your hair. It's full of mud."

Jeriah swore and crawled away. He opened a tap from the cistern and washed his hair, arms, legs, and feet, shuddering at the cold water. He dried himself roughly with the blanket, which Cogswhallop must have carried down, and threw on his clothes. The ladder's rungs clanged under his feet. It was easier to go fast climbing up.

Jeriah did take the time to peek out and make sure the corridor was empty. He didn't think anyone had noticed him on the way down, and it would be stupid to risk his alibi now.

No one in the spring room corridor, or the one beyond. If he could make it up the tree without being seen, the guards would swear he'd been with the Hierarch all the time Nevin had been gone. Jeriah ran lightly to a servants' stairs that would take him to the third level, then froze with his foot on the bottom step.

"This way is quicker." Nevin's voice, coming down from

the stairs above him. Nevin's voice and dozens of shuffling feet. The council was ahead of Jeriah, blocking the servants' stairs. They'd reach the Hierarch's room in minutes!

Jeriah ran back toward the terrace. He had to take the main stairs to the third level, then get up the tree and into the Hierarch's room before they did—and Nevin was right, the servants' stairs were quicker.

The corridor seemed to stretch beneath Jeriah's racing feet. He skidded onto the terrace and dashed up the open stairs, skidding again as he shot onto the third level and ran for the tree.

Miraculously, he hadn't passed anyone. The court was still dancing, but even so . . . *Please, St. Cerwyn, help me now.*

Jeriah climbed the tree faster than he'd climbed the ladder, swarming through the branches like a squirrel, heedless of the leaves that lashed his face.

He'd left the shutters open. Jeriah glanced into the room— no one had come in! The Hierarch slept peacefully. Jeriah leapt through the window, tripped on the sill, and fell painfully to the floor. He had no time to nurse his bruises; Nevin was demanding entrance from the guard.

Staggering to his feet, Jeriah ran his hands over his hair and clothing, straightening, searching for leaves. He found three, plucked them off, and tossed them out the window. He was pulling the shutters closed when the latch clicked.

"Please be quiet, my lords," Nevin said softly. "The Hierarch is asleep."

No reason to close a window on such a mild night. Jeriah opened the shutters and turned, trying to control his breathing.

One glance at their grim faces told him the landholders had more on their minds than an open window. They filed silently into the room. Of the fourteen lords of the council Nevin had gathered ten, along with his father and Master Zachiros. Nevin was carrying the jars from Master Lazur's cabinet. *Good!*

Most of the landholders looked first at their sleeping ruler, but Lord Brallorscourt's eyes went straight to the table where Jeriah had prepared the drugged tea, observing everything. A chill crept down Jeriah's spine. He was glad he'd been opening the window when they came in, glad he'd thought to search for leaves, to slow his breathing. It looked like Lord Brallorscourt already knew about the drug. This was the man who held the evidence against Jeriah's father, and he was far too intelligent. Jeriah shivered.

"Bring those things," Lord Brallorscourt told his son. "We'll talk in the sitting room."

They filed out again. Jeriah followed and stood by the bedroom door, not saying a word. Just an innocent bystander. Lord Brallorscourt glanced at him, then looked away.

It was Lord Brallorscourt who took charge of the questioning, trying to control the situation, Jeriah supposed. But as Nevin revealed his findings, the landholders' outrage soon carried the situation beyond anyone's control. When Nevin told how Chardane had spilled the drug on him, Lord

Brallorscourt held up his hand for a moment's pause and went to the door.

"You," he said to one of the curious guards. "Find the herb-healer Chardane, and bring her here." Then he gestured for Nevin to continue.

The landholders' shock at learning that the Sunlord was being drugged was almost equaled by their anger when Nevin told them about finding the jars hidden in Master Lazur's office. It was the first time Jeriah's name had come into the story, and Lord Brallorscourt's gaze became very sharp. Several landholders testified that they'd witnessed Nevin taking the jars from Master Lazur's cabinet. Jeriah, heart beating in his throat, simply confirmed what Nevin said.

Lord Brallorscourt's attention returned to Nevin, and there was a hint of baffled fury in his expression. It would be maddening to have your own son bring your schemes to naught. But it worked to Jeriah's advantage; even a man as cynical as Lord Brallorscourt wouldn't want to believe his son was being manipulated.

Chardane hadn't arrived by the time Nevin finished his tale. Jeriah began to worry, and had to restrain himself from fidgeting under Lord Brallorscourt's observant eyes. What could be keeping her?

The landholders chattered like starlings—most of them denying any association with Timeon Lazur as fast as they could. Lord Brallorscourt watched Jeriah, who stayed where he was and said nothing.

A light tap sounded on the door and Chardane hurried into the room. She wore a night robe, and her braided hair hung down her back.

"Is he ill?" She was moving toward the Hierarch's bedroom as she spoke. "What are the symptoms?" She became aware of the council's presence and stopped, looking from one of them to another. "What's going on?" It was a beautiful performance. Jeriah could have kissed her.

"You took a long time coming here," said Lord Brallorscourt. "What kept you?"

"It likely took a while for the guard to find me. I was in the dungeon, tending a prisoner who'd taken ill."

Lord Brallorscourt waved it away. "Do you recognize these?" He pointed to the jars.

Chardane went to the table, sniffed one of them, and stiffened—her shock was so realistic, for a moment Jeriah feared something else had gotten into the jar.

"Bright Gods!" Her eyes went to the Hierarch's door and widened. "He hasn't been taking this stuff, has he?"

"What is it?" Brallorscourt demanded.

"It's . . . it smells like green vervallen. No, I've worked with enough of it lately to know; it is green vervallen."

"My son tells me your workshop is full of this poisonous stuff. *Healer.*"

Oh Bright Ones, it could be taken as a sign of Chardane's guilt! He hadn't thought—

Chardane snorted. "I told you that myself. I ordered a bag of it three days ago, and you know very well why—you were one of the ones who asked me to find a drug to use against the barbarians."

Master Zachiros stepped forward and laid a hand on Lord Brallorscourt's arm.

"Mistress," said the secretary gently, "why this drug?"

"Because the biggest problem with using poisoned water as a weapon is that as soon as the first fall ill, no one else drinks it. Green vervallen doesn't kill, it just fuddles the wits. I thought we might get the lot of them with it."

"It wouldn't kill them?"

"Not until they went into battle unable to form a sensible plan, or to decide whether to duck or strike back—then it'd kill a fair few."

Brallorscourt shook himself free. "How do we know the drug in these jars didn't come from your workroom?"

"Well, there's two ways. I only have one sack, and I haven't used much—if you dumped what's in all those jars on top of my vervallen, you wouldn't be able to close the sack. But you don't need to bother with that."

"Why not?"

"My vervallen was picked fresh, a few days ago. This stuff is long dried." She held out a handful, but no one looked at it. "What could Kerratis be thinking, giving him this?"

"Kerratis?" said Lord Brallorscourt sharply.

"Who else could order medicine for him?"

The landholders broke into impassioned comment, but Nevin's voice overrode them. "It's true, it was Kerratis who ordered it. But what was it doing in Master Lazur's cabinet?"

Jeriah's heart plummeted. *Could Master Lazur put the blame on Kerratis?*

Lord Brallorscourt glared at his son. "We'll ask them. Guard, bring Master Kerratis and Master Lazur here."

While the landholders questioned Chardane about the drug's effect, Brallorscourt paced, looking first at his son, then at Jeriah. Nevin was intent on Chardane's answers. Jeriah pretended to listen, but he was always aware of Lord Brallorscourt, as if the man were a buzzing wasp.

Soon he heard Master Kerratis' voice in the corridor. "I saw the Hierarch at dinner, and there was nothing wrong with him but normal weariness. I demand that you tell me who summoned me. I demand—"

The door swung open and a guard pushed Master Kerratis into the room. The healer priest's gaze flashed across the landholders' faces. Fear dawned in his eyes, but his voice didn't reveal it.

"What in the Bright Ones' name is going on here? Who summoned me?"

"I summoned you." Lord Brallorscourt stepped forward. "But as to what's going on, we're hoping you can tell us." He held up one of the jars.

Master Kerratis stiffened. "It's yellow vervallen. I

recommended it to help the Hierarch sleep. It's quite harm-less, I assure you. Is someone questioning my judgment as a healer?"

He was talking too much. Could the landholders hear the guilt, the terror under his arrogant words?

"I knew you were a feckless ass," Chardane snarled. "Aye, I'm the one daring to question your sacred judgment. And it's *green* vervallen, fool."

"It can't be!" Kerratis snatched the jar and peered inside. "The two look similar, but I can't believe the herbalist who supplies it could make such a mistake. Even if he did, it's not my fault. It was yellow vervallen I recommended."

"What I'd like to know," said Master Zachiros, "is why Timeon Lazur had these jars in his office."

Surprise whisked over Kerratis' face. "I have no idea. But if Master Lazur's the one who had these jars, then perhaps you should question—"

A knock interrupted him, and a guard brought Master Lazur into the room. He looked around, wariness flickering in his expression for a second before he composed it.

Master Kerratis glared at him. Repudiation or warning?

"What's going on?" Master Lazur asked calmly. "You sent for me?"

Lord Brallorscourt gestured to the jars. "Do you recognize these?"

"No. Should I?" Master Lazur barely glanced toward Jeriah, but Jeriah flinched at the grim promise in his eyes.

If this didn't work, his family would be destroyed. But he'd known that when he started. He lifted his chin and stared back defiantly.

"Two of these jars were found in a cabinet in your office," Lord Brallorscourt told him.

"I don't know how that could be. I've never seen them before. What's in them?"

"A drug, I'm afraid," Master Zachiros interposed. "One that may have been responsible for the Hierarch's tragic condition all these years."

Master Lazur stiffened. He did it almost as well as Chardane. "Are you telling me that the Sunlord is being *drugged*? That his mind's all right?"

"We can't know that for certain," said Master Zachiros. "But it might be. The problem is—"

"The problem," Lord Brallorscourt interrupted, "is how jars of this drug came to be in your office."

"I don't know," said Master Lazur truthfully. "I can only guess that one of my enemies planted them there. Who discovered the Hierarch was being drugged? That might be a clue." He was careful not to look at Jeriah.

"My son Nevin, whose devotion to the Hierarch is well known, discovered it. But even if someone doubted his loyalty, he's not old enough to be the author of a plot that began seven years ago."

That startled the priest. His eyes flicked to Jeriah, then away. "In that case I can only suggest Master Kerratis might know something. He's responsible for the Hierarch's physical well-being and orders all his medicines."

"I recommended a mild sedative!" Master Kerratis' face was crimson. "If something was substituted, I suggest you look to the man in whose cabinet the drug was found! I won't be held responsible for this, I warn you!"

He glared at Master Lazur's impassive face, and Jeriah held his breath. How could the priest look so calm? He was only a breath from destruction! Surely under that confident facade his nerves were shredding. Surely he could be driven to make some mistake.

Finally, Master Lazur stirred. "My apologies, gentlemen. I didn't want to make accusations before I had proof. I'd already begun questioning the efficacy of this 'medicine,' and I took the jars to try to learn what it was. That's why they were in my cabinet. I was trying to find an herbalist I could trust, and searching for evidence that Master Kerratis might have—"

"Oh, no you don't!" Kerratis lunged for Master Lazur, but the guards caught his arms. "You're not getting out of this! He came to *me*, masters, seven years ago. I'd been . . . It was a mistake. An indiscretion! But if it had become known, I'd have been finished. All my learning, my power, wasted! But Master Lazur came to me! He was the one who suggested a drug. He was the one who wanted him kept helpless but alive. He was the one who planned it all!"

Master Lazur shook his head sadly. "He seeks to save

himself by casting blame elsewhere."

The landholders' expressions were full of doubt and confusion, and Jeriah's heart sank. *It was going to fail.* It was going to fail, his family would be ruined, and Tobin would die.

"Seven years," Master Zachiros mused. "I find it hard to believe any plot could remain secret so long. What motive would either Master Kerratis or Master Lazur have to do such a thing?"

"Is there another explanation?" Lord Brallorscourt snapped.

"Well, perhaps it's a recent plot on the part of Master Lazur's enemies, as he suggested. If you gave this drug to a man whose mind was already damaged, the effect might not be noticeable."

"I'd have notice—" Nevin started to protest but his father's hand clamped down on his shoulder, silencing him.

It was all coming to naught. Master Zachiros' gentle logic would bring Jeriah's whole scheme tumbling down. And then . . .

"Or it might be an accident," the secretary continued. "If the herb seller confused some similar plant with the dangerous one—"

"Confused them consistently, for seven years?" asked Master Lazur. "I grant you, yellow verval—"

He stopped in midword, but it was too late.

"Truly, yellow vervallen looks much like green vervallen," said Master Zachiros. "But it seems you did know what was in those jars, Timeon. Without having found an herbalist to tell you."

The room was still.

Master Lazur hesitated a second and tried again. "Someone mentioned the name of the drug while we spoke."

"Not since you came in, Lazur." Kerratis grinned savagely.

Master Zachiros shook his head. The landholders glared their condemnation. The frustrated fury on Lord Brallorscourt's face needed no words.

Master Lazur took a deep breath. "The relocation is more important than anything else. No matter what happens to me, it *must* be completed." His gaze darted to Brallorscourt, to Master Zachiros, to Chardane. The landholders knew a confession when they heard it and broke into clamorous exclamations, cursing Lazur for a traitor, calling for the guard.

"The relocation must continue or we're all lost!" The guards grabbed him, dragging him out with Kerratis. The priest's eyes sought desperately for someone who might understand. They fastened on Jeriah, and the desperation, the truth in those eyes held him, trapped, unable to look away. "Don't let this stop the relocation! It can save the Realm!" He was speaking to Jeriah alone, now. Demanding. Begging. "All our lives, everything is at stake! Don't let anything stop—" The door closed behind him.

Jeriah's quaking nerves eased a little as the landholders

rushed about. Nevin was asking them to leave lest they wake the Hierarch. Master Zachiros was the first to depart; he had a lot to organize.

It had worked. Whatever the cost, it had worked. But how could a villain show such courage, such selflessness?

Could the relocation really fail because of this?

Jeriah shivered. Surely someone else would step in and take command. Make sure the Realm was saved.

Lord Brallorscourt was silent, no doubt reordering his own plans. He would still have his council seat, in spite of Master Lazur's fall. And perhaps more power. He looked at Nevin, who was politely pushing the last of the landholders out of the room. He looked at Jeriah and stiffened, his eyes raking over him.

"Why is your hair wet?"

"M-my hair?"

"It's still damp. It was wet when we came in. Why?"

"Ah, I'm sorry, my lord. I drank a little too much at the dance. When the Hierarch fell asleep, I began to get sleepy too, so I poured water over my head."

It sounded plausible, didn't it?

Brallorscourt began to pace. "I don't believe in coincidence. I suppose this could be an accident. Perhaps the Bright Gods had a hand in it. But perhaps . . ."

"Father, what are you talking about?"

"Coincidence," said Lord Brallorscourt, gazing at Jeriah. "Or not. But there's one way to be sure."

"Sure of what?" Nevin asked.

"Come with me, both of you. We're going to the vault to check on some papers."

Jeriah felt the blood drain from his face. Lord Brallorscourt saw it and smiled. "If the papers are there, then this is the Gods' will and I won't tamper with it. If they're gone . . . I have a promise to keep."

They had to wait for the Hierarch's servants to arrive. Nevin refused to leave him unattended, and Lord Brallorscourt wanted his son to act as a witness—though to Nevin's frustration, he refused to tell him what he was supposed to see.

Jeriah said nothing, but he prayed the servants would be out of the palace or drunk, anything to delay them. The goblins had just started working on the wall when he left—they couldn't be finished by now. It seemed like an eternity had passed, but it was really little more than an hour.

The servant came in all too soon. They descended to the vaults, Lord Brallorscourt clasping Jeriah's arm. Nevin was babbling about the possibility that the Hierarch might recover, happier than Jeriah had ever seen him.

Jeriah's mind spun. He should try to delay them, but anything he did would confirm Lord Brallorscourt's suspicion. Would that be worse than catching the goblins with Master Lazur's notes in their hands? Delay them how? His plan was in shambles.

Three pairs of guards were stationed in the wine cellar— and they weren't there to guard the wine. As they passed the spring room door, Jeriah remembered his muddy clothes lying on the floor inside. Damning evidence. As damning as the evidence Lord Brallorscourt held against his father?

There was a slight delay outside the vault as the keys were fetched. Did the goblins know they were there? How thick was this door?

"Lord Brallorscourt." Jeriah spoke as loudly as he dared. "I don't know why you need me. Surely Nevin can witness whatever this is."

"I wouldn't dream of doing this without you, Jeriah Rovan. Do you mind being here?"

"Of course not, my lord." He could say nothing else, but perhaps that was enough to give the goblins time to escape. Perhaps . . .

A guard trotted up with the keys. As the door swung open, Jeriah's eyes flashed around the room. No goblins, thank the Bright Gods! The vault's floor had been sunk deeper than the rest of this level to provide more space for the racks and shelves that lined its walls. The greatest treasures in the Realm were here, disappointingly concealed in crates and chests.

Jeriah didn't care if the floor was carpeted with gold—nothing mattered except the gaping black hole halfway up one wall. The goblins hadn't had time to close their entrance! It was partially concealed, near the edge of a set of shelves, but someone was bound to notice it soon.

It can't end like this! Not now!

Lord Brallorscourt went down the four narrow steps and over to a small chest at the opposite side of the room.

Jeriah strolled to the opening, forcing himself to walk slowly despite his screaming nerves. Cogswhallop's grim eyes met his—the goblin had been sliding the stone back into place, but he didn't dare move now. Jeriah turned and leaned against the wall, blocking the hole with his body.

Lord Brallorscourt had opened the chest and was sorting through some documents. "They're here." Astonishment was clear in his voice. "They all seem to be here."

"What's all there?" Nevin asked. "Never mind. Since it's there, can we go?"

Lord Brallorscourt turned to Jeriah, who tried to control his expression. He didn't think he succeeded. The cool draft against his back felt like the breath of a tomb.

Lord Brallorscourt looked at the papers, then back at Jeriah. "Very well. You can relax, Rovanscourt."

"Thank . . . I don't know what you mean, sir." Jeriah was surprised he got the words out without stammering. His teeth were trying to chatter. He clenched them shut and followed the others out of the vault without a backward glance.

"What were those papers?" Nevin asked his father. "Can you tell me now?"

"Just some notes Master Lazur will no longer be needing. They'll go to the justices." Malice flickered in the glance he cast Jeriah, but no real enmity. "They'll probably destroy them when they're through. A traitor's papers."

Emotion began to return, and Jeriah fought down an impulse to laugh hysterically. He wondered if the justices would realize that some of those documents were copies. He doubted it. Master Hispontic struck him as a very careful forger.

It was nearly dawn before Jeriah was free to seek his own bed. And he'd be rising again shortly, for Master Zachiros had promised to get Senna out of the cells "as soon as I can manage it."

After leaving the secretary, Jeriah had gone back to the ravine to make certain Koryn had found her way out. She'd either done so or she was both hiding and refusing to answer his calls. And angry though he knew she'd be, Jeriah thought Koryn was more likely to rage than retreat. Though if she never wanted to speak to him again, Jeriah could hardly blame her.

The sky was a shade lighter in the east, and birds were beginning to twitter when Jeriah left the ravine and made his way back to the palace. But as he circled around the terrace toward the corridor that led to his room, a gray lump that had settled on one of the planters stirred, and a white face turned toward him.

"Koryn!" In the paling torchlight the shadows under her eyes looked like bruises, and scratches showed red on her skin. Marks *he* had put there.

"I'm so sorry. I shouldn't have—"

"Do you have the slightest idea what you've done this night?"

She could have been referring to so many things, Jeriah's only safe course was to ignore that question entirely. "I shouldn't have left you there. I was angry, but that's no excuse."

"They'll hang him!" Koryn stood swiftly, abandoning her usual deliberate care, and wobbled as her crippled leg gave way.

Jeriah reached out to steady her, but she clutched the wall and went on. "They'll try him for treason and hang him. I don't know how you did it, but do you have any idea—"

"I didn't do anything," said Jeriah. "He was drugging the Hierarch. I know—"

"I don't care who he drugged or what he did! He was the only one—"

"Well, I do care!" Jeriah snapped. "I know you liked Master Lazur, but you have to face the facts. He's guilty of treason. If they hang him . . ."

Jeriah fell silent. Master Lazur was guilty, but the thought of sending anyone to the gallows sent cold horror creeping though his belly.

"As it happens," Koryn said, "I didn't like him much. But it wouldn't matter if I'd hated him, you moron, because he was the driving force behind the relocation! With him gone, it will fail. The barbarians will sweep over the whole Realm, and all the blood, all the thousands of deaths to come, will be on your hands, Jeriah Rovan!"

"Look, I didn't—"

"Yes, you did. I can't figure out how, but I know you're behind it. You might even get your precious brother back. I hope you do. I hope his presence consoles you when a barbarian spear goes through your father's heart, and your sisters are hacked to bloody rags by barbarian knives. I hope his presence consoles you then, because I promise you, nothing else will!"

Was that what she had seen? Jeriah wanted to put his arms around her, but he didn't dare. He grasped her hand instead. "We'll stop the barbarians somehow. The threat is clear to everyone now, and we'll find a way to stop them. I promise."

He wouldn't have been surprised if she'd slapped his face again, but she only pulled her hand from his.

"You're a fool."

She turned and limped away.

Makenna

"WHY DIDN'T YOU CALL ME?" Makenna whispered.

She probably didn't need to whisper; Tobin was too deep in his feverish sleep to hear.

"Because you need rest too," said Charba tartly. "You'll do the lad more good applying your mind to those spell books than holding his hand. You can't understand more than one word in ten, anyway."

That was probably true, but . . .

"You should have called me."

A shadow of grief slipped over Charba's sharp features. "Maybe I should. But you need a sharp wit for those spells now, mistress. Because if you don't get him out of this world, he's going to die."

Makenna had lived in dread of those words ever since Tobin had fallen ill, but the cold struck all the way to her soul.

"It's just a fever. People recover from all kinds of fevers. You said so yourself. If we get enough water into him, keep his body cooled down, then surely . . ."

Charba was shaking her head. "This isn't a normal fever. Far as I can tell, just being in this world is causing it. If we don't get him out, he's going to die here."

Sweat shone on Tobin's white skin. His face was too thin, and dark circles ringed his eyes. Makenna's mother was a healer. Young as she'd been when her mother died, Makenna had seen the look of death before.

She straightened her shoulders and summoned her command voice. "How long does he have?"

"Several days," said Charba. "Maybe a week. Not more."

"Then I'd best get to it, hadn't I?"

Makenna left the tent without looking back—it wasn't good for the goblins to see tears in their leader's eyes.

Makenna was almost certain she knew how to create a gate, but nothing could be cast without magic. And Master Lazur's books held not even a hint of how to keep this terrible place from draining their magic away.

Without magic, she couldn't even do the experiments that might help her figure it out herself.

"You should have called me," Makenna whispered. "I'd have come."

CHAPTER 15

Jeriah

"THOSE WEREN'T THE COPIES, WANT-WIT. Even Bookerie ink doesn't dry that fast. The copies are here." Cogswhallop ruffled the sheaf of spell notes. "We had to go back after you'd left to get the rest of them, and make those forgeries."

Jeriah started to reply, but a rumble of chanting distracted him. The priests had begun the gate spell. It was Chardane who'd chosen the deserted farm, at the far edge of the tilled land around the city, and then found a dozen priests willing to cast the spell—now that it was safe for them to do so.

The setting sun of the day after Equinox gilded the ragged outbuildings with golden light. His conversation with Koryn had left him too unsettled to sleep, so Jeriah had gone back to attend the Hierarch. After several hours watching the old man, he'd dozed off himself, in a chair beside the bed. He'd awakened to find sky-blue eyes regarding him brightly.

"Jeriah. Good morning."

The memory still warmed him—maybe enough to counter-act the nightmares that mad night would surely bring. The

Hierarch's mind hadn't miraculously healed, but he was better. He even seemed to understand when Jeriah explained that he had to go away for a while.

The Hierarch's healing mattered; Koryn was wrong about that. But had she also been right?

"Seems a pity," said Cogswhallop, recalling him to the present, "for that Nevin lad to get the credit for all your work."

Jeriah suppressed a twinge of envy. "Maybe." Nevin had also served the Sunlord, not heroically, but with seven years of unfailing patience and respect. "In a way, I think he earned it more than I did."

Cogswhallop started to reply, but Daroo dashed up to them.

"They're all ready, Fa." He beamed at Jeriah, bouncing with excitement.

"We're almost ready too," said Chardane, coming up behind them.

"Go fetch the others, lad," said Cogswhallop, and Daroo raced off again. "Humph. Thinks he's going on a grand adventure, he does. There's no guarantee, even with half a dozen Finders, that we'll be able to reach the gen'ral and the others."

"I know that." Jeriah's heart contracted with grief and fear. Tobin would have been ill for days now.

But the goblin Finders were the best chance they had of reaching him quickly, and Chardane said that even a hedgewitch should be able to cast the spells that would stop the sickness.

There was nothing Jeriah could do to make any of this happen faster. His part had already been done.

At least Master Zachiros had finally gotten Senna out of the cells, where she'd been frantically worrying . . . about Jeriah. She claimed his reassuring notes had frightened her more than any threats Master Lazur made. Jeriah had rousted his friend Harell out of bed to escort her, mounted her on Fiddle, and sent her home—before anything else could happen!

The priest in charge of casting the gate had chosen the entrance of a pigpen as its anchor. He'd said it was the largest gate those gathered could make, and covered its weathered wood with glowing runes. Light poured from the priest's hands as they approached, filling the opening. Beyond the light Jeriah caught a glimpse of something else. He knelt and peered through at the undergrowth and tree trunks of a dense glade. It looked perfectly ordinary, until Jeriah realized he didn't know the species of any of the trees. A chill crept down his spine.

"Aye, a bold venture. Those going with us have kin they want to join. Since that cursed Decree will soon be revoked, most chose to stay." Cogswhallop's gaze turned to Chardane.

She smiled in return, serene in spite of the dark circles beneath her eyes. "It will be revoked as soon as we can arrange it. Probably this week. Since everything Master Lazur supported is now considered suspect, we shouldn't have any problems. There'll be goblin bowls at the back steps any day now."

"Those staying will be glad of it," said Cogswhallop. "Some of them will be too busy to forage for a while. Paying their debts, I understand."

Chardane's brows lifted curiously, and Jeriah grinned.

"He's talking about Master Hispontic and the rest of the Bookeries. I gave them permission to copy the palace library, and they're repaying that favor by searching Lord Brallorscourt's home till they find the evidence Master Lazur had against my father. When they find those documents, they'll replace them with a record of the bribes my father paid the tribunal to get Tobin off. That's illegal too, but everyone already knows about it and half of them have done it themselves. So it won't matter if Brallorscourt decides to open that envelope."

Jeriah enjoyed a moment of perfect peace. This, at least, he'd done right.

Then Daroo hurried up, followed by a mob of goblins. There were women and children among them and they all carried packs—several of which made a familiar jingling sound.

The Bookeries' swift reading of Master Lazur's spell notes had revealed that many of the experiments that dealt with protecting people in the Otherworld had been based on the amulets that protected the barbarians from their gods. Unfortunately, the notes didn't explain *why* the priest thought those amulets were relevant. But Cogswhallop claimed that the bargain was for "as many over fifty" as they could get—and the amulets weren't helping anyone stored under the chorus steps.

One of the approaching goblins was familiar—Jeriah had seen him in the culvert last night. The small man smiled shyly, and Jeriah smiled back with a pang of loss. But his decision was made.

"Either get in or get out of the way!" Cogswhallop told them. The goblins filed through the shimmering gate and into the world beyond. Jeriah could see them examining the strange trees. One flushed a bird, and jumped as it flew.

"You'd better fetch your pack," Chardane told him. "They can't hold it forever."

"I know." Jeriah's eyes stung with unshed tears. "I'm not going."

"What!" They all stared at him, but it was Daroo who spoke. "But your brother's there. You've got to save him!"

"You can save him as well as I can. Maybe better. Once the sorceress has Master Lazur's experimental notes, she'll know more about gates and the Otherworld than anyone." And because Brallorscourt had left those notes in the vault, the Bookeries were able to copy every page. "There's nothing I can do in the Otherworld that the rest of you can't do without me," Jeriah went on. "And my family needs me here.

I'm the heir until Tobin comes back."

"That's pigdung." Daroo scowled. "What's your real reason?"

"It's not entirely pigdung. My father may not need me, but he and my mother would be pretty upset if both their sons vanished into the Otherworld."

Chardane was frowning too. "Since the palace folk believe you left for the border, your parents wouldn't know where you were till you came back and told them."

"I am going to the border," Jeriah said. "I need to see for myself whether the relocation is as necessary, as urgent, as Master Lazur said."

"I see." She didn't look surprised.

Neither did Cogswhallop. "Seems to me, hero, there's plenty could attend to that."

"Yes, but will they? Master Lazur put the relocation *first*. He sacrificed anyone who got in his way, and that was wrong. But it was because he put it first that his plan got as far as it did. It's not a popular idea, especially now. And if he was right . . ."

Koryn's personal tragedy was enough to influence any-one's judgment; but if she'd told the truth, if the barbarians couldn't be stopped, then he had to do something about it. The harm you did in this world mattered. Master Lazur had taught Jeriah that. If bringing down the priest put a stop to the relocation, and the relocation really was necessary, then it was up to Jeriah to fix it.

"In a way," he told Daroo, "it's a matter of indebtedness. I'm the one who stopped him. If no one takes his place, I'd be the one responsible for all the deaths when the barbarians come. I may not be a hero, but I certainly don't want that on my conscience!"

"But why do *you* have to do it?" Daroo protested.

"It's . . . it's a matter of priorities. Chardane's first priority is to put her own people on the council, to reform the laws and correct abuses. Am I right?"

Chardane nodded slowly.

"It may be a long time before the Hierarch can take command. Mistress Koryn would do anything for the relocation—but with Master Lazur gone, there's nothing she can do. Master Zachiros just wants to keep the Realm running and help the Hierarch recover. And the only thing Lord Brallorscourt cares about is increasing his own power. Which leaves only me."

Had Master Lazur realized that, as the guards dragged him away? He wasn't a fool. Jeriah was betting on that. Betting that the priest would go through his trial without ever accusing Jeriah or any member of his family of any crime—so Jeriah would be free to advance the relocation.

Even a nongoblin could understand that kind of debt.

"It seems to me," said Cogswhallop, "that you've no more power than that Bookerie girl of yours."

"She's not my girl," Jeriah said stiffly. "And lack of power hasn't stopped me yet." He gestured to the shimmering gate.

"But you can't not come," Daroo wailed. "You can't!"

"Yes, he can," said Cogswhallop. "And I'm not letting you stay, either."

"But . . ."

"That's final."

"Humph!" The boy folded his arms, like a miniature version of his father.

Jeriah gave him a commiserating smile and turned to Cogswhallop. "It's up to you to reach Tobin and make sure that sorceress sends him back. If you have to, you could use the notes to bribe her. Or—"

Cogswhallop snorted. "If he's in danger, she'll send him back no matter what I do."

"Maybe," said Jeriah. "But I don't trust her. I'm trusting you." They'd earned his trust over this last wild week. Enough trust that he was willing to put Tobin's life in their hands. "Will you do it?"

"Well, that depends on what for, now doesn't it?"

On the other hand, goblins *were* goblins.

"Fa . . ."

"Quiet, lad. This is bargaining."

"You can't trade for that. Not with the way you're indebted." There was a vengeful gleam in Daroo's eyes.

"I told you to be quiet."

"Indebted?" asked Jeriah. "How?"

"'Cause you're the one who put him in command," said Daroo over his father's outraged sputter. "With the mistress gone, none of the others would obey another goblin."

"They never have," Cogswhallop growled. "Bookeries don't obey Finders, Finders won't obey Greeners, on and on. It's the curse of our kind. If the fools would accept a leader and unite, we could have driven out your kind, human. Long ago!"

"Fa wanted them to follow him," Daroo continued. "'Cause he's got plans. So he bet them you could find a way to open a gate to reach the others. And now you have, so he's in command—and he's indebted for it!"

"Blather. That's an entirely separate matter. No debt owed," said Cogswhallop.

"No, it's not. It—"

Cogswhallop started toward his disobedient offspring. "If you don't get through that gate, I'll throw you through."

"But Fa—"

"No buts. Go on."

"You'd better go," Jeriah told him. "Thank you, demon brat."

Daroo glared at all of them. "I'll come back," he assured Jeriah. "You'd best take care, and promise not to do anything stupid, because I'm coming back as soon as I can."

"Tobin made me promise not to be stupid too. What is this? I never . . . Well, almost never . . . All right, I promise." He tried to look sober and reliable, but his lips twitched.

"Humph!" Daroo stalked through the portal.

Even through the laughter, Jeriah's heart cracked. He

would have given anything to join his friend, to rescue Tobin himself. But his place was here, at least until his debt was paid.

The goblins had taught him something.

Cogswhallop must have read the decision in Jeriah's face, for he bent and picked up his pack. "So, hero, this is good-bye."

"Oh no, it's not. You have to bring my brother back, remember?"

"Well . . . since you seem to have done me a small favor, even though you didn't intend it—"

"That's an entirely separate matter—just as you said! And you owe me for it, goblin. Saving Tobin is part of what you already owe me for getting the Decree reversed. . . . You'll save him, won't you?"

"You have a worse memory than a new-hatched Flichter! Stealing those notes paid for the Decree's . . . Oh, all right! I'll find him and deliver those spells to the gen'ral, and she'll do her best to save him. But after that I make no promises!"

"That'll do," said Jeriah. "Tell Tobin . . ."

Ever since he'd realized he couldn't go, Jeriah had been thinking of messages to send to his brother—dozens of them. Now that the time was on him, it was simple.

"Tell Tobin I love him."

"Aye, I'll do that." The goblin shouldered his pack and walked to the portal. "For free."

Jeriah decided to stop by his home before going on to the border. It only took two days out of the way—and if he was now in charge of the relocation, he'd better stop his mother before she raised any more resistance against it!

Was Koryn right, that the barbarians couldn't be stopped? That moving the entire Realm to a defensible position was the only way for them to survive? Jeriah prayed with all his heart that she and Master Lazur were wrong—because if they'd been right, Jeriah had no idea what to do next!

He set out from the deserted farm that night. He couldn't possibly sleep, so he might as well get a start on the journey. By the light of the waxing moon he saw that the crops had grown in the last month. All the trees had leafed out. Summer was upon them.

It was hard to be going home without his brother, after all. Defying his father's banishment, and with all the bitterness of the flooded village awaiting him. It was so easy to believe you had to sacrifice others to your own cause. Master Lazur would go to his death begging those around him to complete the relocation. Like a knight of legend, selfless and courageous. Jeriah shuddered. It was the priest's own choice.

Just as Jeriah had chosen to try to save Tobin, and all the choices that followed. Just as Tobin had chosen to save the goblins. Master Lazur had been right about that; even if Tobin died, it wouldn't be Jeriah's fault. Any more than the responsibility for Jeriah's choices and mistakes was Tobin's.

Around dawn Jeriah realized he no longer cared about

being a heroic knight. Nevin was the hero, and Jeriah was content with that. Well, almost content. It would be nice to have won his father's respect.

He unsaddled Glory, to let her rest while he ate breakfast. He was getting sleepy, but the need to be home drove him on. Though why he felt so much urgency to face to the villagers' hatred and his father's anger was a mystery. He had to deal with his mother, but he didn't need to race home for that. He'd probably passed Senna already—she'd have had the sense to stop at an inn for the night, instead of pressing on like a lunatic.

At midafternoon Jeriah stopped for midmeal and fell asleep in the meadow after he ate. When he woke several hours later, he decided to press on; his need to talk to his father was growing. But it wasn't the perfect father he'd tried so desperately to please who he wanted to see. It was the man who'd traded his own honor to save his son. The man who might understand some of the choices Jeriah had been forced to make—if his son could find the courage to tell him the truth.

Somehow during the long ride Jeriah had made up his mind without realizing it. Master Lazur wasn't the only person to whom he owed a debt.

Jeriah arrived at Rovanscourt several hours after dark, but there was a light in his father's office. The groom who stabled his weary mare glowered at him, but it wasn't the intense fury that had assaulted Jeriah when he left.

As he walked the familiar corridors to his father's door, Jeriah's heart was pounding in spite of his resolve. He knocked quickly, before he could lose his nerve.

"Come in." His father was frowning over a pile of tally sheets. "Jeriah!" The flash of surprised pleasure was instantly replaced by sternness. "What are you doing here? You were banished till I gave you permission to return."

"I know. I'm sorry to disobey you, and I'll explain it later. But first . . . Father, there's something I have to tell you."

A Chronological Glossary

of the

History of the Realm

of the

Seven Bright Gods

BRIGHT GODS: Very early in the history of the Realm, its humans began to organize themselves in a way that valued those who had magic above those who didn't. This organizational process ultimately resulted in the Church of the Seven Bright Gods, who were held to be the source of priestly magic. These priests were eventually ranked in circles, at first according to magical ability and later more according to political power. Seventh-circle priests are the least powerful, usually representing the church in small rural villages. There are only three first-circle priests, who govern the Northlands, the Midlands, and the Southlands, respectively. Above all of them is the Hierarch, who is chosen by the Seven Bright Gods—who conveniently express their will through the Priests' Council, which consists of all priests third circle and above.

THE DARK ONE: According to the church, the Dark One is the source of any magic that doesn't come from the Seven Bright Gods. Because if someone who isn't in the church has magic, then it has to come from some evil source. Right?

THE LESSER ONES: These are those humans whose magic isn't strong enough for them to enter the church. They know perfectly well that their magic isn't evil, and they do a lot of good, healing and helping people in small villages who don't have access to healer priests. Or those in the cities who are too poor to afford healer priests.

THE GOBLINS: They are the other people whose magic is supposed to come from the Dark One. The goblins know this is nonsense, but not being human, they don't have to care. The church has tried to drive them out of the Realm in the past—the great Goblin Wall in the north is a remnant of that effort. But goblins were so ubiquitous, and so stubborn, that the priests failed. Goblins sometimes help the common citizens of the Realm, usually in exchange for a bowl of milk set out at the back door—but they've also been known to work mischief.

Goblins organize themselves by the type of magic they work:

BOOKERIES: whose gifts have to do with reading, writing, and the gathering and use of information.

FINDERS: whose gift is to locate things.

FLICHTERS: small, winged, and only half material, the light-minded Flichters don't do much except make a nuisance of themselves. But they do that really well.

GREENERS: whose gifts work on live plants of any kind.

MAKERS: who are the craftsmen of the goblin world.

STONERS: a subset of Makers who deal with rocks.

THE DECREE OF BRIGHT MAGIC: This brings us to the time in the Realm's history when the barbarians, a very different human culture that lives on the other side of the Great Desert, attacked the southern border of the Realm. When the barbarians first started raiding the Southlands, a priest named Timeon Lazur paid attention to the reports from the army that was sent to defend the Realm. Master Lazur soon realized that the Realm's army wouldn't be able to defeat the barbarians unless the army was in an extremely defensible position—like defending a very small border from behind a very high wall.

Unfortunately, the Goblin Wall was on the far northern end of the Realm, and the barbarians were invading from the south. Master Lazur decided that the only way the Realm could survive was to move everyone north of the wall. But this decision would be so unpopular that even the church would be unable to enforce it . . . as long as the common people had other sources of magic available to them. If they could still be healed by hedgewitches and herb-healers, and assisted by goblins, the Realm's citizens would probably defy the Hierarch's command and stay where they were. So before the great relocation was announced, the church, at Master Lazur's behest, passed the Decree of Bright Magic, which commanded that anyone, human or goblin, whose magic came from the Dark One be put to death.

THE CONSPIRACY: At about the same time the Decree of Bright Magic passed, and the relocation was decreed, the Realm's government started going downhill in other ways. Master Lazur and the Priests' Council were looking out for the relocation. The lords on the Landholders' Council were looking out for themselves. And the Hierarch, who usually stopped abuses by corrupt landholders and priests . . . wasn't doing that anymore. So some of the better landholders and a few priests got together and tried to overthrow Master Lazur's political cadre, which they saw as the source of the corruption. They failed, and most of them were hanged.